Anna Starr

Anna Starr

DULCIE GRAY

Michael Joseph
LONDON

First published in Great Britain by Michael Joseph Ltd
44 Bedford Square, London WC1
1984

British Library Cataloguing in Publication Data

Gray, Dulcie
    Anna Starr.
    I. Title
    823'.914[F]   PR6013.R364
    ISBN 0-7181-2281-X   915878

Typeset by Alacrity Phototypesetters,
Banwell Castle, Weston-super-Mare.
Printed and bound in Great Britain
by Billing and Sons, London and Worcester

PART ONE

~

Susannah

CHAPTER ONE

Susannah looked up from her book and forced herself to breathe more calmly. In forty minutes she would be giving her first professional performance as an actress. She was about to appear with Marilyn de la Roche in a new comedy, *Jack of Hearts*, in Shaftesbury Avenue — one of the two most famous theatre streets in the world. And she had an important part to play. Already dressed and made up, she was sitting tensely on the only chair her tiny dressing room provided, pretending to read. She felt sick with nerves.

Susannah had done her own make-up (a skill she had learned from Marilyn), and her mother, Muriel, had dressed her; but Muriel had now disappeared to the wardrobe room and Susannah thought she was unlikely to see her again before the play started. Already, although they had had only one dress rehearsal the night before, her mother and the wardrobe mistress had become great friends; Muriel had also endeared herself to the rest of the cast by making constant cups of tea throughout the rehearsal, and by making herself useful to anyone who was of the slightest importance — except for Marilyn.

Marilyn de la Roche and her mother didn't get on. Muriel pretended enormous admiration and affection for Marilyn, but Marilyn didn't even try to hide her dislike of Muriel. This saddened Susannah, because she loved her mother dearly, although she was frightened of her; and she adored Marilyn.

It was through Marilyn that she had got the part. Five years ago, when Susannah was only ten, they had done a film together: then, as now, Susannah had played her daughter. Marilyn had taken her completely under her wing, which had

3

upset Muriel — partly because Marilyn had had no time for Charlie, Susannah's brother, who was the apple of Muriel's eye, and partly because she was jealous. Muriel was always jealous if Susannah made a success. Sometimes Susannah wondered if her mother even liked her, but she suppressed this doubt, believing it to be disloyal. It could cause trouble, and she had already had enough of that.

The half-hour call came through on the tannoy. 'Good evening, ladies and gentlemen. This is your half-hour call. Half an hour, please. Thank you.'

Susannah looked at the watch which Marilyn had just given her as a first-night present: six twenty-five. The curtain was to rise at seven o'clock. She noticed with dismay that her hands were very slightly shaking. She tried out her voice, and found that, with concentration and determination, she could keep it steady. Thank heavens for that!

Marilyn had explained that all the calls — the half, the quarter, the five, and Beginners — were called five minutes early, so that the performance should begin punctually. All actors had to be in the theatre by 'the half', otherwise they would be reported to the management. Tonight, Susannah and Muriel had arrived a whole hour and a half early. As they passed Marilyn's door on their way up to Susannah's dressing room, right at the top of the theatre, Susannah had heard her friend's voice and had gone in to wish her luck and to give her the little posy she had bought for her. Marilyn had already started her make-up, and the room was a bower of flowers and telegrams.

Marilyn had kissed her lovingly and given her the watch, with a message attached: 'To darling Susannah, my favourite daughter, to wish her a huge and well-deserved success.' Susannah had been so touched that she had felt like crying. She looked at her friend in the brilliant lights of the dressing room and thought she had never seen anyone lovelier. Indeed she felt almost overawed by such beauty ... the flaming red hair, the huge blue eyes, the perfect little nose, and the wide and generous mouth. 'Good luck, darling,' said Marilyn. 'You're wonderful in the part, so don't be frightened.'

Muriel had pursed her lips disapprovingly. As they were climbing the stairs together afterwards, with Susannah now in a kind of euphoria of happiness, she said sharply, 'Don't let what that woman says go to your head, Susannah. Tonight is only your start in the theatre. No need to get conceited.'

In Susannah's room there was one large bouquet of flowers from the management, but here, too, had been a telegram from Marilyn. She must do her very best tonight, no matter how scared she was, for Marilyn's sake. Marilyn herself had a wonderful part, but the play was still an important test for her as she was best known as a film star, and would have to prove herself again for the critics as a stage actress. Susannah must do well for her mother's sake, too. She realised only too clearly that Muriel lived out her dreams and ambitions through her daughter. It was she who had pushed Susannah into becoming an actress, because she had wanted to be one herself before she had married. Besides, Susannah's small success in the films and broadcasts she had already made were an important part of the family income.

Her mother had dressed her carefully, looked at her critically, kissed her on the cheek, told her to remember everything she had been told, and vanished ...

There was a knock on the door. It was the Company manager. He was a kindly man, who would have seemed quite attractive had there not been something indefinably seedy about his appearance. Surprisingly he had a pot belly, which, because he was otherwise quite thin, seemed to have been added on as an afterthought. His hair was greasy, and flattened down on his head, and he had hazel eyes and a slightly artificial smile. He liked Susannah, and she liked him. He was devoted to children — especially well-behaved and talented children. He had gone out of his way to look after Susannah. Susannah, recognising this, was duly grateful.

'Anything bothering you?' he asked.

'Only nerves,' replied Susannah, smiling anxiously.

'Everyone has those,' he said firmly, 'and you're very good in the part, so don't worry.' He gave her a kiss and left her.

The director of the play came next, and he also had encouraging words for her. Lastly came the manager of the theatre itself, and Susannah's employer, the manager of the play.

By the time she was once again left alone, the quarter had

been called and, quite clearly over the tannoy, she could hear the first-night audience arriving.

Susannah had been nervous before. Now she was panicking. Somehow she must pull herself together. She breathed again deeply, several times. It would have been very nice, she thought wistfully, if she had had a cosy mother who would come in this minute and comfort her. It was no use expecting that from Muriel. Susannah had a 'brother' in the play, and the part had not been given to Charlie. In some mysterious way, this was deemed to be Susannah's fault. 'He would have done it beautifully,' Muriel had fumed. 'You're a very lucky girl, Susannah! I wonder if you know how lucky you are!'

Susannah had assented meekly, but hadn't liked to remind her mother that Charlie got bored very easily with acting, and when he got bored, he behaved like a little monster, so perhaps it was just as well he wasn't in the play. Charlie was a year younger than Susannah. He had the face of an angel and the disposition of a demon. Susannah also hadn't liked to tell her mother that she herself had never wanted to be an actress; that it had been entirely Muriel's idea, and that, although she enjoyed rehearsing for the stage more than she had ever enjoyed acting in films, she could have lived without either.

'Five minutes, ladies and gentlemen. This is your five-minute call.'

Susannah buried herself in her book and tried to shut out the roar of the audience.

Throughout her short life, books had often provided an escape. Her grandmother had been a schoolmistress, and Susannah's bookishness and introspection had probably been inherited from her. Muriel had no time for either. She had been a 'Daddy's girl', adored and spoilt, and Daddy was no intellectual. He had, however, been intensely proud of Muriel's leanings towards the theatre, and was inordinately disappointed when his only child finally gave up her career for marriage. Perhaps Muriel's ambitions for Susannah were merely a reflection of her own father's ambitions for herself. In the circle in which they moved, the theatre was exotic, and the family gained kudos from Susannah's success.

Muriel was still pretty — much prettier, Susannah thought

gloomily, than she was herself. Muriel was fair, with large blue eyes a little like Marilyn's but paler, and less heavily lashed. She had naturally curly blonde hair, and a dimple in her left cheek. She was petite and moved gracefully, and she looked as if butter wouldn't melt in her mouth.

In fact, she had a will of steel.

Susannah stared at herself disparagingly in the dressing-room mirror. She was so very different, and her reflection dissatisfied her today as it always did, and probably always would. She had straight dark hair, now carefully arranged in a page-boy bob. Her grey eyes were set far apart, her nose was slightly and amusingly turned up, and she had a delicately chiselled mouth. Her face was oval, and in fact very lovely, but years of coming a poor second in her mother's affection made her think of herself as plain. Her usual expression was one of great gravity.

Supposing she didn't make a success tonight, what then? She would have upset Marilyn and enraged her mother. Her heart plummetted and she felt weighed down by the responsibility.

There was a thunderous knock on her door and her stage 'brother', Tony Falk, appeared.

'How's tricks?' he asked cheerfully.

He was chewing gum and was the picture of self-satisfaction and bonhomie. He looked slightly different from usual as he was now unnaturally tidy. His great mop of hair had been plastered carefully to his head, from which his enormous ears protruded like question marks; and his portly little frame had been enclosed in a brand new navy-blue blazer and a clean grey shirt and shorts. His orange tie was beautifully tied.

'I'm scared!' said Susannah.

'Phooey!' exclaimed Tony, his small brown eyes twinkling. 'There's nothing to it. Children aren't meant to be good actors, though I must say you're not bad, considering it's your first job in the theatre. If you'd done as many plays as me, you wouldn't worry. Kids fall between two stools. We're not really actors, we're performing animals, so if we do well, everyone drools, and if we don't, it's only what they expect. Cheer up! The end of the world is not nigh. And anyway, when I'm grown up I shan't dream of earning my living in such a soppy way. I'm going to be a vet, and live in the country, and have fun.'

'I shall have to be an actress,' said Susannah, drearily. 'Mummy wants me to.'

'Haven't you got a mind of your own?' demanded Tony.

Susannah was surprised. She considered the question carefully. 'No,' she said at last. 'I suppose I haven't.'

'More fool you!' replied Tony heartily. 'Anyway, good luck. My Mum said last night's rehearsal wasn't half bad, and that we should be a success. She ought to know. She's been in the business all her life. Oh well, I'd better tootle. Mum says she wants me back in the dressing room until we go down on stage, so that she can be quite sure I don't get myself mussed up. Cheery-bye!' He breezed out, slamming the door.

The 'overture' was called on the tannoy and Susannah heard the sudden hushing of the audience. The national anthem was played to a thunder of uptipped seats, after which she could hear the seats banging down again. The music stopped, there was a total silence, then the sound of the curtain being raised and applause for Marilyn's first entrance.

Marilyn sounded cool, clear and confident. Her first laugh came immediately and explosively, then her second, then her third. The audience seemed prepared to enjoy itself. Good!

Susannah opened her script to reassure herself of her opening lines. She sang a tremulous scale, cleared her throat, looked at herself once again to see that she was indeed correctly dressed and that nothing had been forgotten, then offered up a small but passionate prayer. 'Please, God, don't let me let Mummy down. Or Marilyn. Please, God, make me give a good performance so that I don't disgrace myself or them. Please don't let me be so nervous that I can't speak. For Jesus Christ's sake. Amen.'

'Your calls, please, Miss Dale and Mr Falk. Your calls, please, Miss Dale and Mr Falk.'

This was it. Now or never. Please, God, look after her!

She heard Tony's door open, and he yelled out as he passed, 'Come on Sue! Into battle, old girl!'

Susannah looked at herself one last anxious time and, with a thudding heart, prepared to follow Tony. Her mother hadn't bothered to come back and wish her luck and, for a moment, tears of self-pity pricked her eyes, then she braced herself firmly, pulled her dressing-room door behind her and started descending the long flights of stairs.

Why had her mother ever wanted to go on the stage?

CHAPTER TWO

Muriel Baddeley, born in 1915 at 10 Victoria Villas, Croydon, was the daughter of a builder's merchant and a prim north-country schoolteacher. At the time of her birth, Ernie Baddeley, her father, was a sergeant in the Royal Surrey Regiment, on the Western Front. He had joined up soon after his wedding, late in 1914; he had been invalided home for a short time, but was now back in the trenches, and sick to death of the war.

In many ways he had been extremely lucky. Most of the men he had joined up with had been either killed or seriously wounded, but apart from a thigh wound and a slight attack of gas poisoning, he had escaped injury. He was an easy-going, usually cheerful little man, but the death of so many of his friends, the all-pervading mud and strench, and the everlasting boredom, alternating with moments of horror and desperate fear, nauseated him.

He and his wife, Amy, had met in June 1914 on one of his rare holidays, in Blackpool, where Amy was also on holiday from her home in Leeds. Her blonde hair, her soft voice and her air of reserve attracted him. That she was clever enough to be a schoolmistress slightly over-awed him, but he felt that he had taken a step up in the world when she agreed to marry him and this made him very proud of her. Amy, in her turn, found his effervescent sociability stimulating after the stolid young men with whom she usually associated, and the idea of going to live in the south of England had seemed an adventure. They were very unalike, but this had so far presented no problems as they were in love. When he volunteered, they still scarcely knew each other.

Ernie had received Amy's letter about the birth of their daughter with intense excitement. His regiment had had four days of shelling and almost unbelievable carnage during the battle of the Ypres Salient, and though the British had managed to hold on to their small pocket of ground, their death toll had shaken them all. As he read Amy's letter by the light of a torch in the dug-out, a little shell-shocked and dead tired, the baby's arrival seemed a miraculous omen of peace. Ernie was instinctively a family man, and he had always dreamed of having a daughter. From the first, Muriel was a good little girl; and, almost from the first, she was pretty. Throughout the war she and her mother lived with Ernie's parents, with whom Amy was on very close terms, and all the adults spoiled the baby outrageously. Very soon she knew how to get her own way about most things, and developed an inflexible will, with an outward appearance of great sweetness. Her doting father's return to civvy street only reinforced these tendencies.

The family lived on the outskirts of Croydon — at that time still very much a country town — in a white clapboard house, with a small garden, which was old Mr Baddeley's pride and joy. Grandma Baddeley sewed and knitted constantly, so Muriel was always beautifully dressed. The entire family felt themselves a cut above their neighbours and kept their distance. On his return from the war, Ernie was taken on immediately by his old employer, but by 1924 he had decided to strike out for himself. Croydon, unlike many other parts of the British Isles, was enjoying an era of expansion and his one-man business soon flourished. He and Amy moved into a spick-and-span house nearer the centre of town, and Amy, who was still a schoolteacher, was promoted to assistant headmistress with a good rise in salary — so they were now doing very well.

By the time she was nine, Muriel had become a show-off — not that her parents minded. To them she was perfection. She had a flair for dancing and had appeared to great acclaim as a soloist in school concerts, shaking her blonde curls and dimpling modestly while taking her frequent curtain calls. Applause was nectar to her and, from these concerts onwards, she wanted more.

In 1924, as though in answer to her prayer, Madame Vronsky, who had been with the Imperial Russian Ballet, decided to retire and live in Croydon as a ballet teacher. She chose a large Edwardian house near the Baddeleys and her arrival caused tremendous excitement. Immediately it became the ambition of Muriel's life to learn ballet and, although the lessons were expensive, Ernie, who could deny her nothing, gave her permission to attend. Amy was less enthusiastic. Her rather bleak Methodist upbringing made her wary of such frivolities as dancing or the theatre. But Muriel, as usual, had her own way, and at the age of eleven she was enrolled as a pupil.

Now she was happy. She was 'different' from all the others at her school. In her own eyes she was an important person, and this sense of self-importance was becoming a necessity to her. She wasn't clever in a scholastic sense, and indeed was an idle pupil, but she was still very pretty, a born leader, and had her own little clique of admirers who needed to be kept impressed.

The ballet classes were not quite what Muriel had expected, however. Madame Vronsky was a good teacher, but a fanatical disciplinarian. The lessons, which took place after school from five to six in the evening, were exhausting, and Madame demanded total silence and total concentration. At first Muriel went twice a week, but this was soon increased to five times; and she was expected to do a certain amount of practice at home, which she disliked. The early lessons were easy, consisting of deportment, with a fair amount of work at the barre, and only port de bras and arabesques in the centre; but the unvarying routine irked her, and her muscles ached severely in the mornings before she had warmed up. Muriel was never one to tolerate discomfort with calm.

Every class started with demi-pliés and full pliés in each of the 'five positions', first with the right hand on the barre, and then with the left; after this there was balancing on the points, and Madame's cried and exhortations to 'Pliss to stop vabbling, Drop shoulters, Pull in SCHTommack', and so on, rang constantly and unpleasantly in Muriel's ears. Last came the port de bras, the tendues, frappés, and ronds de jambe, which Muriel found exceedingly dull. In her imagination she had seen herself on points, in a tutu, and, with only a minimum of rehearsal, entrancing huge audiences of wildly enthusiastic fans. Instead she practised, with almost no dancing, day after day; and her costume was a wrap-around tunic made in crêpe or satin, which stopped just short of the knees. Her blonde curls were covered in a thick hair-net, with a flat band of ribbon over her ears, which she thought singularly unattractive; and she found it hard to look happy when her muscles were aching, and when the exercises designed to arch her insteps and perfect a good 'turn out' were so exceedingly painful. She soon tired of sitting with her feet hooked under a small wooden bench, straining backwards to straighten her knees; and of kneading her feet with her hands (again to perfect those wretched arched insteps); and of sitting for what seemed like an eternity, cross-legged, pushing her knees down to touch the floor. Madame also carried a stick, with which she hit her pupils sharply on the back of the legs if they were doing the exercises wrongly.

Muriel enjoyed doing high kicks (called grandes battements — words she relished) but Madame complained that she 'placed' them incorrectly, and also told an astonished Muriel that she was not really musical. Muriel was immediately resentful. Madame recognised the symptoms, and neither of them was distressed when the doctor suggested that Muriel 'wasn't quite strong enough' to be a ballet dancer.

The year at ballet school had, however, given her a cachet in the eyes of her school friends, and her 'delicate state of health' alarmed her parents enough for them to indulge her in even more attention. She had performed a few sham faints to keep up the myth of fragility, and charmed the doctor into submission with her dimpled smile. Her father was much more disappointed than she was at the turn of events but, with a sad, brave little smirk, Muriel told him that Madame had suggested that perhaps the stage was a more suitable outlet for her talents — also, less physically exhausting. This happened to be quite untrue, but it laid the foundations of a 'need' for future dramatic training and Ernie Baddeley became very keen on the idea.

When she was sixteen, Muriel left school and went up to London to try for an audition at three of the best-known dramatic schools — RADA, the Central School, and the newly founded Webber-Douglas. Each gave her its prospectus and told her what would be expected of her, but Muriel was most impressed by the Central, which was housed in the Albert Hall.

She managed to scrape by at the audition three months later, chiefly on her looks and the fact that she moved well, and soon after her seventeenth birthday found a room at a girls' hostel approved by her mother, near the Cromwell Road. There she settled down to a heady new life. She had never dreamed that the world could be so exciting.

But it was the world of social opportunity in which she revelled, not the world of the theatre, and in Elsie Fogerty, the Central's famed and formidable Principal, Muriel found a teacher no less exacting than Madame Vronsky.

Muriel didn't do very well at the school. She had no talent, and still disliked hard work, but she loved calling herself a 'student' and relished the reflected glory of being a budding actress.

By the second year, she was once again becoming disillusioned with the training she had chosen. The parts she was asked to study were very obviously becoming smaller and smaller, and her reports (which she never showed to her parents) were not at all encouraging. Her voice was still 'too weak', they said, and her 'slight cockney accent' still showed. She had 'only a small emotional range' and, though 'never a trouble maker', was 'inattentive' during all the classes that 'bored' her. Muriel was worried at the denigrating tone of the reports but, with the slip-shod optimism of youth, hoped that once she had left the school she would manage to get by.

In those days the course was for two years only, and by her fifth term she began to wonder what kind of job she could fall back on if she didn't make the grade as an actress. She couldn't pretend to frailty again as far as her family was concerned, as she now wanted to live away from home; if she was 'delicate', they would object. On no account, though, would she admit to failure: so what should she do?

What she did was to fall headlong in love with Freddie Dale, a handsome, irresponsible, raffish car salesman. How he had been included in the particular party at which she had met him, neither Muriel nor anyone else seemed to know, but Muriel fell under his spell immediately. He had sleek black hair, dazzling white teeth, grey eyes and a slight swagger as he walked. He was tall and broad-chested, made bad jokes at which he himself laughed uproariously, and had beautiful long white hands, with nails that he kept immaculate. He dressed loudly, and had an air of boisterous self-confidence. Muriel at once divined that he was, in fact, a basically insecure young man, but his physical magnetism for her was far too great for her to have any real criticisms of him.

Freddie boasted a bright green second-hand MG with a leather band around its bonnet, and he drove well, but too fast. Going for a 'spin' with him seemed to Muriel the height of ecstasy.

From the moment she met him, all thoughts of a dramatic career vanished. Freddie was similarly 'smitten', as he called it, and very soon they were seeing a great deal of one another.

Muriel's parents didn't like him. They realised that he was a serious threat to the 'great career' they had envisaged for their beloved only child, and his livelihood seemed to them, at the very best, precarious. Just as Muriel had divined his insecurity, they divined his innate irresponsibility, and they begged the young couple not to get 'too serious' until Muriel had finished her course at the Central. This suited Freddie well. He had no wish at all to get serious — which in the language of those days meant becoming engaged. Muriel, although she always hated any restrictions on her desires, also agreed to wait. Perhaps subconsciously she too had nagging doubts as to his character. Prudently she refused to go to bed with him, as she had no wish for children either legitimate or illegitimate, and knew that an abortion would shock her parents beyond recall.

Her insistence on remaining a virgin kept Freddie surprisingly faithful. Sentimentally he took her to see the aunt who had brought him up since his parents had died in an accident when he was a little boy, and the aunt approved wholeheartedly of the match.

Muriel left the Central at the end of the Spring term. Two months later, she and Freddie were married. After the honeymoon, they settled in Coulsdon — conveniently near Croydon and the Baddeleys on the one hand and Freddie's work on the other — in a small modern detached house in South Road, on which Ernie had made the first down payment as a wedding present.

Muriel was completely happy, and Freddie seemed so. They had two children in quick succession — Susannah, and Ernest Charles, who from the beginning was known as Charlie. Muriel resented the arrival of Susannah, as she was still after all only twenty, but from the moment Charlie appeared, she adored him.

Just as Ernie Baddeley had escaped the worst effects of the depression and unemployment after the war, so Freddie managed to escape the worst effects of the depression of the Thirties. Ernie was always on hand to help out financially when the going was rough, and became as doting a grandfather as he had been a father; and Amy was the perfect grandmother. She loved nothing better than visiting Muriel and the children bearing a cornucopia of clothes and food, and on her arrival she always set to, helping with the housework and the cooking — though, to do her justice, Muriel was herself a good house-keeper. Muriel nonetheless enjoyed her mother's visits, and between them the family seemed to blossom in the brightly curtained, everlastingly scrubbed little house. The only cloud on Muriel's horizon was that Freddie's job seemed to demand his travelling very frequently — even on various slightly mysterious missions at weekends. In all other respects, the marriage seemed to her ideal.

As the Thirties progressed, Freddie became more and more excitable about the possibility of another war. He became increasingly nervous, and had some quite unpleasant argu-ments with Ernie Baddeley about Fascism. Freddie admired Hitler and Mussolini, and Oswald Mosley, and he saw no reason to fight against regimes which he believed posed no threat to Britain. On the other hand, he was fanatically anti-Communist. Ernie was a Socialist, and disapproved violently of dictatorships. Muriel, who took no interest whatever in politics, couldn't see what all the fuss was about. She was happy. She didn't think a war likely and was distressed to see that their ideologies were tearing apart the two men she loved best. Freddie was angry with her for not taking his side against her father; and the children, in the suddenly strained atmosphere, became querulous and difficult to handle.

World War Two broke out when Susannah was four and Charlie three, and quite soon Freddie was called up. On the day of his call-up he vanished without trace ... and neither Muriel nor the Army ever saw him again.

Muriel was utterly bewildered. It was true that he hadn't been acting himself lately, and that he had been impatient with her quite often, but she had believed that the tensions would pass in the course of time, and had also genuinely believed that he was a very happily married man. It took quite a while for her to accept the fact that he had left her and, during her period of hope, her parents were a great solace. Her finances became a severe problem; without regular assistance from her parents she would never have got by on what Freddie had given her, and now even that pittance had stopped. Muriel had no wish to join any of the Services; but she got a job working part-time in a café down the road and, in order to appear 'patriotic', spent a couple of mornings a week in the town hall, turning worn sheets into bandages and collecting clothes for the child evacuees due to be sent into the country to escape the bombing.

Her salvation came unexpectedly through an old school-friend, Sheila Goring, who was now in advertising in Croydon and engaged in propaganda work for the Government. Remembering that Muriel had trained as an actress, Sheila offered to use her as a photographic model. Muriel was still very pretty, so it seemed a good idea.

Muriel turned up rather nervously for the interview, flanked by Susannah, now nearing six years old, and little Charlie. Both were extremely decorative children and the three of them together made an enchanting picture. Charlie was as fair as Muriel, with huge blue eyes, a small nose and a wide, full-lipped mouth. He laughed often, and on his best behaviour looked like an Italian *putto*. Susannah had the jet-black hair, oval face and grey eyes of her father. She also had his beautiful hands. Her expression was more serious than Charlie's, but very sweet.

Sheila introduced the three of them to her photographer, who was so impressed that he took several studio stills of them all; they passed this test with flying colours. On later sessions, however, Charlie became bored with modelling, and his manners were so abominable that he was used less and less. Muriel's prettiness was not enough for her to be given a great deal of work, and finally it was Susannah who began making a steady income.

CHAPTER THREE

Muriel's reactions to Susannah's success were fiercely ambivalent. That Susannah should be preferred at work to Muriel's angelic Charlie seemed an impertinence; that Susannah should be preferred to Muriel herself was a profound personal rebuff. Also, Susannah had been Freddie's favourite. This now counted against the child, as did the fact that in many ways she was disturbingly like her father. On the other hand, the money Susannah earned was extremely useful.

Although Muriel knew in her heart that she would never have made an actress, she gave herself the airs and graces of a success blighted only by a too-young marriage — which, indeed, was how her parents regarded her. That she, in such circumstances, should be passed over for Susannah (who in Muriel's eyes was neither pretty nor interesting) was something else for which, for the rest of her life, she would never forgive her daughter.

Susannah became a minor celebrity through the propaganda pictures that were used of her, and this too angered Muriel; though, again, since she herself automatically became a celebrity by proxy, she thoroughly enjoyed her 'fame'. To add to Muriel's fury, Susannah herself enjoyed none of it. She was an obedient child, so she did as she was told, but she was by nature studious — though from where she had developed such a propensity, Muriel simply couldn't imagine, refusing to admit that her mother, the former schoolmistress, had been cleverer than Ernie. Susannah was at her happiest reading. She loved school, too, and very early excelled at literature and languages. She realised sadly that, by a fluke, it was she who was keeping the family afloat; as she loved her mother dearly

19

(although constantly hurt by Muriel's obvious preference for Charlie), she did her best to please.

During the Blitz, the combination of modelling after school hours and losing sleep reduced the child to exhaustion. Muriel recognised this, but it didn't placate her. In her eyes Susannah was a very lucky little girl who was too spoilt to realise it. Here she was, a celebrity already, and all she did was worry about falling behind with her schoolwork! How ridiculous she was! With a career already mapped out for her, what use was conventional learning to Susannah? She would become a famous model, and marry some rich and eligible man after the war was over, and with luck she would support Muriel and Charlie to the end of their days. So what use were literature or languages? A girl who was famous could get along well enough speaking only English.

Though highly-strung in many ways, Muriel was behaving throughout as though the war didn't exist. Since she had no man in the Services, she was uninvolved emotionally, and except for the air-raids, which all civilians living near London experienced, she tried to ignore the 'crisis', as she called it. She was brave about air raids, and, to the indignation of her neighbours, refused to take to the air-raid shelters; but in a curious way, this became reflected in her children, and it calmed them. Like everyone else she lived on sparse rations — dried eggs and, sometimes, as a treat when she could get it, whale meat as a substitute for steak — but, because of Susannah's fame, she managed to do well on the black market; and though the little house had the now required dreary black-out curtains, and most of the necessities of life, like soap and clothes, were in short supply, she still managed to keep the place surprisingly bright and cheerful, and her children smart and self-respecting.

Once or twice, Susannah protested mildly at her work load. She had a passionate wish to live as normal a life as any child could during the war, but when she said so, her mother flew into such ungovernable rages that she found it best to carry on as before. Endlessly her mother rammed down Susannah's throat the fact that she was lucky. She screamed about her own self-sacrifices for the children. 'But for you two, I should have been a star of stage and screen,' she said. 'Freddie didn't mind my being an actress at all. He was proud of me, and in fact I believe he would have been with me still, if I hadn't started a family so early. He met a budding actress, with the world at her feet. He had a family far too soon, and so did I, before either of us had begun to make our way in the world. Not that I'm complaining, mark you,' here Muriel would sigh the heavy sigh of martyrdom, 'but it's a fact. You, Susannah, now have the responsibility of realising all my hopes and dreams.'

Muriel became greedier and greedier as the jobs for her daughter multiplied. Susannah became the family drudge. She realised that, no matter how hard she worked or how much money she earned, her mother would always prefer Charlie, and grew increasingly unhappy. Her grandmother was an ally, but even she was too firmly caught up in the reflected glory of Susannah's career to be of much practical help. Her grandfather always took Muriel's side, as he had done ever since she was born. Charlie tormented her, knowing only too well the exact state of his mother's feelings. No matter how badly he behaved, or how idle he was at school, he was sure of his mother's support, and he only had to pretend to cry a little at the fact that he 'didn't lead as glamorous a life as his sister', to bring Muriel's wrath down on Susannah's innocent head. He also tormented Susannah physically, pinching her and punching her at will, always entirely without punishment. All this bred in Susannah a life-long diffidence and lack of confidence.

The war ended at last, and, when she was ten, Susannah was offered her first film part by Gainsborough Pictures. She was to play the daughter of Marilyn de la Roche, Britain's favourite film star. Because Muriel took Charlie along to the interview, he too got a tiny part. Muriel was ecstatic. The most perfect thing of all, she thought, would have been if all three of them had been engaged; but that Charlie was to make his 'debut on the screen' was almost enough.

The film was made at Gainsborough's main studios at Lime Grove, near Shepherd's Bush. Susannah was given a dressing room to herself, but the presence of Muriel, who was naturally expected to look after her, and of Charlie on the days he was called, made rest of any kind impossible.

Susannah took to filming like a duck to water, and she found in Marilyn a firm friend and ally. Marilyn loved Susannah at

sight. She was happily married to a theatrical agent but had no
children of her own, so was inclined to mother Susannah in
spite of Muriel's constant presence. Marilyn saw at once that
Muriel loved only Charlie, and realised also that Susannah had
a strong desire to learn. Her husband, Jan, was too old to be
called up, but he had volunteered for the Observer Corps. He
spent hours with Susannah, talking about his passions —
books and paintings — and though this aroused Muriel's
jealousy, she pretended to the de la Roches that she was
grateful to them for 'looking after my wonderful little
daughter.' This deceived no one but it did allow the de la
Roches to take Susannah home from time to time, and to give
her a startlingly fresh outlook on life.

Susannah fell in love with Marilyn's house at Denham. All
the rooms had an elegance and charm that delighted her
instinctively. Cautiously and carefully, Marilyn and Jan taught
Susannah the beginnings of taste; they also gave her lessons in
voice production, and in return discovered a quick and eager
pupil. Marilyn helped her, too, with her acting on the film,
with the result that the child played her part well and sincerely.

Charlie, on the other hand, in his usual perverse manner,
made enemies wherever he went. He was rude and intractable.
He never learned his words, and frequently arrived on the set
late, all of which his mother indulgently put down to a natural
envy of his sister's perennially 'good fortune'. His career in
British films ended as soon as it began.

After excellent notices for her performance in the film,
Susannah was sent the following year to Aida Foster's, the
famous dramatic school for children in Golder's Green. It had
started with five pupils (one of them Jean Simmons) in 1941,
originally only for dancing and drama; soon it had included
general education in its syllabus, since with wartime travel
difficulties its pupils found it impossible to combine Aida
Foster's classes with conventional schooling. From then on,
numbers snowballed. It was not a boarding school, so
Susannah was boarded out with Sheila Goring's sister, who
lived near by.

Susannah was a good deal happier here than at home, and she
managed to obtain quite a lot of work, modelling, broad-
casting and filming small parts. This was encouraged at the

school, and Aida Foster became her agent. Muriel and Charlie settled down very comfortably without her, and Susannah's health greatly improved with the silent nights and slightly better food that the end of the war provided.

Muriel had never evacuated her children away from Coulsdon, on the grounds that she didn't want to stand in the way of her daughter's career. She and Charlie had just had to be 'extra brave for Susannah's sake'. Now, with Susannah billeted in Golder's Green, Muriel decided to take in paying guests, mostly travelling salesmen, with whom she often had transitory affairs. If an affair looked like being more permanent than the others, the man was known as an 'Uncle', and, though both Charlie and Susannah (who returned at weekends,) recognised the situation for what it was, Muriel was able to preserve a kind of decorum in front of her neighbours and her parents.

Susannah hated this new turn of events but, as she was away most of the time, was able to shut her eyes to what was going on. Charlie liked it. He quickly learned how to turn the situation to his own advantage, earning tips for his discretion in the early stages of the affairs, and accepting expensive presents for keeping out of the way when an affair was steadying into semi-permanency. Charlie was sharp, but inclined to be crooked; and Charlie knew how to enjoy himself.

CHAPTER FOUR

When Susannah was fifteen, to her great excitement and anxiety, she was offered the part in *Jack of Hearts* — excitement because she would be working with Marilyn again, anxiety lest she should let her down. Marilyn had been in Hollywood for the last three years, and Susannah had never expected to see her again.

One day, out of the blue, Marilyn had telephoned her and invited her to lunch the following week, telling her that it was very important that she should look her best. At lunch she had met Max Parker, the director of the play, and Stephen Wallis, the manager, who was putting it on. Afterwards, at Marilyn's flat, she had read a scene to them and had got the part.

As in the film world, a child actress in the theatre has to have a chaperone, and Muriel at once eagerly volunteered. Charlie went to stay with his grandparents in order to be 'properly looked after', and Muriel and Susannah commuted daily; Muriel from Coulsdon, and Susannah from Golder's Green.

The rehearsals, for some strange reason, took place at the Bedford Ladies College in Regent's Park. Muriel would meet the current 'Uncle' each lunchtime at the Volunteer pub in Baker Street. As Susannah was too young to be allowed into a pub, her lunchtimes were spent, no matter whether the day was wet or fine, standing outside the Volunteer with a couple of sandwiches and a glass of orange squash in her hand, while her mother and 'Uncle' enjoyed themselves indoors. Driving past one day, Marilyn saw Susannah leaning wearily against the wall of the pub, and was furious. She immediately arranged that she and Susannah should be provided daily with a picnic lunch in the rehearsal room, and although Muriel, in turn, was angry (realising that Marilyn had noticed her treatment of Susannah) she allowed the situation to persist, as at least it left her free to spend her own lunch-hour as she wished.

Susannah enjoyed acting for the stage. She found the difference from film work to be mostly a matter of projection; the quality of sincerity had to be the same in both mediums. Marilyn gave her a mass of valuable advice. She taught her about performing with truth and integrity, while yet learning to listen for the audience's reaction. She showed her how to 'kill' a bad laugh, how to win a silence for her emotional moments, and how to achieve her own laughs either by 'building them' (that is, 'asking' for them in an acceptable manner) or by a combination of timing and clarity. 'Belly-laughs are belly-laughs the world over,' she said. 'It's the other laughs which one has to work for, and it's these techniques which add up to the creative side of a stage performance. An understanding of the part and character, an original mind, a sense of humour and perfect timing make up a pretty good performance! Plus, of course, the capacity for hard work. But that hard work is worth it. The public isn't really fooled by idleness and short-cuts, though some critics are.'

Susannah was an apt pupil, and the technical side of her work gave her, for the first time, a real satisfaction. Marilyn's theories about acting in the theatre fascinated her and kept her utterly absorbed during the run of the play. Unlike many actors, who get bored if they are in a long run, she found that working out the techniques for gaining her effects, at the same time as living the part with an intensity seldom encountered in real life, gave her a goal to strive for each night; and since each night the audience was different, each night was a new excitement. The perfect performance eluded her, as it eludes every actor throughout his life (even excepting the one or two magical evenings when everything seems to go the actor's way); but she was happy searching it out.

Another bonus from her point of view was the inclusion of Tony Falk, the fat little boy who played her brother. Precocious, talented, sophisticated beyond his years after a whole lifetime already spent on the stage, he had a zany, outrageous sense of humour, and made her laugh more than anyone she had ever known. The fact that there was another child in the cast with her took much of the strain off working so intensively in an adult world.

The play opened cold at the Globe Theatre, to surprisingly good notices — 'surprisingly', because critics seldom see plays which haven't been on tour for several weeks. Susannah herself got a good press (*The Times* said that she was sincere and moving — and the *Evening Standard* praised her comedy) and Marilyn an excellent one. Muriel enjoyed having a 'West End star' as she called her, for a daughter, and for a while Susannah basked gratefully in maternal approval.

Presently, though, being away so much from home in the evenings made Muriel restless; and when she was restless, she became bored and bad-tempered. On these occasions she would go into her usual routine of telling Susannah what sacrifices she was making for her daughter's career. Her trouble was that one of her affairs at home was settling down to a steady relationship, and Muriel, who had really fallen in love once again, was frightened of losing her man. As it turned out, however, her frequent absences actually did make Jacko Brunswick's heart grow fonder. He had always before found 'easy market' (his own words); as in the case of Freddie, the enforced waiting made him comparatively faithful.

From Susannah's point of view, her mother couldn't have chosen a more unsatisfactory lover. All that Jacko stood for, Susannah detested. He was a braggart, drank too much, was a compulsive womaniser, and told lies. Susannah was sure that even his name wasn't genuine, but had been made up to give him the pretence of good family connections. He was in his late forties, and said he had been in the RAF in the war. His language, when it didn't consist of four-letter obscenities, was littered with words like 'wizard' and 'prang' and 'old boy'. His hazel eyes were slightly watery, his nose was beginning to be bulbous, with blue veining starting to become prominent, and his mouth was slack and surprisingly red. His hair was dark on top and white at the temples, and Muriel thought him very handsome and the 'perfect gentleman'. Certainly, his easy manner, deceptively constant laughter and complete assurance with women seemed to be irresistible.

Jacko's 'jobs' were mysterious. Sometimes he was in the money, sometimes he was broke, but he always paid the rent regularly. Susannah's private belief was that he was an addicted gambler on the horses; but Muriel believed his claim that he played the Stock Exchange.

In spite of her fears of losing Jacko, Muriel was unwilling to give up her rôle as Susannah's chaperone. Her jealousy of the child was so profound that in some odd way it was a necessity for her to be near her. Besides, she was paid for it, and the money meant a great deal to her; she would have had to pay for a substitute in any case. Perhaps because Freddie's defection had made her feel chronically insecure, or perhaps only because she was greedy, she had a powerful urge to collect and keep money. 'When you come right down to it,' she'd say, 'money is what life is all about.' Nevertheless, Jacko's lure became increasingly strong; and since Jacko too needed her more and more (although somewhere there was a deserted Mrs Brunswick, so he couldn't marry her), he and Muriel had an 'understood marriage', as Jacko described it, and Muriel started calling herself Mrs Brunswick.

From the moment he had 'married' Muriel, Jacko's manner in the home changed. He was no longer a lodger and a supplicant. He was the man of the house, and a swaggering bully. He insisted on being called 'Father' by both Susannah and Charlie, and he took to spending more and more time in the house, being waited on hand and foot by a besotted Muriel. Surprisingly, since he had a genuine affection for Muriel, however casual, he began drinking too much, and drink made him quarrelsome and tiresome. It also made him amorous, so Muriel tolerated it. Charlie, still billeted with his grandparents, was spared the worst excesses of his new 'father's' behaviour; but Susannah, at home for the school holidays from Aida Foster's, was disgusted, and this became another bone of contention between mother and daughter. Muriel called Susannah a snob, and told her that she was giving herself airs just because she was a 'star'.

Susannah denied this hotly. She also, without success, tried to explain to her mother that stardom was a technical term, which denoted having one's name above the title of the play, which Susannah hadn't yet achieved. Muriel neither understood nor was satisfied with this explanation. Susannah knew that her mother was seeking an excuse to find fault with her again, and she also understood that, now that Muriel and Jacko were 'married', Muriel was nervous that he might once again begin to stray.

Susannah was nervous too. She was fully aware that, although she was so young, Jacko found her attractive. This terrified her. Jacko was always under her feet at the house. He pretended to be something of an invalid who needed waiting on. The stomach ulcers which he claimed to have contracted in the RAF and.to have been responsible for his being invalided out, had started playing him up again, he said. Muriel nannied him anxiously, and both of them expected Susannah to nanny him, too. Susannah tried to keep out of his way, and Jacko, seeing it, was furious. She was maturing fast, and showed every sign of achieving an exceptionally good figure. She was also growing into an outstanding beauty, and although she herself disparaged her looks, she was fully aware that Jacko did not.

Susannah had no idea how to cope with the situation. Although in her panic she tried to ensure that she was never with him alone, Jacko was wise to her, and found ways to outwit her. Suddenly he took to lying in bed on Sunday mornings, and ordered Susannah to bring him his breakfast in bed — 'in order,' he said, 'to save Muriel trouble'. Unfortunately Muriel agreed to this, as in fact it was a help to her to have him out of the way at a time when she had her hands full feeding the other lodgers.

When Susannah reached his room, Jacko used to make her sit on the bed while he was eating his breakfast, and he made suggestive remarks about her figure and pawed at her breasts. She saw to it that the breakfast tray was always between them, but she knew that if Jacko really meant business it would take more than a tray to protect her.

One day, her nerves getting the better of her, Susannah told Muriel something of her fears. It was a disastrous thing to do. Muriel was angrier than Susannah had ever seen her. She refused to believe any evil of Jacko, and, because Susannah had criticised him in such terms, her natural jealousy of the girl assumed titanic proportions. Susannah's life became more difficult than ever — especially as Jacko was aware of what had happened and was delighted at the result.

At the theatre, Marilyn worried for her young friend, but Susannah was too loyal to her mother to tell Marilyn the whole truth. All she could do was to long for the time when she could leave home altogether.

CHAPTER FIVE

Eventually the play came to an end, and Susannah was out of a job. Muriel told her that, as she was now a big girl, and no money was coming in, she would have to live at home and commute to Golder's Green during the week. Aida Foster was still her agent, so Susannah went to see her to ask if there was any new work for her. Aida explained to her gently that, from now on, just 'any sort of work' was out of the question: it had to be a job of some quality, she said, and for the moment nothing suitable had made itself known. Susannah must be very careful what she chose to do next; she had made a good start, and it was stupid to throw away what she had achieved so far.

'But Mother needs the money!' exclaimed Susannah anxiously.

'Not many mothers are so dependent on the earnings of their teenage daughters,' replied Aida grimly, 'and you can tell Mrs Brunswick that, in the long run, you and she will do better if you are patient and wait until the right job comes along.'

Worried, Susannah returned home, where her mother, all icy contempt, treated her once more as the family drudge.

From the moment that mother and daughter were freed from the necessity of going to the theatre every night, it was possible for Charlie to return, and he came back full of bounce and bad behaviour. Susannah could never make out why he was so tiresome when he already had so much of his mother's doting attention but, on his return this time, the presence of Jacko seemed to send him berserk, and even Muriel became slightly exasperated. Quite soon, though, he saw the advantages of having Jacko permanently installed, so, pulling himself together, he capitalised on the situation. He carefully reconnoitred Jacko's weaknesses, and perhaps only he fully realised the extent of Jacko's need for drink. For money, cash down, he saw to it that Jacko was amply supplied, without Muriel's knowledge. He and Jacko often played two-handed poker, in Charlie's bedroom, and Charlie soon became good enough to fleece Jacko of a tidy sum each week. Jacko was less than pleased, but gambling was an addiction; he either had to stop playing, and accuse Charlie of the cheating he was sure went on, or go on playing and let Charlie cheat. He went on playing.

Muriel loved having the two men under her roof. The other lodgers gave little trouble, and with Susannah's help in the evenings and at the weekends as housemaid and kitchen maid, she was positively sunny-tempered.

One of the perks that Charlie demanded from Jacko was his complicity when Charlie wanted to spend an evening away from home. Although he was only nearing sixteen, Charlie was exceptionally attractive to women and appeared far older than his years. He had already become adept at a great many grown-up sports, as he called them, and liked being out until very late some nights.

So, unexpectedly, did Muriel. Once having 'married' Jacko, she liked one or two evenings away from her lodgers.

Initially, Jacko was happy enough to stay in, provided that there was a sufficient amount of drink, a good fire if it was cold, and the wireless to listen to, and provided that Muriel came back cheerful and compliant; but Susannah hated the evenings when her mother and brother were both away from home. The trouble was that the outings never appeared to be pre-arranged, so she was often caught out, with no invited girl-friend to protect her from the increasingly lecherous eye of her 'step-father'. It was not safe to go to her bedroom at all on these occasions, because Jacko's intentions only too evidently included bed. There was a sofa in the living room, but she knew that would prove too inviting; and since the drink and the music on the wireless inflamed Jacko's need for 'romance', as he called it, and since she had already confided her fears to Muriel and suffered for it, she was trapped.

'I only want one little kiss from my lovely li'l step-chile,' Jacko would implore drunkenly. 'Your mother would gimme li'l kiss. Your mother is a gran' ol' lady and the love of ol' Jacko's life. So her daughter sh'd be kine. Step-daughters sh'd alwiss be kine. Thass wha' step-daughters are for.' Susannah would try and laugh the situation off, but the thought of Jacko mauling her about so scared and horrified her that her laughter sounded as false as it indeed was; and Jacko, hearing it, resented it.

Susannah was now nearly seventeen; but, despite her growing beauty, she didn't find it easy to date boy-friends. To begin with, she was shy; to go on with, her mother's unswerving preference for Charlie made her in her own eyes unlovable and undesirable; and, further, her mother's chosen career for her was having its effect and she was feeling the first faint stirrings of ambition. On their side, the local boys found her 'fame' slightly intimidating, her mother frankly frightening, and Susannah's own gaucheness unattractive. So the evenings passed with Susannah rather guiltily encouraging her 'step-father' to drink himself into a stupor before his desires became impossible to fend off; and Jacko, on the whole, obliging.

Before long, however, Jacko began to resent Muriel's habit of leaving him at home when she went off to join her cronies at the pub. One evening he asked if he might accompany her but, to his surprise, Muriel refused. He hadn't really wanted an evening with a 'bunch of old hags', but her refusal rankled all the same. How could she prefer their company to his? What's more, she was leaving her handsome Lothario night after night in the house with her young and beautiful daughter — certain that Susannah wanted nothing to do with him! This was another major blow to his self-esteem.

When he remonstrated with Muriel, she laughed and said that, when she was indeed his wife, then she would consider staying at home. This unnerved him slightly. Was she getting tired of him? Would he have to marry her after all in order to keep her with him? He didn't want to. He was through with marriage. Her house was comfortable, and she and Susannah cooked well and kept the place clean and tidy. As Muriel's 'husband', he had a free and cushy billet which he had no intention of losing. What could he do, other than offer marriage, to be certain of keeping it?

Make her jealous ... ! Go out himself ... ! (Not often enough to upset her, but enough to make her jealous.) Of course, that was it! In his younger days he'd been out on the prowl most nights looking for crumpet, and getting it. Now he was older, and lazier, and Muriel satisfied him; but if she wanted competition, she could have it! He'd get hold of some young bird and show Muriel he wasn't the type of man you could neglect. She'd see the error of her ways, and come running back to him. Wizard idea! Good-oh!

A few days later, therefore, he told a surprised Muriel that he, too, had a date. He knew the pub she always went to, so swaggered his way to The Feathers, further down the road. One of the lodgers had been there a few evenings ago and had told him about some bird who was there nearly every night, looking for trouble. Well, Jacko would see that she got it!

Jacko was surprised to find how much he enjoyed the feeling of being out and about again, on his own. Muriel was perhaps on to something when she insisted that freedom had its merits; but then Muriel was not out for sex, only to have a break from routine — or so she said. Jacko was confident of success, his pockets jingled with the money he had won the day before on the three-thirty, and he had enjoyed smartening himself up. He was ready for anything.

At least he thought he was.

The Feathers was cosy and warm. A good fire blazed in the grate. The glasses were brightly polished. The barmaid gave him a flatteringly lingering look when he ordered a double Scotch and soda, and he noticed immediately the bird who was looking for trouble. She was a stunner. She had on a scarlet woollen dress which hugged her ample figure. She wore black silk stockings on her beautiful long legs, and had fair, glistening, well-brushed hair. She'd got class, that was evident, so what was she doing here? She looked little more than a child but she was knocking back her drink as though there was no tomorrow, and the barmaid obviously knew her well. She spoke in an affected drawl, and it fascinated Jacko that she couldn't pronounce her r's.

There was a stool beside her, so he sat down on it, and gave her the eye. She stared back at him coolly. A wonderful mouth to kiss, he thought gloatingly; generous, and beautifully shaped. He waited a bit before attempting to talk to her. It had suddenly become important to him to succeed with her. She might be out for trouble, and indeed get it, but she wouldn't want trouble from just anyone. He licked his lips nervously, then sneered at himself — Jacko, the great lover, being nervous of a tart!

He cleared his throat. 'Good evening,' he said, and gave her a flashing smile. 'I don't think I've seen you around before.'

He saw that the barmaid was looking amused, which irritated him.

'I'm talking to you, Miss,' he said loudly.

She suddenly seemed aware of him as a fellow human being, and said, as though surprised, 'Mrs.'

This threw him. 'Mrs?' he asked, floundering. 'You look a little young to be married.'

'I am,' she said, expressionlessly, 'a little young.'

He pressed on.

'I'm Jacko Brunswick,' he said. 'My friends all call me Jacko.'

'I wonder why,' she replied, deadpan, and he flushed.

'Have a drink?' he asked.

'Why not?'

'What's the tipple?'

'Vodka and tonic,' she said. 'Double.'

He ordered her a double, and a whisky for himself. 'Cheers,' he said.

'Mud in yours,' she replied.

Conversation languished while his brain raced for something to say that might interest her. Then he remembered that he hadn't asked her name. 'Have *you* a name?' he asked roguishly.

'Oh, yes,' she replied. 'I have a name.'

'What is it?'

'Mrs Maltravers,' she replied.

'Really?' he asked. It sounded a stupid sort of name. He wondered if she was laughing at him.

'Weally,' she replied.

'And a christian name?'

'Certainly. My mother is a devout Catholic.'

He thought he heard one of the customers snigger.

He went on doggedly. 'So what's your christian name?'

'Emelda,' she said.

'Emelda,' he repeated. 'That's a very unusual name.'

'Not in our family,' she answered.

He decided to be bold. 'I hear you're in here every night,' he said. 'A dicky bird told me.'

'Fascinating,' she drawled, but there was an edge to her voice, and he heard it.

'If you're married,' he said, slightly unpleasantly, 'where's hubby?'

'Under the sod,' she replied.

'Dead?'

'Oh, dear me, no!'

'Is that supposed to be funny?' he asked, suddenly belligerent.

'Tragic,' she replied tersely.

He brooded over his whisky. Was his pursuit of her worth it? She would certainly be no push-over. He hated her arrogance, and he dreaded rejection. All the same, a conquest here would certainly boost his ego, and he needed a boost. Besides, he could sense that the whole clientèle of the pub were watching their contest, and he wasn't going to be beaten by a young girl. Strangely, too, they seemed to be on her side.

He eyed her again, and to his annoyance felt his pulse quicken and his mouth go dry. She'd be good in bed, he was sure, and he'd never laid one of her kind before.

'Feeling peckish?' he asked tentatively.

'Where were you thinking of taking me?' she demanded in reply.

'Hey! Not so fast!' he said. 'I'm not thinking of taking you anywhere, but I want a snack and I wondered if you'd join me?'

She considered this carefully. Finally she said slowly, 'OK. Suits me.'

He felt good. It was a start. 'So what's the ticket?'

She smiled briefly and ordered a salad.

'And another drink?'

'Please.'

'You shouldn't, you know,' he said, and he was astonished

to find that he was feeling almost paternal suddenly. 'Too much drink isn't good for a girl like you.'

'Maybe not.' She shrugged her shoulders.

The food was handed over the bar, and Jacko led her to a small table by the fire, gallantly drawing out her chair for her. She seemed amused, but said nothing.

All the time they were eating he stared at her, but she didn't seem to notice. Finally he said, 'Not much of a talker, are you?'

'No.'

'Makes a change in a woman.'

She was silent.

'You want to tell me about yourself?'

'No, thank you.'

'I'd like to hear. I bet it's a good story.'

'No thanks.'

'Want to hear about me?'

'If you wish.'

'I was in the RAF.'

'You and several others,' she said.

He didn't like this, but he said, 'Yeah. I enjoyed it. Funny isn't it? I was dead scared most of the time, but I enjoyed it.'

'Good.'

'Still, I'm glad it's all over.'

'Quite.'

Once again he was non-plussed. He changed the subject. 'Is it true that you come here most nights?'

'Yes.'

'Not got a home to go to?'

'Oh, yes, I've got a home.'

'But you don't like it?'

'I like it very much.'

'Then why come here so often?'

She shook her head. 'Why are *you* here?' she asked.

Jacko puffed out his chest. 'I've been a bit of a stay-at-home these last few months, and it was beginning to pall.'

'I see.'

In desperation after a further silence, he said, coaxingly, 'Go on. Tell me about yourself. You interest me. Really you do.'

She answered slowly, as if each word was very important.

'OK. I was born in Japan, but came back a couple of years before the war. I liked Japan.'

'You *were* on our side, during the war ...?' he quipped.

'Oh, yes,' she said. 'Very much so. But my stay in Japan taught me a great many useful things.'

'Such as?'

'Such as how to look after myself, if the need arose.'

'Has the need arisen?'

'That sort of need, yes. For my other sort of need, I'm not so good at taking care of myself.'

Jacko looked at her deliberately. 'A beautiful girl like you shouldn't have to take care of herself,' he said. 'That's what men are for.'

She laughed shortly. 'I've often wondered,' she answered.

He frowned. 'Doesn't hubby mind you being out every night?'

'No.'

'He's a fool.'

'I'm inclined to agree.'

'You going home after this?'

'Yes.'

'Straight home?'

'After another couple of drinks, yes.'

'Hubby there tonight?'

'No.'

This was better. 'May I see you home?'

'Why not?'

He was encouraged. He didn't like her. He thought her a bitch, and, truth to tell, a bore; but she had something which drove him wild for her physically. He straightened his shoulders, and flashed her his most ingratiating smile. 'You don't want another drink,' he said. 'I'll take you home now.'

'I want another drink,' she said. 'A double. Come to that, I want two doubles!'

She seemed to be getting excitable, so he anxiously calmed her. 'OK, OK,' he said. 'Two doubles, and then I take you home. It's a deal?'

'It's a deal,' she said.

He studied her again, this time slightly worried. She had drunk a great deal, but, except for an inner tension which she evidently couldn't quite control, had remained, as far as he could see, completely sober. She must have a head like teak! Unless she was one of those silly bitches who looked OK until they hit the cold air outside, then passed out! Well, there was nothing he could do about it. She wouldn't go home unless he gave her two more drinks, and, unless she agreed to go home with him, he couldn't lay her. And to lay her he was determined, or his name wasn't Jacko Brunswick! . . . which in fact it wasn't, so this made him laugh.

She looked surprised. 'What are you laughing at?' she asked. 'You're not plastered are you?' She peered at him, frowning.

Jacko was hurt. 'Plastered?' he demanded. 'Plastered? I haven't drunk one tenth of what you've drunk!'

'That doesn't mean you're not plastered,' she answered calmly.

She drank the two vodkas quite quickly, and neither of them seemed to have the smallest effect. Jacko's two whiskies, on the other hand, had certainly had an influence. The world seemed a more indefinite, but definitely more inviting place. He felt good-tempered and relaxed; capable of anything. He was a King and a Conqueror. He was the nice neighbourhood chappie from next door. The world was wide open for a brilliant man like Jacko. The world was also a closed-in bedroom, where he seduced Emelda Maltravers endlessly. Yet at the same time he felt eternally bound to his 'old lady', Muriel. He felt sentimental about her, almost maudlin.

'Well,' said Mrs Maltravers suddenly, breaking into his fantasies. 'Who's for hitting the trail?'

For a moment he was bemused.

'You said you'd see me home,' she said.

'Oh. Yeah, yeah. I'll see you home.' He snapped his fingers for the bill, reeled when he saw what he had spent, added an unnecessarily large tip and lurched towards Mrs Maltravers's chair. 'C'mon, Emelda,' he said. 'We're hitting the trail.'

She rose quickly, found a fox stole from somewhere, fastened it around her shoulders and headed for the door. Jacko followed her.

The night air came as a shock. Jacko staggered from the amount of drink he had consumed. Emelda was walking quickly ahead and he almost had to run to keep up with her.

When he was alongside her, he took her arm, and she allowed it. 'Where do you live?' he asked.

'At the Manor, in Norwood East Fields.'

'Christ!' he said. 'We'll need a taxi!'

'That's right.'

'It's about five miles out.'

'Slightly more,' she replied pedantically, and her voice jarred on him. He nearly asked her if she had the money to pay, but, remembering he was going to lay her, decided against it.

A taxi suddenly cruised up beside them and they got in. How would he get home? It would be the devil and all to walk! Again he wondered if this bloody little bitch was worth it. Again he decided that she was. Just.

He put his arm around her in the cab, and though he thought she shifted a little away from him, his arm was still around her shoulders — just. The taxi was being driven at a tremendous pace. It swerved, throwing her against him, and he took the opportunity to drag her towards him and kiss her on the lips.

The kiss excited him enormously, and the feeling of her body pressed against his made him feel so randy that he wanted to take her there and then. He fumbled with her skirts, and she drew away at once, but the taxi was still cornering so she was still lying against him. He kissed her again, and again he began to fumble. She struggled, but he was much stronger, and his hand was exploring the top of her silk stockings. Now she was fighting, but he held her without effort. His senses were swimming, but he was enormously intent. Either by mistake or design she eased her breast against him, and this momentarily diverted him. His hand left her skirts and began undoing the buttons of her dress. His lips were still clamped to hers, and she was still struggling. It was wonderful! She was fighting with all her strength, but, compared to his, her strength was nothing. His tongue was probing the inside of her mouth. He found her left nipple and squeezed the breast savagely. He flung a leg across her and began to pull down her pants. Her arms were flailing weakly, and she was groaning. He felt exultant. Christ, this was the life! She couldn't escape him, and once he'd had her in the taxi, he could take her as often as he wanted, in bed! She'd be mad for him. They all were.

He began to undo his flies. Immediately she gave him a kick which sent him sprawling to the floor, and in a second she had pulled back the glass partition and was screaming, 'For God's sake! Help me! He's trying to rape me! Stop this bloody cab. Oh, God, help me!'

The driver stood on his brakes, and she managed to get out. The driver leapt out, too, and hauled Jacko, dazed and bewildered, on to the road at their feet.

'Get back in, lady,' he said.

.But before Emelda could move, Jacko made a desperate lunge for her. She let him get unsteadily to his feet, and then, to his utter amazement, picked him up and threw him over her shoulder.

'There,' she said grimly, as he lay groaning on the road. 'Don't try anything again. I told you they taught me many things in Japan. That was one.' Her face was bruised and bleeding, and her dress was torn.

The driver was as amazed as Jacko. 'If they taught you how to take care of yourself like that in Japan or wherever, why didn't you do it in the cab?' he asked.

'No room. I couldn't get a hold,' she replied. 'Besides, you were driving much too fast.'

The driver looked disapproving, but said gruffly, 'Well, what do we do now?'

'Take me home,' said the woman. 'Without that scum.'

'You can't leave me here!' shouted Jacko. 'You were begging for trouble. Egging me on, she was,' he added, appealing to the driver. 'You can't leave me!'

Emelda Maltravers climbed into the taxi, and slammed the door. 'He tried to rape me,' she said tersely. 'He'd go to prison if he had succeeded, so take me home.'

Leaving Jacko dishevelled and dirty, bruised and considerably hurt, the cab drove away.

CHAPTER SIX

Muriel was still out when Jacko got back, although it was three o'clock in the morning. There was a note from Susannah to say that Muriel had suddenly been called to her parents, because Amy had developed pneumonia. She wanted Jacko to know that she was sorry, but she might be away some days. Susannah and Charlie were in bed.

Jacko knew he had had a lucky escape, in that neither Muriel nor Susannah had seen him in the state he was in, but he nonetheless felt aggrieved that two women in one evening had stood him up — three, if one included Susannah. He was extremely angry; physically sore, and mentally humiliated.

During the rest of the week, his sense of grievance grew. Muriel he didn't blame so much: her parents were a damned nuisance, but she really loved that terrible old Pop of hers, and was fond of her prissy and irritating mother. Although he grumbled about it, her loyalty was reassuring. (Besides, he had tried to two-time her, so his punishment was strictly justified.) No! It was the others he had the grudge against. And a grudge it certainly was!

Susannah's dislike of him was a daily insult. But for her, he could still have thought himself irresistible to women. Emelda's treatment of him seemed to confirm that his attraction was on the wane, and he couldn't bear it. One day he'd have his revenge on her, but not yet. For the moment, the whole business was too close for him to be dispassionate ...

Susannah was a different matter. She could be punished now. She was a stuck-up little prig and needed to be taken down a peg. What's more, she actually lived in the house: it was her duty to recognise who was the master there. Like

Emelda, she was asking for trouble. And she would get it. She wasn't much younger, either ...

On the Saturday night, there was nothing on the wireless to amuse Jacko — Charlie was out, so they couldn't play cards. He had tried to talk to Susannah but she had gone into the kitchen to avoid him, and he was bored and bad-tempered. He'd had too much to drink already, but he was prepared to drink a good deal more. Tonight he felt he needed a binge.

He supposed that Muriel would be away until Monday at least, and the other lodgers were, in his eyes, an insignificant lot. Now that he was no longer one of them, he found it demeaning to fraternise with them. Besides, he had the uncomfortable feeling that the story of his come-uppance on Tuesday night had got around. He was getting some pretty peculiar looks, and he didn't like it.

Drink didn't suit him either physically or mentally: after his first randy period, he became maudlin, then violent, and the following day he felt terrible. But he wanted to forget about Tuesday. He couldn't face himself now with his usual bravado and self-satisfaction — although he knew that this self-satisfaction wasn't real, just a cover-up for a deep-down dislike of himself. His lies and tall stories were a cover-up too; they filled a curious emptiness in his ego. He was — what had someone once called him? — a hollow man. Well, there wasn't much he could do about it! He wasn't young any more, and wasn't likely to change. He'd got away with it pretty well until now, and women liked him; at least, they always had until recently. And he liked them too; like drink, they made him temporarily forget his inadequacies. But on that one night, Emelda had rammed down his throat that he was a no-hoper. And Susannah found her own way of doing it all the time — the little bitch! He'd show her!

He went into the kitchen, where Susannah was peeling some potatoes. She looked pretty in her blue apron with her dark hair falling about all over the place.

'You all right, then?' he asked. 'Like me to give you a hand?'

She shook her head. 'No thanks,' she answered politely. 'It won't take long.'

'When you've finished, come and listen to the wireless with me,' he said. 'I get lonesome when your mother is away.'

He saw the slight look of dislike, but she said, 'OK. Where's Charlie?'

'Out, as usual,' said Jacko. 'Beats me what he finds to do at his age.'

Susannah didn't answer.

Jacko swaggered to the door. 'Ta-ra, then,' he said. 'See you later.'

Susannah sighed heavily after he'd shut the door. She'd smelt the drink on his breath, and prayed that Charlie would be back soon. She peeled the potatoes as slowly as she could, then prepared the carrots and onions for the pie she was making. She rolled out the pastry, put the finished pie in the oven, then sat down to read while it was cooking.

The door opened again. Jacko was considerably drunker. His face hardened when he saw that she was reading.

'I thought you were coming in to keep me company,' he said. 'You said you would.'

'I have to see how the pie is going, first, don't I?'

'Do you? Is a pie more important than me?'

'You won't enjoy it if I ruin it.'

'How long will it take?'

'Quite a bit,' said Susannah.

'Ten minutes? An hour? What?'

'An hour at least.'

'You don't have to do anything to it while it's cooking, do you?'

'Not really. But it's better to be here.'

'That's where you're wrong,' retorted Jacko. 'It's better to be with me when I ask you, even if the pie isn't quite perfect. Your mother knows how to look after a man, and she wouldn't like me to be lonesome.'

'She can't help being away when Gran is ill.'

'No, *she* can't help being away, but *you* can help me not to be lonely,' replied Jacko. 'If you're frightened of burning the damned pie, turn the oven off, and you can finish it tomorrow.'

'Unfortunately, I can't,' said Susannah anxiously. 'I've got this thing to do on the wireless tomorrow.'

He mimicked her: '"I've got this thing to do on the wireless!"' It was a parody of her voice. 'Oh, aren't we grand! Very exhausting, too, I'm sure.'

'No, it's not exhausting. Actually I quite enjoy broad-casting. It's simply that I want to help Mummy, and to see that there's something in the house for everyone to eat while she's not here.'

'Little Goody Two Shoes.'

Susannah flushed, but she didn't answer. Suddenly this reminded him of Emelda Travers.

'Turn the oven off, and come into the living room with me,' he ordered unpleasantly.

'I can't. Really I can't.'

'Oh, yes, you can.' All at once he was violently angry. He strode to the oven, turned it off himself, then spun her round and pushed her ahead of him. 'You'll bloody well do as you're told and like it, my girl!' he shouted.

He thought he heard a door open somewhere, and this made him even angrier. He almost threw her into the living room, slamming the door behind them, and hurled her towards the sofa. 'Now then,' he said. 'Sit there, and shurrup.'

Susannah hastily sat down as she was told, but took care to see that she was at the extreme end of the sofa.

She was frightened. Jacko had often tried to sneak up to her and give her a kiss, he had pinched her bottom and fondled her furtively; but he'd never manhandled her before, and, though she'd often seen him drunk, she'd never seen him so morose. His behaviour had been worrying her these last few days. He seemed to have been in some sort of a scrap on Tuesday night. He limped a bit, and his face was scratched and bruised.

When she had mentioned it to Charlie, he'd roared with laughter. 'Good old Step-Dad!' he'd said. 'He met his match, as anyone could have told him!'

'What does that mean?' asked Susannah.

'Never you mind,' replied Charlie, and roared with laughter again.

The living room was hot and stuffy, and the air was stale with beer. Susannah hated this room. Almost every row she'd ever had with her mother had taken place here, and always to the background of the wireless turned up full-blast, as it was now. Except for Marilyn's home in Denham, she hadn't seen many well-furnished houses; nonetheless, the decor here gave her a feeling of immense depression. The colours were too garish on the upholstering, and the brown-papered walls with the green bordering near the ceiling seemed to make the already small room seem even smaller. The clock on the mantelpiece was large and ugly, and it ticked too loudly; and even she could tell that the two pictures on the walls were badly painted, and sentimental into the bargain. The gas fire had a nasty habit of popping loudly, and hissing when it was lit, and there were pieces chipped off some of the bars. On the other hand, as Jacko has recognised with such pleasure, the room was kept fanatically clean, and the pewter mugs and brass fittings on the cupboards shone with polished care.

The wireless was blaring out one of the latest hit tunes, and Jacko, now slumped at the other end of the sofa, began tapping his feet to the rhythm. He had poured himself another pint and was staring into space. Susannah sat hardly daring to move. Finally he seemed to become aware of her, 'Join me in a drink,' he slurred.

'No thanks,' answered Susannah.

'Why not?'

'I told you, I have to work tomorrow.'

'Ah, yes. So you do. The broadcast! Our own little personal idol of millions is going to broadcast. Tell me, girlie, how exactly do you broadcast?'

Susannah was surprised. 'What d'you mean?'

'I mean, what do you do, exactly?'

'Well, for a play, which this is, you read off a script,' said Susannah.

'You don't have to learn anything?' asked Jacko.

'No. You just read.'

'And they pay you for that?' He sounded exaggeratedly surprised.

'Yes.'

'Just for reading off a sheet of paper?'

'Yes, but you have to do it well, or they wouldn't have you.'

'They pay you just for reading off a sheet of paper!' He whistled.

'Yes.'

'Well! Well! What are things coming to? Not what we in the RAF thought, when we risked our lives so that you and your kind could lie safe in your beds. No, indeed, that isn't what we thought the Brave New World was going to be like! Paying good money to someone to read off a sheet of paper!'

As Jacko's much-vaunted career in the RAF had been strictly a ground job, he had been in little more danger than Susannah herself, so there seemed no reply to this.

Jacko now turned and stared at her without speaking for a moment or two. Then he said, 'Tell me, Susannah, when your mother told you she was going to make me your step-father, were you pleased?'

Taken by surprise, Susannah hesitated fractionally before answering, which Jacko noticed. 'Of course!' she exclaimed, over-heartily.

'I see!' he sneered. 'Simply delighted.'

'Yes.'

'Good. I'm glad. You thought I'd make her happy?'

'Yes.'

'Why was that?'

'I don't understand.'

'Why did you think I'd make her happy? ... Go on, you interest me! Have a drink.'

'No thanks.'

' "No thanks." Well, why?'

'Because she's very fond of you.'

'Why do you suppose that is?'

'I don't know. She just is.'

'Do you suppose she thinks me good-looking?'

'Yes. I'm sure she does.'

'And do you?'

She hesitated again. 'Yes.'

'Good. I never knew that. How many men have you kissed, Susannah?'

'None.'

'Liar! You've kissed me.'

'Yes, but not like that.'

'Like what?'

'Like you and Mummy kiss.'

'How do we kiss?'

'Like people who love each other, I suppose.'

'Don't you love me?'

'That's different.'

'What's different?'

'You're in love, and you're grown-ups.'

'So you've never had a grown-up kiss?'

'No.'

'Don't you think you ought to get started? I mean, you're a big girl now. Don't want to get left on the shelf, do you? You ought to learn how, you know.'

'There's plenty of time.' Susannah laughed uneasily.

'I think not,' said Jacko, his voice becoming menacing. 'I think you ought to learn now.'

'I'd rather not,' said Susannah. She noticed that beads of sweat were coming out of the enlarged pores on his nose, and felt sick.

'Oh, indeed? You'd rather not! I thought you said you thought I was good-looking!'

'You're my step-father.'

'Not a blood relation. Not even your real step-father, if it comes to that.'

'Mummy wouldn't like it.'

'Mummy need never know. Unless you told her, and you wouldn't do that, would you? For your own sake as well as mine!'

'Charlie might come in.'

'You know as well as I do how Charlie spends most nights when his mother is away.'

'Yes,' said Susannah, 'and it worries me. Mummy would be terribly upset if she knew. After all, he's only a teenager, and it can't be right for him to get so dissipated so young.'

Jacko laughed. 'Dissipated!' he exclaimed. 'Oh, *aren't* we smart to use such long words!'

With a flash of spirit Susannah replied, 'You don't like me, so why do you want to kiss me?'

'Now, now, my dear. That's very naive,' answered Jacko. 'Men often get attracted to the women they dislike.'

'I'm not a woman,' retorted Susannah.

'You will be very soon.'

'Yes. But not yet.'

'Tonight,' said Jacko. 'You'll be a woman by the time I've finished with you, tonight.'

Susannah made quickly for the door. 'Good night, Jacko,' she said. 'I'm going upstairs.'

'There's no lock on your bedroom door,' said Jacko. 'You'd be asking for trouble if you undressed and went to bed after the kind of conversation we've been having.'

'I didn't start it, and I don't want it,' said Susannah.

'Come here,' said Jacko.

'No thanks.'

'I said, come here,' said Jacko. 'Do you want to disobey your father?'

'It depends on how he's behaving,' said Susannah.

With tremendous speed Jacko hurled himself towards her. 'Don't you bloody well talk to me like that,' he said, 'or you'll get what's coming to you!'

'Please!' begged Susannah. 'Let me go upstairs and stop this silly nonsense.'

'Silly nonsense, is it?' shouted Jacko. 'I'll silly nonsense you!' He slammed her hard across the face, nearly knocking her off her feet, and, before she had time to recover, picked her up in his arms and carried her across to the sofa. As he straddled her, she began screaming.

This seemed to send him mad. He put one hand across her mouth and with the other jerked her head back by her hair, then, removing the hand on her mouth, began kissing her savagely. She kicked and struggled as he tore at her clothes, punching her brutally in the stomach as she twisted and turned under him. She began to cry, and he slapped her face so violently that she thought her neck was breaking. Then he began ripping her dress. Her lips were bleeding and one eye was closing. Her cheeks were puffy and wet with tears, and she was half-naked. He was like an animal now. All the pent-up rage he'd been harbouring against Emelda Maltravers was spending itself in an orgy of revenge against all womankind, and Susannah's uncovered breasts aroused a lust in him that was uncontrollable. He bit her neck hard over and over again, then bit her lips and her breasts. He began undoing his trousers.

Nearly silly with fright and horror, Susannah struggled gamely. Every time she opened her mouth to scream, he hit her; and when she whimpered with terror, he laughed.

By the time he had raped her, she was nearly unconscious with fear and pain. He took her again and again, and in between times he gave himself more to drink. She thought she had never seen anyone so contemptible or degraded. She herself felt humiliated beyond recovery — and unclean, filthy, in her agony of pain.

At the end of what seemed light years, Jacko suddenly passed out. At first she couldn't believe her luck; then, when she tried to shift him off her, he was so heavy and she was so weak that she thought she would never manage it. Eventually she was free. All at once, he was at her feet on the floor, and he lay there snoring peacefully. No lodgers had come to her rescue. Charlie had not returned. Gasping and sobbing, she telephoned Marilyn, begging her to come straight down to Coulsdon to help her.

Marilyn, woken from a deep sleep, heard the terror and urgency in her voice and promised to start immediately.

Shamed, bleeding, in such pain that she found it difficult to move, Susannah crept to the front door to wait for Marilyn's arrival. Then, like the child she really was, she slept on the hard chair she had put beside the door.

When Marilyn came, Susannah awoke with a wild jerk. Shivering with cold, and almost out of her mind with horror at the recollection of the experience through which she had just passed, she let Marilyn in. Jacko was still unconscious on the floor of the sitting-room. Marilyn changed Susannah's clothes, wiped the blood from her face and breasts, dressed her carefully and gently in clean clothes, and took her away. She wanted to go straight to the police station, but Susannah, hysterical with fright and horror, asked her to take her back to her own home.

'After we have been to the police,' said Marilyn gently.

'No! No! Never! Mummy would never forgive me! She'd kill me! She loves that horrible, horrible man, and she'd kill me!' Susannah was screaming wildly, and the tears were pouring down her cheeks.

'Hush, darling. Hush. We have to report him. He can't be allowed to get away with it!' replied Marilyn. 'Rape is a crime, and he must be punished.'

'Oh, please, Marilyn! Please! I just can't stand anything

more tonight! Everything seems so filthy and vile. I'm in terrible pain, and so terribly tired!'

'Tomorrow, then,' said Marilyn. 'We shall *have* to go to the police tomorrow. And I'll get hold of the doctor right away.'

'All right. Tomorrow. But not tonight, Marilyn. Not tonight. I simply couldn't bear it!'

'You must see a doctor tonight, and that's final,' said Marilyn firmly.

CHAPTER SEVEN

Susannah slept on until nearly one o'clock the next day, and when she woke up, Marilyn and Jan were at her bedside. She was bewildered to see them, and it took some moments before she remembered the terrors of the night before.

'You're safe now,' said Marilyn gently. 'We're here, my darling, and we'll look after you. Don't try and talk. Lie there, and I'll get you some hot soup.'

Only too thankfully, Susannah did as she was told. Her face was stiff and swollen. Her breasts hurt agonisingly and scabs were forming over the mauling they had received. Between her legs there was an area of unbelievable pain.

Sunlight blazed through a long window beside her, and the room she was in was light and beautifully furnished. The sheets between which she lay were soft, and the mattress more comfortable than any she had ever known; but then she remembered with agonised humiliation not only the rape, but the doctor's visit, and she blushed scarlet. She could hardly look at Jan, who had been present after the examination. The examination had been bad enough, but what had followed had been a nightmare. Although he didn't say so, the doctor gave the impression that he believed that Susannah must have done something to encourage Jacko. She had protested vigorously, but he had remained unconvinced. And Jan had been in the room! Susannah had been so shocked, and in such pain, that she hadn't found the right words to disabuse the doctor, but his reaction had made her more certain than ever that she didn't want to go to the police. Could Jan perhaps believe that she had encouraged Jacko? His face betrayed nothing ... She had heard that the police were wary of rape, and that girls trying to get help after being raped often had a hard time. And in Court it was even worse. She couldn't go through a court case! The publicity and the shame would kill her! Surely Jan could understand that?

As well as making her frightened and miserable, the doctor's disbelief had made her angry. She was still angry now when she thought about him. But Jan was a different matter. He and Marilyn were her ideals in a far from perfect world.

Jan patted her arm and, in spite of herself, she winced at his touch. He understood immediately that it was because he was a man, and was dismayed. He again showed nothing on his face, however, but said kindly, 'Feeling a bit better?'

'Yes, thank you.' She tried to smile.

'Good. Well you're going to stay here, where you'll be safe, for just as long as you like. Marilyn is going to Coulsdon to see your mother tonight.'

'That's wonderful of her! Thank you both so much. I hope I shan't be a nuisance.'

'You won't,' he said. 'She thinks of you as the daughter she never had, you know.'

'You're marvellous! Both of you!' said Susannah.

At least she managed to say what she wanted to.

'Jan, *you* don't think I egged Jacko on, do you? Like the doctor did?'

'Good God, no!' exclaimed Jan. 'I know you far too well.' He smiled reassuringly. In spite of herself, she began to weep with relief.

'Take it easy, my dear. Just lie there and relax.'

Marilyn, returning with the soup, saw the tears at once.

'Drink that up,' she said firmly, 'and then we'll have a good talk.'

Susannah nodded but, as she tried to drink between her battered and swollen lips, the tears still ran down her cheeks and she choked.

Marilyn's expression was stern. 'Drink, darling. It will do you good.' She watched as Susannah struggled to obey, then went on, 'As soon as you feel up to it, we've got to go to the police.'

'No!' said Susannah, panicking at once. 'And if you take me I shan't say anything, so it won't do any good!'

'Your step-father can't go around raping people,' said Marilyn firmly. 'He's got to be punished. He's a dangerous man.'

'Not really. Just weak, and frustrated,' said Susannah, shuddering.

'He's got to be punished,' insisted Marilyn.

'I wish he could be,' said Susannah, 'but, if we go to the police, what do you suppose will happen to me? The police may think I encouraged Jacko. The doctor last night was sure I had. Wasn't he, Jan? He didn't say so, but I saw it in his face. And the police and everyone else may think so too. Life won't be worth living at home! The story will get round everywhere ... even perhaps into the papers ... and my career will be finished. I can't win! Everyone will think it was my fault except you and Jan. And it wasn't! It wasn't!' She was working herself into hysteria again.

'Of course it wasn't!' exclaimed Jan staunchly. 'We know that!'

'But you see, even you are protesting a little to much!' said Susannah, suddenly older than her years. 'You are reassuring yourself, as well as me, that you at least are on my side. I can see it — you believe me, but, as you said, that's only because you know me.'

Surprised by her perspicacity, Jan said slowly, 'Perhaps you're right. There's a good deal in what you say.' He looked at Marilyn.

'Nonsense!' exclaimed Marilyn. 'It's our duty to tell the police.'

'Then I'm sorry,' said Susannah wildly, 'but not only will I say nothing, but as soon as I'm well enough, I shall leave you for always. You think that your duty as a citizen is important. I think my life is important. If you want to humiliate me even further, then take me to the police station. If you love me, leave me alone!'

'That's not fair!' retorted Marilyn. 'You know as well as I do what we should do, and you know as well as I do how much we love you.'

'Look,' said Susannah. 'Last night was the most disgusting and frightening night of my life. I even heard the doctor saying that it was lucky I didn't have to go to hospital for the damage to my insides! You rescued me, and Jan says I can stay here until I'm well again. I want to get better, recover from my pain, and try and forget the whole frightful business. If I thought it would do anyone any good — me, the world at large, or even Jacko — I'd go to the police like a shot. But it won't. Mummy dislikes me as it is. If we humiliate her by exposing Jacko, then I'm done for. I don't know why she dislikes me so much, but she does. Perhaps because she wanted to be an actress so much, and I stopped her by being born! Oh, I know it wasn't my fault — I didn't choose to be born — but the timing wasn't right.'

'The timing was up to your father and mother,' said Marilyn briskly. 'And if your mother had had any real talent, she'd have had a career in the theatre if she'd wanted one, with or without children. Other people manage. We've only got Muriel's word for it that she was any good at all. And my bet is, she wasn't.'

Susannah was shocked by this. She was too indoctrinated by her mother to allow such a heresy — but she didn't argue with her beloved Marilyn. She thought for a moment, then shook her head. 'We still can't tell the police about Jacko, Marilyn. It really would be more than my life is worth.'

Jan nodded. 'I'm inclined to agree.'

'But Jan!' exclaimed Marilyn. 'It was you who told me it was our duty.'

'I hadn't quite seen it through Susannah's eyes,' said Jan.

'Oh, thank you Jan!' said Susannah. 'I'm so glad someone understands.'

'Then what do we say to your mother?' demanded Marilyn. 'She'll expect us to do something about it, surely! You can't possibly go back home, and she'll have to be given a pretty good reason or she'll refuse to let me keep you here.'

'What precisely have you said so far?' asked Jan.

'What I told you — that Jacko attacked Susannah, and that he hurt her so much that I've brought her back here.'

'Nothing about rape?'

'No.'

'Why not?'

'So that Muriel couldn't forestall us with the police.'

'Then don't tell her,' pleaded Susannah. 'Please don't, Marilyn! Make up some sort of story about Jacko getting so drunk that when I annoyed him he lost control, or something. But not rape! Please! Mother would think it was my fault, or pretend to. She was furious with me when I even said that Jacko was pawing me about. Jacko is a fearful liar, too, and he'll have go round her already, as you'll see when you talk to them. Whatever he's told her has happened, the fault will be mine, you'll see. But *you* believe me, don't you? Please say you do. Jan does, and I couldn't bear it if you didn't too. You know how much I love you! And I hate Jacko. I always have. You *do* believe me, don't you!'

'We both believe you, darling, utterly and completely. He's a ghastly little man, and I hate him, too.'

They argued the pros and cons of going to the police for so long that Susannah, exhausted, collapsed again in helpless tears.

The doctor called again at tea-time. After he'd examined Susannah and approved of the progress she was making, he said, 'I'll testify, of course.'

'Thank you,' answered Marilyn, 'but we still haven't made up our minds about going to the police. Susannah is terribly against it.'

Immediately the doctor's mouth tightened. 'You'd have to have an open-and-shut case ...' he agreed.

Susannah understood what he meant at once and said steadily, 'What does that mean?'

He looked embarrassed, clearing his throat. 'The case wouldn't stand up if you'd been leading the man on.'

'You see?' demanded Susannah of Marilyn. 'Just what I told you! That's what I'd have to go through, and I don't want to!'

'All the same,' said the doctor, 'it doesn't do to hide these things. The man is a so-and-so. Lucky for him you're sixteen.'

Susannah flushed, and Jan came to her rescue. 'What's the sense in adding to Susannah's humiliation, when, if the police see her, she'll refuse to prefer charges?' he said.

'Whatever the girl did, the man is a menace!' shouted the doctor.

'I did nothing,' said Susannah. She was shaking with anger.

Marilyn now came firmly down on Susannah's side. 'The child's mother is in love with the man and living with him! What do you suppose her home life would be like if we succeeded in putting Brunswick away? Susannah is right.'

'I don't like it. It's my duty to report to the police.'

'Susannah is already quite a well-known actress,' said Marilyn firmly. 'We can't subject her to publicity of this sort.'

Very reluctantly the doctor agreed. He did, however, suggest that Susannah would see a psychiatrist. 'Rape is a deep trauma,' he said to Jan and Marilyn as they saw him out. 'It could well have disastrous consequences for the rest of her life if she is not helped now.'

CHAPTER EIGHT

That evening Marilyn went down to see Muriel. She found her in a belligerent mood. As Susannah had warned her, Muriel appeared convinced that Susannah had deserved any trouble she was in; but Marilyn had a strong conviction that Jacko had confessed the entire story and that Muriel was putting on an act. Muriel affected to believe that Jacko had hit Susannah because she had angered him when he had drunk too much. She did also, however, seem quite glad to allow Marilyn to take Susannah off her hands for the time being, although she said she couldn't afford to pay Marilyn for her.

'We don't have your sort of money,' she sneered.

'That doesn't matter,' answered Marilyn evenly. 'We neither need nor want payment, and if after all there are any little extras that are too much for me, I can always get your authority to draw on Susannah's bank account, can't I?'

Muriel put her hands on her hips and stuck out her chin. 'What does that mean, when it's at home?' she asked, furiously; but she looked scared.

'Susannah has been earning money pretty regularly for years!' replied Marilyn. 'She must have some sort of a bank account.'

'Well, she hasn't!' snapped Muriel. 'She's been to Aida Foster's and been fed and boarded out — and dressed far above her station, I may add — because of this career that she has insisted on making, and anything she's earned has gone into all that. She hasn't a brass farthing!'

'That's daylight robbery ...' Marilyn exclaimed. 'You should be up in court!'

'Careful, now. Careful!' warned Muriel. 'I don't like that

sort of talk, and one more word of it and I'll fetch Susannah back home.'

'Just you try,' replied Marilyn dangerously. 'If you do, you and that revolting little man you call your husband will be in bad trouble. You're damned lucky that I haven't been to the police — so far.'

Muriel changed her tactics hurriedly. 'Well, I've said you can borrow my daughter for a bit, haven't I?' she wheedled. 'No need to get unpleasant! You're fond of her. You haven't any children, and she earns a bit from time to time, which I shall find difficult to do without, but she'll be a companion for you, and she's fond of you, so I'm willing to let her go.'

Susannah stayed away from school for several months. During this time she went to a psychiatrist twice weekly. For three weeks she was in terror of a pregnancy, but she was lucky. Her physical wounds healed, and, as she was happy with Marilyn and her husband, she soon seemed to have recovered in every way. But the psychological scars were never to disappear completely, and, had it not been for a lucky chance, she might have turned against all men from then on.

At Aida Foster's she had already made friends with a talented boy two years older, called Dickie Franklyn. Dickie showed great tact and gentleness during her 'illness' and they soon became inseparable. They even swore to marry when they were old enough.

' ...when I'm established enough as an actor to support a wife and child,' Dickie had added rather grandly.

'I can support myself,' retorted Susannah. 'I always have, and although I didn't start by wanting to be an actress, I do now.'

'We'll see!' said Dickie.

Susannah was astonished at the ease of their relationship, which was so unlike her usual awkwardness with boys.

Dickie laughed when she told him this. 'You and I are the choosey type,' he said cheerfully. 'We don't fall easy.'

Dickie came from the same sort of South London background as Susannah. His father was a bricklayer in Norwood, and his mother had always been keen on the theatre and had encouraged him when he had shown signs of wanting to be an actor. This helped them to confide in each other, and soon they were keeping no secrets at all. Finally Susannah told Dickie about Jacko. He was appalled and extremely angry — so much so that he threatened to take the story to the *News of the World*. Susannah only stopped him by saying that, if he did, she wouldn't confirm the story. However, she was deeply touched by his reaction which, together with the constant kindness and love she received from Marilyn and Jan, went a long way to restoring her faith in life.

That winter, Jan died. He had had chronic bronchitis even before he had been in the Observer Corps in the war, and a succession of damp huts, and the outdoor life he was forced to live in order to do the job, had taken their toll. He had never been strong. Now he caught a severe chill trying to dig his car out of a drift during a blizzard, and the chill turned to pneumonia. To Marilyn's unbelieving despair, he didn't recover.

Susannah too was heartbroken. Jan was a father-figure, and she adored him. She did everything in her power to comfort Marilyn after his death, but the marriage had been an extremely happy one and Marilyn, though grateful for Susannah's presence, was inconsolable.

At last one day she called Susannah into the drawing-room for what she described as a 'very worrying talk'.

It transpired that she had been offered a film contract in America, and wanted to sell up in England and emigrate. 'I can't go on living here, Sue darling. Please understand. Everything reminds me too much of Jan, and this contract is a wonderful opportunity to get away and start a new life.'

'Of course!' agreed Susannah warmly, but with a sinking heart.

'I asked your mother if I could take you with me,' said Marilyn. 'I said I was quite willing to adopt you formally, but she wouldn't hear of it. She reminded me that you are only a minor, and that she has rights over you, and since you wouldn't go to the police, I'm afraid she has a cast-iron case. I don't quite know what to do.'

'You must go to America,' said Susannah firmly. 'It would be madness to turn down such a chance. It's wonderful of you to care about me, and I'm terribly grateful, but I wouldn't dream of standing in your way.' Marilyn began to protest, but Susannah continued, 'I should feel guilty every minute of every day. Don't be sorry for me, Marilyn. I'm older now, and I can handle things at home, I know I can. I've got Dickie's family on my side and they know the whole story, so I shall be all right.' She sounded confident, but she was frightened.

'You can't possibly go back home, but God knows what else we can arrange,' said Marilyn.

'I must go home,' said Susannah simply. 'Don't worry.'

Marilyn went down to Coulsdon to see Muriel again. It was an understatement to say that she was worried about Susannah; and if indeed the child was to be forced to live again in the same house with Jacko, then Marilyn wanted to be sure that Muriel understood the gravity of the situation. Muriel pretended to be offended by such an 'intrusion', so Marilyn told her outright about the rape. When Muriel flushed angrily and pursed her lips, Marilyn said menacingly, 'Perhaps you'd better know that quite a number of other people know about Mr Brunswick's behaviour, and if he lays one finger on her again, he'll go to gaol. And not before time.'

'Susannah's a fibber!' exclaimed Muriel. 'Jacko would never do a thing like that!'

'Perhaps you'd better see the doctor who saw her that night at my house!' retorted Marilyn. 'Or my cousin, the Chief Constable of Norfolk,' she lied wildly, in her effort to save Susannah. 'Anyway I've warned you, so he'd better behave. You can't shut her up here, away from everyone, if you ever want her to earn for you again — so if I were you I should take a little more care of her.'

Muriel controlled her temper with extreme difficulty, and smiled. 'Of course I'll take care of her!' she exclaimed sweetly. 'She's a clever child, and this is her home.'

Marilyn was not reassured by this, but felt powerless to deal further with the situation.

She returned to Denham feeling worse than ever and quite unable to conceal her anxiety from Susannah.

'There's only one thing for it,' said Dickie, when Susannah brought the problem to him. 'We'll go to Gretna Green tomorrow and get married right away. I won't let you go back to Jacko.'

'But we're both too young!' protested Susannah 'And I might ruin your career.'

'Of course you wouldn't,' said Dickie. 'You'll probably earn much more than me anyway.'

'Your life, then.'

'How could you do that? If the marriage doesn't work, we can get a divorce.'

'We shouldn't be talking about divorce before we even get married,' said Susannah. 'Getting married should be wonderful.'

'It'll be OK,' said Dickie.

'What about your family? They'll never forgive me!'

'They like you, and they'll understand.'

Strangely enough, the marriage worked surprisingly well. As Dickie had predicted, one or other of them was always in work and, although neither was really in love, their friendship was unshakeable. It was a long time before either became attracted to anyone else.

In some ways, it was precisely this lack of passion that made sleeping with Dickie possible for Susannah. He was immensely patient and understanding. Sometimes after their love-making she woke up screaming, but he was never offended or angry. He wisely insisted, though, that they continued to live as man and wife: he was convinced that she might fear sex for the rest of her life if she let the past with Jacko dominate her.

Dickie's parents, although horrified at their son's ridiculously early marriage, liked Susannah and, as Dickie had expected, understood the reasons for it. Muriel, on the other hand, was so angry with both of them that after one terrifying descent on the Franklyn family, when she screamed and ranted and behaved so rudely that she finally and for ever lost their sympathy, she retired to Coulsdon swearing never to speak to any of them again.

Back at home, licking her wounds, Muriel felt resentful and impotent. She didn't want to face the fact that she had lost Susannah for ever. She knew in her heart that she had always behaved less than generously to her daughter and deserved to lose her, but the indulgence with which she herself had been brought up was a bad training for self-criticism, or indeed restraint, and for the moment she preferred to think of herself as the wronged one. She blamed the 'interloper who couldn't mind her own business' — Marilyn de la Roche. She didn't blame Jacko. His physical hold over her was still strong, and her dislike of Susannah was too ingrained for her to allow herself to believe that it had been Jacko who had made all the running. Nevertheless, she was worried about the future. She had an instinct that her daughter would one day become famous, and she knew that she would like to be there when it happened. She knew, too, that no one else would supply the extra perks that Susannah had made possible almost from the moment she had first become a photographic model.

She wryly recognised that neither Jacko nor Charlie would ever even try to help her financially, and saw the irony in her situation — that she, who craved security so much, should love and tolerate both of her men so blindly and care so little for the only one of the family who earned good money. However, there it was and it couldn't be helped. She'd bide her time and see what she could do to repair the damage with her daughter later, if circumstances made her wish to do so.

For her part, Susannah was only too thankful to be rid of her mother. A creature of habit, gentle and deeply conservative, she still loved Muriel in spite of everything that had happened; but she had found a diet of rejection too exhausting to bear consistently, and the thought of not having to meet Jacko again was like a blessed reprieve. Susannah's feelings towards Charlie were more ambivalent. Her affections, once given, were never totally withdrawn, but she knew him for what he was: a selfish, spoilt, marred young man ... untrustworthy and callous, however attractive. They'd never seen much of each other when they were at home, so she didn't really miss him when she was away. But she thought about him, often.

CHAPTER NINE

In February 1954, at the age of nineteen, Susannah had her big break. She tested for, and landed, her first starring part with an American film company, in a film to be made in Rome, called *Roman Summer*. It would start in April and she was to play opposite William Blandford, one of the hottest properties in Hollywood at that time. Also, she would be earning a considerable sum of money. The entire Franklyn family was wildly excited for her, and Susannah was touched to find that Dickie was not in the least jealous of her success.

Impressed by her test, the film producer told her that, if she did well on the film, he would see that she was signed up for a three-year contract. He also decided that her name should be changed before the film started.

'Susannah Dale does nothing for you,' he said. 'We must find something more glamorous.'

After much discussion, he and the director settled on 'Anna Starr'.

The subsequent blaze of publicity in the papers quickly brought Muriel to the scene, in the belief that there might be money in it for her somehow. She sought out the producer and told him that she strongly objected to the change. 'Dale is our name,' she said. 'If Susannah's going to be famous, why should she change it?'

She was bought off generously by the film company in return for a letter promising that she would not interfere further in her daughter's career.

Muriel banked the money as a contingency fund, which she anxiously feared might be needed later, and for the time being, to augment her regular income, took up dressmaking. Jacko was more or less self-supporting, even paying for his own drink now, but he contributed nothing to the household; and Charlie, who hadn't yet found a steady job since leaving school, got through every penny he was given, and more. He had also already been in one or two scrapes with the police, and Muriel was frightened. To make matters worse, Amy, who had not been well for some time, died suddenly one night in her sleep, and Muriel thought it quite likely that Ernie might want to come and live with her. Though they could then sell his house, which would bring in some money, it was possible that he too would be a financial burden as he grew older.

She wrote to Susannah (who was due to leave for Italy very shortly) to tell her her troubles, and Susannah, saddened by the death of her loving grandmother, immediately suggested to Dickie that they should make Muriel an allowance.

Dickie was adamant. 'She has brought you nothing but unhappiness,' he said. 'She's a bitch and deserves all she gets. I won't hear of it.' Reluctantly, Susannah let the matter drop.

Now it was Dickie's turn to be offered an excellent part in a play in London's West End. 'So we're on our way, Sue!' he exclaimed jubilantly. 'Life's pretty good, isn't it?'

Susannah agreed.

Ever since landing the part, she had been studying her film script meticulously, as she wanted to be word-perfect before she left for Rome. Dickie was now rehearsing daily, and loving every moment of it, so the two of them were extremely busy.

'The director is smashing!' said Dickie. 'So is the cast. And as for the juvenile who is to play opposite me — you should see her, darling! If you and I didn't get on so well, you might be in trouble!'

They both laughed. It was the peak of their happiness together.

Rome was a revelation to Susannah, who had never been abroad before. A wartime childhood, followed by years of postwar austerity, had ill-prepared her for the oppulence which surrounded her.

A friend who had made a film in Italy in 1946 had often described her own amazement at the dazzling capital of this defeated nation, in contrast to shabby victorious England, which was still at that stage bound by stringent rationing. In England she could buy just two outfits a year, if she didn't bother too much about underclothes, nightclothes, or silk stockings; and her food coupons allowed her one-shilling-and two-pence-worth of meat. In Rome, she and everyone else who could afford it could buy all the silks, satins and high fashions they craved, and the steaks were so enormous that she could hardly face them — 'slightly shocking,' she had called it.

Susannah's emotions, eight years later, were almost identical. Clothes were now easier to buy back home, though they were still on the drab side and made of poor materials, but food rationing was only to be ended finally in July that year, with the de-control of meat and bacon. She was stimulated by the elegance and panache of the Roman women, and the city itself totally enslaved her. Its beauty almost disorientated her. She felt elated by it, but that the same time profoundly lonely. On the rare occasions when she wasn't filming, she wandered up and down the great shopping streets, or through the narrow alleyways, gazing and gazing, as though she had spent her life half-blind before.

Like so many millions of others, she visited the Vatican, marvelling at the Sistine Chapel, and wandered round the magnificent interior of St Peter's — awed by a vastness which reduced all humans to midgets, but enchanted by the amount of light which poured in through the great windows. The soaring grey stone seemed to turn to silver and, on the altar, Bernini's *baldacchino*, forty feet high, blazed in golden splendour, its huge canopy supported by serpentine pillars. Susannah fell in love instantly with Michelangelo's *Pietà*. So astounded was she by his work that she returned again and again to the Capitol, also designed by him, which she thought was the loveliest place she had ever seen.

It was heady springtime, and everywhere in Rome there was laughter and singing. To her surprise Susannah found a house where Keats had lived, at the bottom of the wide Spanish Steps down which multitudes of brilliant sweet-smelling flowers cascaded from the stalls of the flower sellers. She enjoyed treating herself to a drink at the chic old Hassler's Villa Medici Hotel at the top, near the lovely church of the Trinità dei Monte. William Blandford, her co-star, also took her to see the

Forum and the Colosseum, and together they visited Trevi, where, like hundreds and thousands of other tourists down the centuries, they threw coins into the Bernini fountain in accordance with the superstition that this would ensure their return to Rome. She was sad that Dickie wasn't with her to share her happiness.

All the stars of the film, as well as the director, the producer and the cameraman, were booked into the Grand Hotel, which lived up to its name and was comfortable and spacious. On warm nights, the actors and the crew often ate out together in open-air restaurants under the brilliant stars. Susannah loved best the Piazza Navona, where the two great fountains, one by Bernini and one by his pupil, splashed musically behind the laughter and chatter of the diners.

Although she felt ashamed of her few British clothes, the Italian men seemed to find her attractive. They murmured 'bella, bella' as she passed, and pinched her behind if they got close enough. They sighed for her, wooed her, sang to her and pestered her, and she revelled in it. It was a far cry from Coulsdon and Norwood.

The film was being made at the Cine Città studios which, unlike most film studios in England, were almost within the city bounds. A car came to fetch Susannah at six every morning, so that she could have her hair set before her make-up; as she now wore it long, it took some time to do. The assistant make-up man made her up, as William Blandford had first call on the head man, and, when she was ready, she would go to her dressing room, where she carefully studied her words for the day's shooting. Her stand-in, meanwhile, was being lit in the various positions that she herself would eventually take up, to prevent Susannah becoming too tired before she started shooting.

All the same, the work was exhausting and the hours long; when summer came the heat in the studios was almost insupportable, especially when the lights were lit on the set. The constant retakes, necessary because the sound had been imperfect, or a light had flared or been wrongly placed, or an actor had fluffed his lines, were frustrating, as indeed were the long periods of waiting while lights and camera were repositioned; but Susannah found her work absorbing

—much more so now that she was an adult, not a child.

She was almost embarrassingly well-cast in the film, as a young girl whose beauty and talent were ruthlessly exploited by a grasping mother and father. As usual, the camera seemed to fall in love with her face; and she was a congenitally hard worker, which pleased her director. Although always diffident about herself, even she was generally pleased with the previous day's 'rushes' which were shown after lunch every day. William Blandford was very kind to her, became a good friend, and was extremely enthusiastic and helpful about her work.

Days in the studio were long, but there were parties every night if they cared to go. Unimaginably grand houses opened their door to the screen 'couple'. Susannah sensed that her naiveté and lack of worldliness amused her hosts, and sometimes even bored them; she in turn was shaken that drug-taking was so prevalent, that husbands and wives automatically expected their spouses to have lovers, and that their recent defeat in war seemed not to have scarred the Romans at all. She was also shocked at the poverty and squalor to be found just around the corner from such ostentation.

It was a bewildering society. The aristocrats behaved with an arrogance she despised, yet cab drivers waited for their passengers in the lounges of the smart hotels, drinking and at ease. Beggars ran after the rich, and were lavishly and cheerfully rewarded; and dressmakers, making up for a pittance the lovely silks she had bought, seemed to yet relish the beauty around them with a quite un-English enthusiasm, and appeared surprisingly content. In this quixotic new environment, Susannah began to relax, almost as if she were on holiday.

Then, inevitably, she fell in love — with the second male lead, an amusing and outrageously attractive Italian called Antonio Fortuno. He was tall and thin, with fair hair and a drawling voice. He came from a very good family, who looked on his acting career as a temporary affliction from which he would soon recover. It was he who introduced her into the most exclusive society of all.

She felt gauche and inadequate in this new set, and was both over-awed and very disapproving of their way of living. The young ones were idle, promiscuous, and enormously rich. As for the older generation, the frail, immensely distinguished old

ladies, accompanied by even more decrepit old men, lived out
their trivial self-absorbed days in enormous decaying palazzos
gorgeously furnished with pictures by the greatest of the Old
Masters, and manned by armies of servants. Their lineage gave
them boundless prestige, since 'the family' was still of
paramount importance in Italy. The mothers still ruled their
elegant sons and daughters-in-law with rigid autocracy. And
not one of them did a hand's turn.

The parties which this social set gave, to which Susannah
was now taken, were even more decadent than those she had
visited before. Drugs were provided by butlers with the
syringes neatly arranged on silver trays. Everyone made love
quite openly, often naked. The quantities of drink consumed
were prodigious, but seemed to have little effect on anyone,
and though Susannah found the whole business distasteful, she
grudgingly admired their poise and sang-froid. Occasionally
actresses and actors were present, but only those who were
considered fashionable, which didn't necessarily mean those
who were especially talented. Rich foreigners were also
sometimes invited, but for the most part the Italians looked
down on them as barbarians.

His family understood Antonio's infatuation with
Susannah. She was young and beautiful, and had started a
promising career. She was a prig — but then she, like his career,
would soon pass. Susannah fully realised that they didn't
accept her into their circle any more than she really wished to
be a part of it; but she was so in love with Antonio that, for the
moment, nothing else mattered. And Antonio, too, had fallen
a little in love.

CHAPTER TEN

In due course the film came to an end. The Americans seemed glad to be going home, but Susannah had no wish at all to leave Italy.

Knowing that she wasn't really comfortable with his friends, Antonio offered to install her in what he described as a 'love flat'. She wanted above everything to accept, but she knew that she must first go back to Dickie. Dickie had saved her when she was in trouble, and she wouldn't desert him if he needed her.

The producer took her out to dinner the night before he left for America. He told her that he was delighted with her performance and would certainly recommend his studio to put her under contract. This excited her very much. He said that, if it had been left to him, she would already be a contract artist, but that the studio would want to see her work first. They might even want to wait until the film had been out on general release and an estimate made of her impact on the public.

Antonio was surprisingly unhappy at the prospect of losing Susannah. Like his family, he had originally thought of her only as a temporary divertissement; but now that she was on the brink of leaving for good, he recognised that he was more deeply involved than he had expected, or intended.

To his fury and frustration he hadn't yet succeeded in seducing her. This was an unheard-of slight to his manhood — he had never waited for any woman for so long. But he was certain that she loved him. He had realised that she was not playing hard to get and was indeed in some very real psychological trouble, but her excuse that she was married to a good and nice man didn't convince him, and Susannah hadn't given Jacko's rape as her excuse, as she instinctively felt he wouldn't be sympathetic. (In this she was right.)

Antonio had pretended to his family and friends that they were lovers, so as not to lose face, and was astonished at himself for taking so much trouble over any woman.

'Come back my little one,' he said. 'I cannot live without you. I shall buy a little love nest in any case, and it will be waiting for you for ever.'

Susannah promised that she would return if she could, and that, if she did, she would become his mistress.

With this he was forced to be satisfied.

So Susannah returned home, to the Franklyns. They seemed delighted to see her again, and, though she missed Antonio daily and hourly, she enjoyed being back among her own kind. England seemed small and ugly and grey and dull, but it was her own country. She was rooted there, and she knew it.

It was soon apparent that it was not only on her side that there were problems with her marriage. Dickie, though as friendly as ever, was noticeably abstracted, and appeared reluctant to make love. His play in the West End was still running successfully, and he had made a small name for himself, which delighted Susannah; but he didn't seem to want to talk about his work, or indeed to make Susannah a part of his theatrical life. She saw him on stage in the play, and realised that he had become a very able actor, with unmistakeable star quality. He had a good stage presence, an excellent voice and great assurance. She felt proud of him. All the same, he seemed to have to be at the theatre surprisingly often for 'rehearsal', which was odd as the play was doing so well; and he didn't invite Susannah to join him at any of the theatre parties. Finally she asked him why.

Dickie hesitated. 'Leave it for the moment, darling,' he said. 'I'm a bit bothered about something.'

'Can't I help?'

'I don't think so. At any rate, not yet.'

Susannah was receiving letters daily from Antonio. She tried to laugh them off, but she was so excited when they arrived that the Franklyns guessed at once that she had fallen in love. When, in due course, she asked if she could go back to Italy for a holiday, as she had 'fallen under Rome's spell', all of them knew what she meant.

Mr and Mrs Franklyn were sad and worried. They believed that Dickie, too, was in love with someone else, and realised that a break-up was all too likely.

Dickie, who had indeed fallen for the girl in his play, had no wish to end his marriage. He wanted Susannah to remain in England and to weather the storm with him. He suggested that having children would help, but Susannah pleaded passionately for her 'holiday', as she called it, and reluctantly Dickie agreed.

She returned to Italy and Antonio.

The apartment Antonio had found for her was magnificent. It was on the third floor of a seventeenth-century palazzo, and filled with gilded Baroque furniture. From one of the family houses he had brought pictures by Murillo, Tiepolo and Guardi. The ceilings were gilded and plastered, and in the bedroom the enormous bed-head was draped in green-and-gold brocade, with gilded cherubs romping above the corona. The dining room had a table which could seat fourteen, and there was a remarkably practical kitchen. Thoughtfully, Antonio had engaged a Swiss couple to look after them.

He was amused by her rapturous delight. Such seduction techniques were second nature to a rich Italian male. 'It is nothing!' he laughed. 'Could I do less for the woman I love?'

'You shouldn't have gone to so much expense!' exclaimed Susannah. 'But I adore it! It is absolutely wonderful!'

Antonio wrinkled his nose. 'Expense!' he scoffed. 'Don't be so *bourgeoise*, my darling. If I want it, I want it, and if you like it, then the talk of expense is absurd.'

Susannah was always very slightly dismayed by him when he was at his most seigneurial, but she was moved by his generosity.

It was early in the New Year, and cold in the city, but in the apartment it was eternally warm, and the Swiss couple cooked and cleaned and attended to their every need. Even though she appreciated everything he had done for her, it was several days before Susannah could bring herself to allow Antonio to make love to her. He reminded her of the promise she had made before leaving for England, and this sincerely distressed her, but she couldn't prevent her fear of close physical contact. His outsized ego resented having to ask for favours, and the situation maddened him; but he carefully bided his time, and was gentle, kind, entertaining and exaggeratedly respectful, until he gradually won her round. When she finally gave herself to him he made love so expertly that she experienced only happiness, and a physical love so profound that all memories of Jacko were banished.

For the present, Antonio, too, was physically satisfied, but he never wholly forgave her for keeping him waiting.

Susannah marvelled at her good fortune. It seemed incredible that she who had been so unwanted in the bleak little house she had called home when she was a child, should have found such a lover. The apartment never failed to enchant her, she was fathoms deep in love, and Antonio seemed to become more and more affectionate as the days went by. He taught her many things; how to dress, how to appreciate paintings and furniture; how to enjoy sophistication.

Making love by firelight in the otherwise darkened bedroom was an unforgettable pleasure. Knowing how intensely selfish Antonio was in everyday life, Susannah marvelled as much at his patience and consideration as at his passion. That he could so completely erase the horror of Jacko made her deeply grateful.

For some months both were content. Gradually, however, the enormous disparity in their natures began to have its effect. Antonio, like most Italian men, expected to have his own way in everything. He regarded her need for independence as unfeminine, and since she seldom wanted to go to the kind of parties he enjoyed, he began going out more and more without her. He only rarely took her to see his family (which Susannah noticed), since both he and they knew that he had no intention of marrying her. When the time came, he would marry a well-bred rich Italian bride, from a family of which his parents approved. So he made no real attempt to make amends. Susannah, still feeling very much a stranger in Rome, enjoyed most the parties which included theatre and film people, so it was to these she went — often, alone (Antonio, strangely, looked down on theatrical occasions). Above all, she hated being so idle, though she enjoyed having no domestic chores. Antonio preferred her to be idle. He liked to think of her as an exquisite, amusing, brainless little doll, whom he would enjoy until he grew tired.

They began bickering, and presently quarrelling; and, behind her day-to-day preoccupation, Susannah was worried that she had heard no more from the film company. Although she was deeply in love, she recognised that she was now firmly committed to a career, and although the break with her mother had at first relieved her, it now saddened her to think that they were cut off from one another entirely. She had Muriel to thank, after all, for the fact that she was now an actress.

Antonio disliked her thinking of her career.

'But you are an actor, youself!' protested Susannah.

'For the time being,' he replied rather grandly. 'But a woman should live for her man.'

'That is absurd!' exclaimed Susannah. 'Why shouldn't a man live for a woman?'

'Man has always been the breadwinner.'

'What nonsense! You have worked in films, but your father has never done a day's work in all his life!' laughed Susannah. 'Wandering round one's estates giving orders is not work in my terms! He has a manager for the business side, and wouldn't know how to do manual work if he tried! And you will be like that, one day, when your father has died and you have inherited. I know it.'

'My father has always provided for his family,' replied Antonio, stiffly.

'On inherited money!' exclaimed Susannah.

'What's the difference?' asked Antonio.

'Well I couldn't possibly spend my life doing nothing,' said Susannah, returning to the original point of the conversation. 'It would drive me mad! I'm trained as an actress, and an actress I want to be.'

'So, if the studio want you, you will go to America and leave me behind,' said Antonio, laying on the pathos.

'You could come too,' retorted Susannah.

'And walk four paces behind you?' He was indignant.

Again Susannah laughed. 'I can't imagine you doing any

such thing!' she said. Antonio laughed too, but he didn't enjoy such conversations.

He went out even more often among his own friends and she among hers; and his mother, hearing of Susannah's determination to continue her career, turned completely against her. Contessa Fortuno had tolerated her before (although she had disapproved of her effect on her lecherous old husband), but now things were different. Susannah was impossible; an upstart and a foreigner. It was time for Antonio to come to his senses and find a suitable wife.

The second spring came and went — still without news from Hollywood — and both became increasingly restless.

Susannah often felt guilty about Dickie. He had so generously allowed her to return to Rome but must now be feeling deserted, perhaps even angry. She found herself comparing him with Antonio, nearly always to Antonio's disadvantage, except of course in bed. She saw clearly that she was behaving badly, and realised that a kind and dependable husband deserved better. Yet it was Antonio she loved — though she knew he could never be her friend, which had always been Dickie's great strength.

Antonio too was critical of Susannah. He was a promiscuous and selfish man, and sincerely considered that fidelity was not only unmasculine but actually injurious to his health. In his eyes, Susannah was not his social equal. He found her simultaneously too independent and too faithful, and he simply had no conception of what she meant when she said that she would leave him if she could not count on some measure of trust between them.

She found his new insistence on a purely physical relationship, which precluded all intellectually stimulating conversation, initially claustrophobic and, in the last resort, frankly dull. Rome, too, was closing in on her. She was astounded that, amid such beauty and luxury, living with the man she loved, she should find life basically unrewarding; but there was no denying that she did.

At this point, unexpectedly, Antonio found the woman who could be his wife — a wife whom both he and the family could consider suitable. She was beautiful, very rich and very stupid, but she was his social equal.

'So you see,' he said, cheerfully, 'you must go home to England for a short while, my little one, until my wife and I have settled down. And then you shall return to me, and all will be as before!'

Susannah was incredulous. 'All will be as before?' she asked in amazement.

'But of course!' Antonio seemed as surprised as she was.

'Have you no intention whatever of being faithful to her?'

'None. Are you faithful to Dickie?'

'That's different. I hadn't met you when I married Dickie,' said Susannah.

'I see no difference,' retorted Antonio.

'Won't Lucia mind?' asked Susannah defensively.

'Why should she? She will find a lover too. Marriage is for children, for inheritance, and for family reasons. Love is for ourselves. Love is for you and me.' Antonio kissed her enthusiastically.

'I find the idea appalling!' replied Susannah angrily.

'But I cannot understand you!' exclaimed Antonio. 'You live like this yourself, yet you wish me to live otherwise!'

She saw his point, but all the same she was horrified. On the other hand, she couldn't yet bear to leave him: her love for him was still the strongest emotion in her life.

Antonio, however insisted. 'Go back to Dickie,' he said firmly. 'Explain to him that all is well. Return, then, to me. Afterwards you will go again for the few months after the wedding, and then, after that, all will be quite well. You'll see.'

Unhappily, Susannah returned to Norwood.

CHAPTER ELEVEN

Dickie's play in London was still running. He was glad to be in such a success, but he was growing bored. He still didn't want it to end, though, as then he would have to make up his mind about marriage with Eileen. He himself was quite content to continue with the affair. Eileen was not.

Dickie was still fond of Susannah, though he had never believed in the fiction of her 'holiday' in Rome and had been irritated by her absence when he was going through such a crisis; but, like his parents, he thought that a divorce might well be the wrong thing, since he and Susannah were such good companions. All the same, the two of them couldn't live in two different countries for the rest of their lives, so he was glad to see Susannah back in England if only to talk things through.

Unfortunately for him, Susannah had outgrown living with the Franklyn family at Norwood. She loved them all, and was immensely grateful for what they had done for her, but England, she now knew, could never be the final extent of her horizons. She needed room to be herself, to expand, and to live an international life. Dickie had no such needs. For him, England, his parents and the British theatre provided all he wanted ... except that he'd have liked a home of his own. Because of this, for the first time, they found it hard to talk to one another.

One thing Susannah realised, above all, was that she had no wish for a domesticated life. She had, by chance, achieved a life free from chores at last, and ideally she wanted to be free of them for good. Eileen was a first-class cook, a good manager and a real home-body, in spite of the profession she had chosen. She was obviously more suited to Dickie than

Susannah. If he married her, they would set up house together and he'd have his own home. And yet, both Dickie and Susannah hesitated to make the final break. Susannah didn't trust Antonio, or the kind of future he would provide for her; Dickie wondered if, by tying himself down to Eileen, he would at some future date regret missing out on those new horizons of Susannah's. So, by the time Susannah left once again for Italy, nothing had been decided.

Rome enchanted her as usual on her return. He apartment was as magically beautiful in fact as it had been in her imagination. The things which had overwhelmed her with joy when she had first arrived in Italy still caught her heart — the sunshine, the laughter, the natural elegance, the gaiety, the constant music and the exhilaration of living in a place where moods and emotions were openly encouraged, and where, beyond all, Antonio still made passionate and wonderful love, love-making which almost blinded her to the extraordinary conditions attached to being his lover.

Plans for the wedding went forward lavishly, and with great social decorum. It was decided that Susannah would not be present: Antonio felt it would not be *comme il faut*. He was constantly at the tailor's and seemed slightly annoyed that Susannah wished to take no part in choosing his new wardrobe. His wife was to have a wedding dress with a three-yard train, hand-embroidered with pearls; they were to be given the family home on the Palatine Hill, as well as a country estate near Monte Bellugia; the honeymoon was to take place at the Palace Hotel in Vienna, and would last six weeks. Understandably, the telephone rang day and night with urgent matters for the bridegroom's attention.

Antonio was well satisfied. He approved of his bride, and adored the fuss that such a fashionable wedding entailed; but, as he had promised, his engagement made no difference to the ardour of his lovemaking — at first. Presently, though, Susannah realised that his attention was wandering from her. He was away more and more, and on the comparatively few occasions that he was in the apartment, he seemed to want to pick a quarrel with her.

At the beginning she put it down to a guilty conscience, then one day the telephone rang, and a girl with a lovely voice asked if she might speak to him. Susannah realised at once that Antonio was being unfaithful. Since he had never agreed to be faithful, she knew that it was absurd to take it so to heart, but an instinct told her that this girl would be dangerous. She was outraged that Antonio not only was prepared to marry while his affair with Susannah continued, but expected her to tolerate his infidelity with another mistress as well! She decided to have it out with him, unemotionally if possible.

It wasn't possible.

Antonio realised that his best means of defence was attack. Even he recognised that he was behaving badly, but he was not prepared to tolerate any restrictions on his freedom. Besides, Susannah was right. His feelings for Gina were indeed stronger than his feelings for most of the girls with whom he had secretly had short affairs while still living with Susannah, and he was not prepared to lose her. The talk turned into an argument, an argument which lasted for several days. Rows and recriminations became daily occurrences, and this didn't suit Antonio at all. In an already complicated relationship, it distanced them still further. Susannah saw him less and less, and she became more and more miserable. Antonio was unrepentant.

Susannah had now been out of work for over a year. For the hundredth time she rang her agent demanding action.

'No, I'm sorry. We can't stir them up,' said the agent firmly. 'We must simply wait, Susannah. The film must be out soon ... heaven knows what's delaying it ... and you were told you would hear something then. Patience, my dear.'

'I could do a play in London to fill in time!' pleaded Susannah.

'Your only offers are small parts in not very good films,' retorted the agent. 'No London plays. But all that will change if the film is a success. Don't worry.'

Out of the blue, Susannah had a letter from Dickie asking for a divorce. Though she was half expecting it, it came as a great blow. Dickie reminded her that they had been ridiculously young when they had married, and that she knew as well as he did that they weren't in love at the time. He said that he was grateful to her for her friendship and affection, but such a marriage had nothing to do with real life, or real fulfilment. He pointed out that her absence had accelerated his dependence on Eileen, and that Eileen was the woman he now wanted above all others.

Susannah acknowledged that she had brought the situation on herself, but in her desperation and loneliness she felt utterly bereft. There was nothing else for her to do but to give him her blessing, but perversely she felt let down. Partly she realised that this was because she had banked on Dickie's ultimate loyalty as a safety net when her affair with Antonio came to an end. This she knew was selfish and unfair, but the fact remained that, should she return to England, England would now prove as lonely as Rome had become. Unless she had work.

It was high summer, and stiflingly hot. This made matters worse. There was no air conditioning in her apartment, yet, until the cool of the evening, there was no temptation to go out into the baking, arid city. Most of her own Italian friends were away at the seaside, and she knew few of the foreigners in Rome that year. As an out-of-work actress, she was now an embarrassment to her 'friends' at the studios. Her old deep-seated mistrust in herself began plaguing her again, and with it came feelings of enormous self-pity. These she alternately despised and gave way to, almost luxuriously.

Antonio was bored by her problems. Mistresses shouldn't have problems. Her impending divorce from Dickie gave him no satisfaction — indeed, the reverse. His plans for sending her back home to England for a while to wait until he might want her again were now likely to be wrecked. The situation increased his guilt, and belittled her in his eyes.

Susannah tried hard to pull herself together, because she knew she was heading for a breakdown.

Antonio still gave her a generous allowance, so she decided to entertain lavishly among the small circle left in Rome; but news of Antonio's new love had already spread, and although this provoked curiosity, she was certainly not an object of compassion. The new girl was popular, one of their own set, and Susannah soon realised that she herself was the target of much joyful and malicious gossip. One or two of the men tried to seduce her, but when they were satisfied that she disliked casual encounters and had no wish for further emotional entanglements, they left her severely alone. Then she received her long-awaited letter from America. It informed her that the studio was pleased with her performance, but that no decisions had yet been taken to put her under contract.

Despair became a familiar — a hopeless hell, where agony and loneliness dogged her constantly. Feebly she told herself that living in the lap of luxury in the world's most beautiful city would seem a dream of perfect happiness to hundreds and thousands of other people. It didn't help. Without Antonio's love, it was death. She suffered from insomnia, and took pills which only increased her depression. The anti-depressants she was given induced a feeling of total unreality and, behind the occasional euphoria, misery waited to engulf her. Was it that her pride had been so bruised that she couldn't crawl towards normality out of the pit she had made for herself? Was it that one more rejection was one too many? Did it matter? Who was she anyway, to care so deeply about herself — just a 'promising' actress, who had no real gift for inspiring the love which she so desperately craved. She was no one. Redundant. Uninteresting. The promise not fulfilled. She thought often of suicide, but while Antonio was still visiting her, even if now so dreadfully seldom, she dragged herself through the long days hoping against hope that she might see him or hear from him; that the situation might change, and he would love her once again.

Then the final blow fell.

Antonio arrived in the best possible humour, with champagne and caviare, and lobsters to be cooked for dinner. He told her frankly and cheerfully that he needed the apartment at once for his new girlfriend.

Susannah was horrified. 'But how *can* you need it now, when you are to be married in a fortnight's time?' she demanded.

'That is just the point,' he answered. 'I must get Gina installed and comfortable so that she will wait for me for the six weeks I am on honeymoon. She's very attractive you know. *Très soignée*. Other people may take her away if I do not hurry.'

'Does Lucia know about her?'

'Certainly not. Why should I hurt the poor girl?'

'Supposing Lucia finds out, what happens then?'

'Lucia will be my wife. I shall be good to her. She will be by my side for the rest of my life, and will bear my children. You English are so so quaint. So silly and romantic, so — if you will forgive me, my dear — so immoral. You only look for love. It does not matter with whom. And the love for which you look is the passion which always dies. Such love is sometimes taken too cheap. The English in love are naive and irresponsible. You, Susannah, are sweet, and we have had a wonderful time together, but you had a good husband. You did not give him children, or prestige in the eyes of others, or make a home for him. You looked for romantic love, and found me. Now this so-romantic love has finished, as it always does.'

Clinging on to the only part of the tirade which she could absorb in such a state of shock, Susannah answered indignantly, '*I* am irresponsible? I? What about *you*? You play with people's deepest feelings, and then desert them. You are going to be married to a woman for whom you have no passion, and whom you have already deserted emotionally. And you call *me* irresponsible!'

'Yes, I do and you are! Life is not a fairy story, Susannah. Human life is no different from all nature. We are born, we grow — straight or crooked — but we grow. We blossom, we fade and we die. But when we are at our zenith, we do our very best to procreate. This is the importance of all nature; that we keep our species, as you call it, alive. It is the single most important fact in nature: that we procreate.'

'You could have fooled me!' said Susannah, feebly, and near a kind of laughing hysteria.

'We fooled each other,' replied Antonio, seriously. 'For a while I believed that it was with you that I should procreate. But my parents were right. Mistresses are for one side of life. Wives are for another, and wives have the most important rôle.'

'Have you told this to Gina?'

'Gina will know. She is not romantic. She comes to me for what I offer, so she will not be disappointed. This apartment is better than she has ever known. The money I give her is better than she has ever earned. She loves clothes and beauty and servants, and sex.'

'And you? What about you?'

'What does that matter? Sex is what I ask from her. She will give it to me. Also she will not wish for independence, nor question where I have been or with whom. She will accept, and I shall give. You could never accept unquestioningly, Susannah. It is a talent which you should learn.'

'I love you, Antonio, with all my heart.'

'This is true, but not with all your intelligence. I can tell. I am clever, and I know these things. I am all you wish as a lover, but not as a man, or as a friend. You will be better off without me, when you have had time to think, and I shall always wish you well.'

'Thank you,' murmured Susannah.

The irony was lost on Antonio. 'So now, you see, you must leave this apartment, and I will give you some money for a month or two. I am not niggard,' he added, puffing out his chest, and looking pleased with himself. 'I do not, as you say in England, boot out my old friends.'

There was a long silence, then Susannah said quietly, 'When do you want me to go?'

'At the end of the week?' he asked. 'I will be generous, and my lawyer will find you somewhere to go for the time being.'

'Very well,' said Susannah. 'At the end of the week.'

After Antonio left, she cried her eyes out, and all night she lay staring into the darkness, thinking of him.

CHAPTER TWELVE

The next few days were a limbo of unreality. Antonio telephoned her every morning to see how she was getting on. His lawyer had found her another small furnished apartment on the other side of Rome, and Antonio told her that she would be getting a good allowance for the next three months only: then the money would cease, and with it all correspondence. He was practical and cheerful, and utterly without remorse. If she tried to talk to him about her distress, he hung up immediately, but otherwise he was not unsolicitous. He said that the new apartment had been carefully chosen to suit her tastes and comfort, so that the months should 'pass conveniently', as he called it. He had arranged for a car to take her to her new home on the Friday.

'I shall come to say good-bye on Thursday evening,' he said. 'Not late, you understand, as I have another engagement. And I have bought for you a little present for you to remember me by, which I think you will like. It is very beautiful.'

'Thank you,' she said feebly, 'but please don't bother to come if it is too much trouble.' She was trying sarcasm again, but as usual it was wasted on Antonio.

'It is not too much trouble to say good-bye, Susannah,' he said sententiously. 'One should always leave one's loves on a good note, you agree?'

She laughed, and he said quickly, 'Why do you laugh?'

'I think you're funny sometimes,' she said.

'I shall see you on Thursday, then. *Arriverderci.*' He sounded displeased.

She packed her things, made arrangements with the porter to forward her mail, and settled all accounts with the local shops. She told none of her friends what was happening. She lived very intensely in her mind, and performed all physical tasks mechanically. The agony of despair still persisted, but alongside it, on another level, she was able to appreciate that a more prolonged stay with Antonio would have led to a total dead end.

Dead End. The words seemed to hover in the air, and the idea of suicide, flirted with before, returned to take purposeful possession of her.

But she would wait until Thursday. Miracles sometimes happened. She would look her best, for Antonio, seek no quarrels with him, be submissive, and somehow — oh God! somehow — charm him back to her.

She constantly turned over the events in her short past, wondering where she had gone so completely wrong and realising with surprise how little she had controlled her life. Things had happened to her, or been forced on her, and she had always given in to stronger wills. She was nearly twenty-one, and still disastrously obedient. She was well known in England, and perhaps would make a small success in America with her film; but, except for Marilyn, no one in the world cared whether she lived or died. No! That was not true! Dickie and his parents would be sad if she died, but only a little sad. Very soon she would be more or less forgotten by them, and Marilyn, absorbed in her new and exciting life in America, had already apparently forgotten her. She hadn't heard from her for several months.

Antonio had said at the beginning of their affair, 'Life is how you want it, sometimes, but only if you make the most of every chance that comes your way. Every chance, every human relationship has its circumscribed end, and during the time such opportunities are with you, you must make of them what you will. Success. Failure. These times are always for just so long. Never take them for granted. Make of them what you need.'

He was right, but she hadn't realised how right he was. She had laughed at the word 'circumscribed' and he had been hurt. But he had seen through her. She had lived her life as a sleepwalker, letting the chances come and go, letting her mother rule her, letting Marilyn take charge of her, and Antonio use her. Well, leopards couldn't change their spots, and nor could she! She was weak, and trained to obedience, and saddled with a diffidence she could never eradicate. Jacko's scars, though dormant, would still plague her, she had no doubt. After all, she had immersed herself in her wonderful love affair with Antonio partly to expunge them, to prove that sex could be wonderful not horrible. Perhaps, then, she had used Antonio, too? Impulsively she reached for the telephone and rang him to tell him that she forgave him, and that she wanted him back; that she would be for ever as he wished her to be — his chattel and his slave, if necessary. She told him wildly that if he left her she would kill herself. He listened politely, then said coldly, 'All women use moral blackmail, Susannah, and blackmail is never nice. I had thought better of you.'

Instantly sorry for what she had done, she begged him, 'But you will be coming on Thursday evening?'

'Of course I will,' he said grandly. 'I have given my word.'

Susannah had been taking sleeping pills for many months now. Feeling increasingly insecure, she returned to her friendly chemist. 'I have been silly,' she said. 'A friend in trouble asked me to let her have my pills, and I have given them to her. Now I cannot sleep myself. What am I to do?'

He shook his finger at her. 'This you should not have done,' he said. 'Such pills are on prescription. You may be doing your friend harm, not good. I can do nothing.'

'I'm sorry! I never thought I might be harming her. But please, please, help me! I have a radio play to do here in Rome tomorrow, and for a week after, and if I cannot sleep, I cannot do the job properly. I am in despair ...'

He softened at once, pleased to hear about the job. 'I shall let you have one more hundred,' he said carefully. 'But only this once, and never never again. It is understood, Signora?'

'Understood,' answered Susannah fervently.

She took the pills back home like a new-found treasure, and put them on her bedside table. One hundred and fifty pills altogether! Enough and more to end her life — her ridiculous, worthless, unhappy, short life. Poor Susannah! Nobody loves you. The world has stopped turning on its axis, and oblivion is just around the corner. Poor Susannah!

Antonio's farewell visit was a disaster. He came looking extremely handsome and excessively well-pleased with himself, and Susannah, too, had dressed to kill. Even she was pleased with her appearance, and Antonio was so appreciative that he became almost sentimental.

He showed her the present he had bought for her. It was a diamond brooch on a gold pin, in the shape of a heart; and beside the heart, on each side, were the letters A and S. 'For us,' he said. 'Then you will always remember.'

She took it listlessly and stared at it. Had he no idea how cruel he was being? She was hardly likely to forget him! What an absurd leaving present. How crassly insensitive! How ostentatious! How horrible!

He was waiting with shining eyes for her gratitude. She saw this, and gave him a wry smile. 'Thank you,' she said. 'How very generous!'

If he had hoped for more, he didn't say so. Indeed, he seemed pleased with her reply. 'Wear it,' he ordered.

She pinned it to the collar of her silk blouse.

'You look beautiful, Susannah,' he said, 'but all good things must come to an end.'

She nodded.

'You wish for one last time, for old time's sake?' he asked, almost archly.

For a moment she was so angry that she almost hit him, then she pulled herself together and said quietly, 'I think not, thank you. The affair is over. Let us not stir dead ashes.'

He was charmed with this reply. '"Stir dead ashes ..."!' he repeated. 'That is beautiful. Like poetry. I must think of this.'

'For next time?' she enquired sarcastically.

He agreed, happily. 'For next time.' He puffed out his chest. 'I wish you all the best Susannah. We have been happy on the whole, haven't we? And one day, I see you in my imagination as a pretty little, good little English housewife, who appreciates her man and has no silly ideas to be an actress. This way you will be content.'

'I'm sure,' she said, to avoid an argument.

'How is Dickie?'

'The divorce is going ahead quite well,' said Susannah.

He frowned. 'This I think is a pity,' he said. 'He was a good husband from what you say, and good husbands are not so usual. I, too, shall be a good husband.' Susannah laughed in spite of herself, and he looked angry. 'Your ways and my ways are different,' he snapped. 'Lucia thinks as I do. She is my countrywoman, and from my kind of society. She understands, and we will do well together. We will have sons ... perhaps many ... and they will inherit the family property and carry on our name.'

'Has our affair meant anything to you?' asked Susannah suddenly.

'Of course,' he replied gently. 'All affairs leave their mark. This was not just a — how do you say? — a one-night-stand. We have made love for a long time.'

'And Gina? Will you love her for a long time?'

'Perhaps. Who knows? Maybe for months. Maybe for years. We shall see how well we suit each other. She is very pretty.' He looked self-satisfied.

'Will you go on acting for a while?' asked Susannah. 'Even after you are married?'

'Who knows?' he said again. 'If they wish for me in Hollywood, I shall go perhaps for the experience. And then, perhaps, if you too do well, I shall meet you there.' He smiled and she sensed the patronage in his tone. 'To be a film star is good,' he went on. 'To be a stage actor in Italy just now is not important.'

'Why did you become an actor?' asked Susannah. 'It seems so unlikely in your family.'

'A film director saw me and he liked my face. He offered me a lot of money, so I say yes. Why not? Estates are expensive to keep up.'

'I'm sure they are,' she said.

He looked at his watch. 'I must go, Susannah,' he said, suddenly brisk. 'I meet Lucia in a quarter of an hour.'

In spite of herself Susannah felt the tears start into her eyes. 'Don't go so soon,' she said. 'I can't bear it.'

'Don't cry, Susannah,' he said, cupping her chin in his hands. 'There is a future for us both.'

'Not for me,' she said. 'There is no future for me without you.'

For a moment he looked put out. 'You are not thinking of this silly business of killing yourself, are you?' His voice had sharpened with annoyance. 'You know this kind of talk makes me angry! It is feeble, and it is irresponsible. Suicide is a crime in the eyes of the Good God.'

'And adultery?'

'Adultery is not a crime. That is also good, as far as *you* are concerned, no? A sin, maybe, but not a crime.' He smiled suddenly. 'Sometimes it is a misfortune, especially if you are married and you are caught, but it is not a very big sin. Only a little one, which the priest will soon forgive.'

'I can't live without you, Antonio. I can't! I can't!'

'You can and you will,' he said. His jaw had tightened and he was looking bored and uncomfortable, but he kissed her on the lips. 'Goodbye, little English,' he said. 'Take care of yourself.'

'How can I, when I shall never see you again?' she demanded.

She clung to him, but he disengaged himself dextrously. '*Arriverderci*,' he said, bowing. 'I wish you luck.'

He went quickly out of the room and shut the door.

Susannah looked at the time. It was seven-thirty. Although the day had been hot and humid, the air was cool now. Perfect. She gazed out of her window down into the lovely elegant square beneath her. Lights were going on, one by one. The waiters were flicking crumbs off the tables, putting on fresh tablecloths and arranging flowers in huge vases. One or two people were drinking. Several more were strolling arm in arm in their beautiful, expensive clothes, and here and there, lovers were kissing.

What a city for love! What a city to live in without a lover! She sighed deeply and wiped the tears from her eyes. She went over to the writing desk in the drawing room, opened her blotting pad and wrote two letters; one to Dickie, and one to his mother. She thought for a long while about whether she ought to write to her own mother, decided against it at last, and propped up the letters she had written against the lamp on the desk. She went into the kitchen, opened the fridge and found a small bottle of champagne. Carefully she made herself some toast, and spread some paté de foie on it. She poured the champagne into an exquisite crystal glass, held it up to the light, and drained it. Nibbling the toast, she undressed, and changed into her prettiest nightdress, brushed her hair until it shone, and poured herself another glass of champagne.

PART TWO

Anna

CHAPTER THIRTEEN

Marilyn rang Susannah's doorbell. There was no answer. The porter had said that Susannah was at home, so she rang a second time. Again there was no answer.

She turned to her new husband. 'What shall I do?' she asked.

'I don't speak Italian, but if you're sure the porter said she was at home, ring again,' he said.

'She's living with an Italian,' objected Marilyn. 'We don't want to disturb them if they're making love, do we?'

'Try once again. If they still don't answer, then we'll go.'

The first ring caught Susannah in the act of putting the pills into her mouth. She had a large carafe of water by her side, now, and a glass. She hesitated. Who could it be? Was it possible that Antonio had had a sudden change of heart? He was an imperious and unpredictable creature. Had he suddenly decided that he couldn't leave her after all? Should she answer the door? Why not? If the intruder wasn't Antonio, no harm had been done. She could take the pills later.

But how stupid! It couldn't be Antonio. He had the keys, so he wouldn't have to ring.

Then who?

At the second ring she did nothing at all. Just listened ... tense. At the third she went to the front door. She was surprised to find that although it was not a cold night she was shivering.

'Who's that?' she called out anxiously.

'Marilyn,' replied Marilyn. 'Have we come at an awkward time?'

'Marilyn!' Susannah was almost incredulous. 'How

93

wonderful! How absolutely wonderful! Come in!' She threw open the door and burst into tears.

Marilyn was shocked at the sight of her and at once took her in her arms. 'Hush, honey!' she said gently. 'Hush! It's OK. I'm here and you can tell me all about it. This is Bob, by the way, my new husband. Bob ... Susannah. Susannah ... Bob. Now take it easy, honey. What's the matter? Where's Antonio?'

'He's gone.'

'For good?'

'Yes.'

'I see. Well, why don't we all sit down and talk about it?'

Susannah found a handkerchief and dabbed fiercely at her eyes. 'My God!' she said. 'What on earth must you think of me? What a way to greet you, and I'm so thrilled to see you! Really I am! Congratulations on the marriage, too. Come on in, and have a drink. What will you have?'

'What is there?' asked Bob, smiling kindly. 'I guess we all need one!'

'Almost anything,' replied Susannah. She led them both in the direction of the drawing room.

'When you didn't answer, we nearly went away,' said Marilyn. 'I'm so glad we didn't.'

'So am I, for heaven's sake!' exclaimed Susannah fervently. 'It's perfectly marvellous that you're here!'

Marilyn smiled. 'When did Antonio leave?' she asked.

'He went finally tonight,' replied Susannah, 'though it has been looming for some time.' She smiled wanly. 'And he's turning me out of the flat as from tomorrow because he's found another girlfriend.' She blew her nose and smiled shakily through her tears.

'Oh, dear! I am so sorry,' said Marilyn warmly.

'Yes. It's all been a bit traumatic,' answered Susannah. She gestured feebly round the room. 'I'm sorry I'm in my night things, but I've been packing, so everything is a bit of a mess.'

'It looks pretty good to me,' said Marilyn. Susannah noticed that her accent had become very slightly Americanised. 'What a beautiful place! You must show me round later.'

'I'll take you round now, then we can settle down properly to our drinks afterwards,' replied Susannah.

'Later,' laughed Marilyn.

'No, now,' replied Susannah, over-emphatically.

Marilyn saw that she was trying to give herself time to pull herself together, so she and Bob allowed her to take them on a tour of the apartment. Her own bright eyes missed nothing — the expensive luggage, heavily labelled; the champagne and water by the bedside; the pile of pills on the bedside table, and the traces of earlier tear marks on Susannah's cheeks.

'I'm starved,' she said, finally. 'Since Antonio isn't here, why doesn't Bob make us some sandwiches while he's mixing the drinks? He's a dab hand at sandwiches. then you and I can have a heart-to-heart. OK, Bob?'

'Sure,' agreed Bob good-humouredly, heading back towards the kitchen.

Marilyn followed Susannah into the long drawing room and threw herself into a comfortable armchair.

'My, how lovely all this is!' she exclaimed. 'And Rome, too! It's the first time I've ever been, and I've fallen in love with it. Isn't life extraordinary? When Jan died I thought my life was over. You know how I was. I'd never have believed in a thousand years that I could find someone to take his place, and of course in some ways I never shall, but Bob is just wonderful, and I'm quite deliriously happy. He's a scriptwriter. The lowest of the low in Hollywood, he says, but he's going to write the great American novel any day now, and it will be a bestseller, and we will be made. Not that we do so badly now, as he's filthy rich! His mother was a starlet who slept around with an eye to real estate, and when she died he inherited a fortune.' Marilyn was rattling on determinedly, to give Susannah time to adjust. 'Now then, darling,' she said strongly, having decided that Susannah had recovered enough to talk rationally, 'tell me what's up. You're looking very pretty, but otherwise in a bad way. I saw the pills, darling,' her voice was compassionate, 'so I can see that you've been feeling terrible.'

Susannah nodded. Tears had welled up in her eyes again, and she didn't speak.

Marilyn waited, then crossed over to her and hugged her lovingly. 'Come on, sweetheart!' she said. 'Tell me! Bob and I came to Rome on our honeymoon especially to see you, so you can understand that I want to help you if I can.'

Susannah began to talk. The relief was enormous. She was immensely touched by Marilyn's concern. That she should be here at all was a miracle, and that on her honeymoon with Bob she had troubled to come and see her, and arrived on this particular night, was a gift from the gods! As she talked, her sense of humour made a welcome but shaky return. She was almost able to laugh at herself. But Marilyn didn't laugh. Presently Bob came in with champagne and sandwiches, and Susannah, surprisingly, took his presence in her stride. Quite without self-consciousness she went on pouring out her story. 'So there you are,' she finished finally, the tears streaming down her cheeks. 'I'd come to a dead end, and life didn't seem worth living.'

'How old are you?' asked Bob quietly.

Susannah looked surprised. 'Twenty-one next Wednesday,' she said. 'Grown up!'

'Yes. You're nearly of age,' he said gravely.

'That's right.' She still sounded surprised.

Marilyn and Bob exchanged pitying glances, then Bob said, 'We must celebrate that birthday of yours. We'll throw a party, won't we, honey? A big one, and you'll ask all your friends, Susannah.'

'Sure,' said Marilyn. 'One hell of a party! Meanwhile,' she went on, 'you're not going to that boring new flat of yours tomorrow. You're coming to stay with us at Hassler's from tonight, isn't she, Bob? You know the Hassler Hotel, Susannah?'

'Of course.'

'You like it?'

'Of course!'

'As I told you, we don't know Rome,' said Marilyn. 'So will you show us around a bit?'

'I'd love it,' said Susannah. And at last she was smiling broadly.

Although she was bewildered by the turn events had taken, she felt, as she always did with Marilyn, comfortable and at home. She was thankful to let her take charge. Marilyn had always put matters right when things had been intolerable, and in an odd way it seemed natural that she was here now. That she herself had been on the point of committing suicide seemed already extraordinary, and Marilyn would somehow take care of the future. Only one thing was certain, though. She mustn't spoil their honeymoon.

'I can't stay with you at Hassler's,' she said. 'I wouldn't want to be a drag on you, on your honeymoon!'

'How could you be a drag when we want you with us?' demanded Marilyn. 'You shouldn't be on your own just yet, darling. You aren't ready for it.'

'But Hassler's is expensive!'

'I told you. Bob is a rich man.'

'But on your honeymoon ...' objected Susannah.

'A six-month honeymoon!' laughed Marilyn. 'We're not wanting to be on our own that long, or we wouldn't have chosen such a long time! Now,' she went on energetically, 'where are we going to eat properly? The sandwiches were delicious, but I'm still hungry. I told you, we're new here, and we need a guide. You're our guide, Susannah, if you'll be so kind, darling.'

'Of course!' Susannah suddenly became emotional again. 'Oh, this is all so marvellous!' she exclaimed. 'A few minutes ago there didn't seem to be anything to live for, and now you're here!'

'Before we go out,' said Marilyn, 'we'd better let Antonio know what's happened to you, as he has a flat waiting for you from tomorrow. From then on, though, he's out of your life, and you're going to start afresh. What's his telephone number?'

'He won't be there,' said Susannah.

'I can leave a message.'

'He might not want to talk about me.'

'Too bad!'

Antonio, however, was at home and, since Marilyn was famous, he used all his charm on her. Marilyn was polite, but wrinkled her nose in disgust while she was talking, and when she put the receiver down she said, 'I don't like him one little bit. I'm sure he's got the fascination of the devil, and he's the best-looking man in town, but he's arrogant and cold and selfish and conceited.'

Bob laughed. 'You got all that from one telephone conversation?' he teased.

'From one telephone conversation and a talk with Susannah,' agreed Marilyn firmly.

They called a taxi while Susannah unpacked a dress to wear and changed into it, and the porter took the suitcases while all of them were having a last look round to see that she had left nothing behind.

'There are two letters here, darling,' said Marilyn. 'We can post them at the hotel.'

'No,' said Susannah. 'I'll take them. I shan't be sending them now ... I don't expect.'

'That's my girl,' said Marilyn. 'Come on.'

When she was ready, Susannah locked the door of her apartment behind her for the last time, gave the keys to the porter and, without looking back, got into the taxi with Marilyn and Bob.

The three of them dined together at Susannah's favourite restaurant in the Piazza Navona. The stars were their magnificent impersonal selves. The air was balmy. It was wonderful to be with Marilyn.

Faintly, her will to live returned.

CHAPTER FOURTEEN

Although she went on feebly protesting that she couldn't stay with them at Hassler's, Susannah allowed herself to be persuaded at last and, once installed, almost in spite of herself, enjoyed showing the two of them round Rome. She was able to see it anew, through their eyes, and the well-remembered sights gave her surprisingly few pangs since Marilyn's and Bob's outlook differed so completely from Antonio's. They gave her a large birthday party at the hotel, to which her friends crowded, and it was considered the most chic party of the season. Susannah found Marilyn's high spirits infectious and, remembering how devastated she had been by Jan's death, she marvelled at her present happiness. It also gave her hope. She didn't forget Antonio, even for a moment, but for the time being was content to live each day for its own sake, and by the time Bob and Marilyn moved on to the next stage of their honeymoon — three weeks in Greece — she was able to go to her new apartment almost with composure, since, at the end of that time, she had agreed to join up with them again in the South of France.

She heard nothing from Antonio, though she certainly heard about him. His wedding to Lucia was the most fashionable of the year. She sent no word of congratulation, but read the newspapers avidly. She was surprised to find that his marriage touched her hardly at all; it was his liaison with Gina which hurt. He'd been right. It had been on a sexual level only that she'd been so passionately engaged, and, on this level only, she missed him.

She lived most of her life at this time like a somnambulist, but thankfully not in the grip of the nightmare she had dreaded.

Marilyn had said hotly that those who, like Antonio, used others — perhaps even destroying them for their own satisfaction — were 'trespassers on eternity', as were those who — again, like Antonio — deliberately chose to be dilettantes when they had the capacity for real achievement. The phrase haunted Susannah, who gradually assimilated it as part of her own thinking.

The three weeks in Antonio's new apartment were a time of introspection and reconciliation within herself. The place was box-like, characterless, adequate; a clear indication of her demotion. But its very difference helped her to obliterate his memory, and in so securely winning Marilyn's love she knew that she had at last succeeded in a relationship. This gave her the strength, and the determination, to face her future with courage. She had youth, beauty and a chance of wide horizons. She must accept them and move on without self-pity, to fulfil their promise. But she had still heard no word from Hollywood.

The time passed swiftly and she set off doggedly for the South of France. She hated leaving Italy; she had lived there so intensely, albeit mostly unhappily. But Antonio was on his honeymoon, and Rome was already her past.

It was September. She went by the night sleeper to Nice. She lay awake all night, then, during her breakfast of hot croissants, cherry jam and coffee, watched the early morning sun finger the alien landscape of the Italian Riviera. It was pretty enough with its colour-washed villas and pine trees, and its sea of picture-postcard blue, but it seemed insipid after the stone glories of Rome.

Marilyn and Bob met her at Nice station.

'You're looking better,' said Marilyn, studying her affectionately. 'Feeling better?'

'Yes, much. And you're looking wonderful.'

'And I'm looking wonderful, too,' laughed Bob, 'and we're mighty glad to see you again, Susannah.'

They piled her luggage into the boot, and themselves into the large chauffeur-driven car, and drove towards Antibes.

'We have a heavenly villa on the coast,' said Marilyn

cheerfully. 'We've run into lots of old friends, so it's going to be rather social, I'm afraid. But that may be a good thing for you. France is very different from Italy, darling, and personally I like it better, but for you it's the difference which is the main thing. We have a couple of house guests, and we're going out most nights, but the days can be your own, for swimming, or sleeping, or reading, or even exploring. I'm a stay-at-home, but Bob will take you anywhere you'd like to go. Make the most of Bob quickly, though, because his freedom is nearly over. He's wrestling with an idea for his great novel, and once he begins writing, he'll be lost to us. He says he must write or die, but I can't say his work seems to make him happy.' She grinned at Bob.

Susannah looked around her curiously as they drove. They had taken the coast road. To their left the sparkling sea wrinkled its way along the white sands which stretched for miles and miles, and were almost empty. On their right there were palm trees and a few white houses with shutters, set among luxurious gardens; and behind these rose the inland hills.

Antibes, with its squat little castle and its grey ramparts, enchanted her. Flowers rioted everywhere in the squares and gardens. Roses, cannas and agapanthus were in full bloom. Geraniums of every colour spilled from the balconies. Yachts by the hundred bounced lightly in the harbour. On the foreshore, fishermen were mending their nets, their catches already displayed on stalls along the waterfront. From other shops tumbled fruit, vegetables, buckets, spades, swimming costumes, toys and sweets. Only the restaurants were shuttered.

Presently the road forked right into a rough lane. Before a huge wooden gate they came to rest. The chauffeur got out of the car and rang a bell, and after a pause the gate was opened by a very old man — obviously a gardener. His face was seamed and creased, and his blue eyes filmed over.

The house came in sight around a bend at the end of a short drive. It was long and low, and on two floors. The shutters were dark green, and the massive front door was up a flight of marbled steps. The lawns which flanked it were an emerald green. Roses bloomed in profusion in the garden, and indoors

they were arranged in huge vases along the walls of a large
marbled hall. To the right a door led into a big, cool, elegant
drawing room. To the left was a high-ceilinged and stately
dining room. Susannah's luggage was already being carried up
to her bedroom, which was light and airy and opened on to a
balcony furnished with a most inviting garden chair. The
windows faced a long lawn at the back of the house, from
which marble steps led quite steeply to the sea. Again, it was a
far cry from Coulsdon!

'D'you like it?' asked Marilyn.

'Adore it.'

'Use it for convalescence,' said Marilyn. 'Tired?'

'Not too tired for a swim.'

'We have our own beach at the foot of the cliffs at the end of
the garden. Or there's a pool beyond that hedge to the left.
You may find one of the others. We have three people staying.
Alex Claverdon — he's a Lord — and the Marmonts. She was
an actress. He's an American businessman.'

'How did you find this lovely house?' asked Susannah.

'Friends in England have lent it to us.'

Susannah changed into a bathing costume and walked down
the steep marble steps to the sea.

The beach was deserted, though she noticed a towel and
some slippers under a striped umbrella. The sea was warm and
calm, and there were no clouds in the sky. She lay on her back
floating on the water, and thought, as always when by herself,
of Antonio. With all her heart she wished he was with her.
With some of her mind she was glad he wasn't. It would mean
misery. She wondered how he was, and if she would ever see
him again. She wondered if she would ever forget him and be
free of his attraction.

A cheerful voice broke in on her thoughts.

'I say! Hullo. You must be the actress, Anna Starr. We've all
been dying to meet you. My name is Alex Claverdon.'

Swimming alongside her was a big fair man of about thirty.
He had bright blue eyes and was very sunburned. Susannah
liked the look of him immediately.

CHAPTER FIFTEEN

Susannah spent a fortnight in the South of France, and Alex Claverdon fell in love with her. She was grateful for his attention, but her affair with Antonio was too close and had been too unhappy for her to want to get emotionally involved. He seemed content to be her friend, which was a relief; and she enjoyed his company. He was a rather serious young man ('with the makings of a tycoon', someone told her) but he had a good sense of humour. He danced well, swam well and played an excellent game of tennis, but his chief passion, it seemed, was gardening. He had a stately home in the North of England which was expensive to run and needed a great deal of repair, as troops had been billeted there during the war. The main staircase had been ruined, lead had been stolen from the roof and dry rot was rampant. He himself had seen active service in North Africa and Greece, but had escaped without injury, and his ambition was to make enough money to look after his ancestral home.

Susannah had not met his type before and was surprised at her ease in his company. A year or two ago, his title would have impressed and frightened her; but he seemed to have no arrogance, unlike Antonio, and she found his thoughtfulness and effortless manners a welcome contrast. She made no attempt to know him better, but on a surface level she was certainly attracted. Marilyn, seeing this, was pleased.

Marilyn was worried about Susannah's future. Now that the child had grown up, she realised that it was too late to take total responsibility for her, even though she loved her dearly — because it might prejudice Bob's happiness, and therefore her own. On the other hand, it seemed heartless to abandon her at such a moment. Fortunately things were soon taken out of her hands.

One morning Susannah received a telephone call from her new agent. 'You've won, my dear!' he announced. 'Congratulations! MGM are giving you a three-year contract. Apparently they were very pleased with your performance in the film, but a bit dubious about your type, which they class as very middle-class British! And they've had an influx of those, lately. Anyhow, they are willing to take a chance, and the money is good.'

'When do they want me?'

'Three weeks.'

'Will they find me somewhere to live?'

'If you want them to.'

'I do.'

'How long will you be in France?'

'I'm going back to Italy in four day's time,' said Susannah.

'Will you be coming to England on your way to Hollywood? You have to sign a contract.'

'I don't think so. I've still got a flat in Rome for a few weeks, and I haven't much money at the moment!'

'I'll cable you an advance.'

'Thank you. But any publicity about the contract and my mother will want to leap on the bandwaggon, and I'm not ready to face that again yet. And especially not Jacko!'

'We won't let the cat out of the bag until you're safely in America!' said the agent. 'Excited?'

'Yes, but I haven't quite taken it in.'

'Well, give me a ring when you do, Susannah, and we'll make all the arrangements. Oh, by the way, you'd better get used to answering to Anna from now on. It's Anna Starr they've put under contract. See you soon, darling. Goodbye.'

Susannah put down the telephone feeling slightly dazed. Immediately she found herself wishing she could tell Antonio. He would be impressed, she knew, and, had she heard earlier, she might perhaps have been able to salvage a little of her pride. He might not have turned her out of the apartment so precipitately, and she might not have tried to commit suicide. Ah, well, it was too late now! Chalk it up to experience, she thought wryly.

She ran to tell Marilyn, who was relieved and delighted. 'Bob and I will be able to look after you a bit in Hollywood when we get back,' she said happily. 'We can show you the ropes, and perhaps stop you feeling too lonely.'

'You're a saint, Marilyn!' exclaimed Susannah. 'What would I do without you?'

Marilyn laughed. 'We'll have fun in America,' she said. 'Oh darling, it's wonderful! Congratulations!'

Alex Claverdon was dismayed. He had been willing to bide his time about Susannah, but had banked on her returning to England. Now he might never see her again. Fully realising that he was heading for rejection, he asked her to marry him. She refused.

Three weeks later, Anna sailed on the Queen Mary from Le Havre. A suite had been put at her disposal, and flowers from her agent, from Marilyn and Bob, Alex Claverdon and MGM were in her cabin. As Anna Starr, contract artist, she was already of some importance. She sat at the Captain's table for meals, and, for the first time for a long while, felt that the future might be on her side.

She was met in New York by the head of her British agency, who was to wine and dine her preparatory to putting her on the plane for Los Angeles the following morning. Her first sight of New York horrified her. She had heard about skyscrapers, and seen them on the movies, but after war-time London — small, dingy and bleak — and the magical beauties of Rome, they seemed bigger and more harshly impersonal than she had expected, and the city itself uglier and much noisier. MGM was at that time all-powerful, so she had been whisked through Immigration and Customs with no trouble at all, and with considerable speed, and a huge Cadillac had taken her to the Waldorf Astoria. There a swarm of bell-hops grabbed her luggage and deposited it in the enormous apartment that had been reserved for her. She went to the window to look out, and felt giddy. Her suite was so high up that the people in the street below looked like midgets, but even so the noise was still deafening; cars, motor-bikes, police whistles, sirens and road drills all shrilled and screamed and buzzed and roared, and on this hot September day the air conditioning, which she had hardly encountered before, hummed loudly.

Her agent was speaking to her.

'I'm so sorry,' she said apologetically. 'I didn't hear. I'm a little bewildered.'

He laughed. 'I was only saying that I wondered if you were hungry. Had any lunch, or would you like to come to the 21?'

'I'm broke,' said Anna. 'I can't possibly pay for all this!'

'MGM is paying. You might as well relax and enjoy it!'

They went to the 21 Restaurant and the place was filled with socialites, but also actors whom she had only ever seen on the screen: Clarke Gable, Myrna Loy, Burgess Meredith and Paulette Goddard. She was thrilled but exhausted at the same time, and when the agent, Garfield Fenn, asked her if she would like to see a play that night, though she agreed enthusiastically, she knew she would have to rest all the afternoon — not only because she was tired, but because emotion, and a feeling of strangeness that she had never encountered before, were sapping her usual resilience.

The trip to the theatre was a nightmare. The New York traffic shocked and amazed her. Cars were bumper to bumper, with their drivers honking, hooting, yelling and cursing. Police whistles were still blowing, and pedestrians darted frenetically and, it seemed to her, dangerously, in and out among the cars. On the pavement outside the theatre, the crowds were churning and screaming and cursing, until she felt suffocated. On the other hand, it was stimulating, and — curiously — she had a faint premonition that one day she might live here, and come to love the city; perhaps even think of it as home.

The play was a musical, and wonderfully staged, but by now she was too worn out to give it the attention it deserved; in fact, to her shame, she fell asleep during the performance.

The drive from Los Angeles airport the next day into Hollywood was a mammoth disappointment. Second-hand car lots, hot-dog stands, hamburger-joints, telephone wires and electric cables, tangling untidily among unattractive, dirty pink and yellow stucco houses and huge billboards advertising everything from Coca-cola to Cadillacs, made the journey depressingly sleazy. In Los Angeles the houses were only one or two storeys high and there was plenty of skyline, but most of the architecture had a temporary, pseudo-Mediterranean, slip-shod quality that appalled her. Could this horrible place really be the Silver City? But as the car drove into the residential part of Beverly Hills, it was different altogether. First there were orange groves in the valley. Then the houses. Her spirits rose. Here, all was luxury and elegance. The enormous and beautiful homes were set among exquisitely manicured lawns bordered with tropical flowers, and bougainvillea of every colour climbed the masonry. The sun shone benignly out of a brilliant sky.

All at once she realised that, if she played her cards right, little Susannah Dale from a small suburb in England had the world of fame and fortune at her feet! She had been sent for to Hollywood because she was talented enough to be groomed for international stardom. She was twenty-one, and perhaps, after all, life was only beginning!

The film company had found a small bungalow apartment for her in Santa Monica. It was well-appointed and extremely chintzy, furnished in what she was to learn later was called the 'English style'. Double frilled curtains framed every window, and the view from her sitting room was of more bungalows, more or less like her own, all with small unfenced gardens, again like her own. The gardens were filled with flowering shrubs and there were giant palm trees everywhere, inhabited, she was also told later, by enormous rats.

Flowers had been arranged in vases in all the rooms, and a card on the mantelpiece informed her that several of the bouquets had been sent by Hans Schwarber, the director of *Roman Summer*, who would be calling that evening at around six o'clock to take her out to dinner. (Again she learned later that everyone dined early in Hollywood, either because they actually *were* working in the studios the next day and perhaps on early call, or because they were pretending to be working.)

She dressed with care and in great excitement and, punctually at the time stipulated, Hans arrived with his wife Estelle, a sharp-nosed fine-boned little woman, with small restless eyes and bony claw-like hands covered in enormous rings.

Hans was delighted by Anna's appearance. The months she had spent in Italy with Antonio had taught her an elegance and chic which charmed him. Estelle too professed her admiration,

but Anna saw that she was watching her with a catlike intensity
and guessed that she would be a difficult woman for any other
woman to please.

They took her to the Brown Derby restaurant on Wilshire
Boulevard, where everyone sat in semi-circular booths. To
Anna's amazement, telephones were brought to the tables,
and plugged in, as the famous and not-so-famous received
outside telephone calls. This she found very impressive. She
also recognised famous faces at nearly all the tables near by.
James Stewart, Loretta Young, Joan Crawford and Cyd Cha-
risse were all within a stone's throw, and a little further off she
could see Joan Fontaine, Ray Milland and Maria Montez.
How excited her mother would have been! To visit Hollywood would achieve Muriel's lifelong ambition! Again she
thought how sad it was that Muriel's jealousy of her had
resulted in a total severance of communication. She sighed
with an unfamiliar pang of homesickness.

Estelle had noticed the sigh. 'What's up, honey?' she asked
briskly. 'Not up to your standards?'

'Good heavens no!' replied Anna strongly. 'I was only sad
that my mother couldn't be here to enjoy such a wonderful
evening with me. She is completely stage-struck; more so than
me, in fact,' she added laughingly. 'She would be in heaven
here!'

Hans, who remembered Muriel clearly from the time she
had so forcefully objected to Anna's change of name, only
smiled politely, but Estelle was genuinely touched. 'Yeah, I
guess it can be lonely at first for you foreigners sometimes,' she
agreed kindly. 'But remember, if you ever get too lonesome,
Hans and I are here to give you a hand.'

Anna's obvious gratitude touched her still further, and by
the end of the meal she and Anna were on the way to becoming
friends.

The food (Cobb salad) was strange to Anna's English (and
Italian) palate, but what astounded her was the beauty of all
the waiters, and indeed of the car 'pick-ups' — the young men
outside the restaurant who parked the guests' cars. (Soon she
was to be equally astounded by the beauty of all the girls and
young men in the coffee shops and drug-stores, the hotel
reception-lobbies, the gas stations and offices.) Estelle laughed

at her. 'They all want to be movie stars, honey,' she said. 'Every single one of the poor slobs! And only one in ten thousand will make it.'

It turned out that Anna had very little time to be lonely in the next few weeks, for which she was thankful. She was able to forget Antonio for hours on end, but saw very little of Holly-wood except the MGM studios, the Wardrobe department, and the Stills department. The enormous Thalberg building, known to actors as the Iron Lung, was her home and her prison. She was introduced to Doré Schary (a big-nosed man with crinkled hair and rimless spectacles, who had just taken over as Head of the studios from Louis B. Mayer), to Mayer himself, and to Bert Thau, but she was too nervous of them to receive any clear idea of their personalities at this time. Their power was too great, as far as she was concerned, and she could only stammer at them helplessly. She was to get to know Schary and Thau all too well in the future. (The legendary Louis B. Mayer died the following year.)

Anna was turned over entirely to the Publicity department which was to manufacture a persona for her. She had endless stills sessions and make-up sessions, during which they tried to find a selling 'personality' for her, and a life story which would have more public appeal than her own. Finally it was decided that she was to be the daughter of high-born parents who had fallen on evil days after her father, an officer in a Guards regiment, had been killed during the war. Her mother had been reduced to becoming a seamstress in order to keep her family afloat and, although Anna had made one film as a child, playing the daughter of Marilyn de la Roche, she had gone back to school and remained unnoticed until Hans Schwarber had seen her in a cinema queue and had decided she was perfect casting for *Roman Summer*. He had had her tested, she had landed the part and, as a result of her success in the film, he had persuaded MGM to sign her as a contract artist. Anna Starr, they predicted, would become a name to conjure with.

At first she hated the stills and make-up sessions. If she had made a success looking as she already did, she thought it stupid to spend days on end trying to make her look different. Her hair was waved, then straightened; she was given a fringe, then had her hair swept back off her face. They bleached it and gave

her colour washes of every hue, then allowed her to wear her
own colour again. They enlarged her mouth, then made it
smaller. They worked at enlarging her eyes and altering the
shape of her eyebrows, and took endless pictures in endless
sexy positions. They took photographs of her alone, and with
up-and-coming young male hopefuls — gazing into each
other's eyes lovingly, or with acute disdain. She was fully
dressed, then half-dressed, showed a lot of leg and bosom,
looked demure and unapproachable; and all the photographs
were sent to the powers-that-be, to be studied and discussed.
Finally it was settled that a 'sophisticated simplicity' should be
her image. Her dark hair was given copper highlights and worn
long and slightly waved. Her eyebrows were to be made up
arched, and left unplucked; and she was urged to dress as a
slightly more elegant 'girl next door'.

During this period she was invited to several quite grand
parties at some of the most famous and glamorous Hollywood
homes, and for these she was lent clothes from the Wardrobe.
There were butlers and footmen with white gloves, swimming
pools and champagne. Surprisingly, too, to an English actress
reared on magazines extolling Hollywood's virtues, there were
drugs at the parties (uppers and downers at this time, and
bowls of drimamyl on the tables) as well as drink.

She didn't always enjoy herself, as many of the male stars and
directors automatically expected her to have sex with them
before the evening was over, and extricating herself from such
situations without injuring their masculine pride was sometimes difficult. She didn't want to be branded as a 'British
prude' before she had even started work, but neither did she
want to be an easy, and therefore perhaps comtemptible, lay.
Besides, always and always, Antonio was in her mind. And
behind him again, was the shadow of Jacko. It was like walking
on a tightrope, because, as she well knew, rejected males could
become angry and vindictive.

She was made to attend several important Hollywood
premières, (often at the Graumans' Chinese Theatre) for
which again she was dressed by the Wardrobe, and to these she
was escorted by young men deputed by the studios to look
after her for the evening. When she objected to such a total
manipulation of her personality, she was told firmly that she

was in competition with thousands and thousands of other, probably equally talented, girls and that she would be sensible to do as she was bidden and to keep her mouth shut.

With the publicity machine in permanent action, photographs of her began appearing in all the film magazines. Now, they told her, she had one toe on the bottom rung of the ladder. When she appeared at the premières, she was even cheered by one or two of the fans on the bleachers (a series of benches on rising steps placed in front of the cinema, from which fans could watch the arrival of their idols) and they clapped her, and shouted her name. Perhaps she really was getting somewhere!

But in spite of the fact that she had been told to keep quiet, Anna began to make enquiries about future films. She was again told to be patient; but with the stills session over, time began to drag.

She went out and about a great deal during the day, driving around Beverly Hills and Bel Air, into the Hollywood Hills, staring like any tripper at the enormous houses of the famous, follies of every kind — Spanish haçiendas jostling vast Scottish baronial castles, Italian palazzos set side by side with French Châteaux, and Mexican ranch houses nudging English 'Tudor' houses of huge proportions. All the gardens were unfenced like her own, and beautifully kept by Japanese gardeners. On Mulholland Drive, with its magnificent views over Los Angeles, the houses were smaller. (Then it was sparsely populated; now it is one of the most expensive parts of Hollywood.)

Anna spent a lot of time on Malibu beach, and learned to play golf at the seaside course at Pacific Palisades. She also learned to play tennis. She had never felt fitter than now, living this open-air life. But she needed to work. Now that she was here in America, she wanted to prove herself ... otherwise what was she doing all these thousands of miles away from the people and places she knew best?

It was at this time that she met Phyllida Mantell, who had been a child star in the Thirties — Hollywood's Golden Age. Like the 'Gang' stars (Matthew Beard, kown as 'Stymie', Darla Wood, a dark-haired little beauty who sang and danced, Dickie Moore, clever as paint and a born comedian, 'Baby Peggy' and

Edith Fellowes, not to mention Jane Withers and Freddie Bartholomew), Phyllida had been gifted, loveable, exploited and indulged. And then, like most of them, she had been dropped because she was no longer a child. No preparation. No explanation. Just dropped. The trauma had been devastating.

'I couldn't believe it!' said Phyllida. 'And I couldn't get over it either. One minute we were rich, fêted, and supporting our families in style. The next we were through. No child should have been subected to such shocks.'

'How did you become a star?' Anna asked her.

'All of us had ambitious mothers — or guardians, or grandmothers — pushing us for the money. I can hardly forgive my mother. I'm working as a private secretary to a scriptwriter now — Neal Kendred — and sometimes I dream that I've been rediscovered and I'll be a star again. Silly, isn't it? Stymie went on drugs and is serving a twenty-year sentence in the Federal Penitentiary. Diana had a bad patch and nearly went under, but she's met a Catholic priest who's helping her. Darla was actually happy when her mother broke the news that her contract was not going to be renewed. Perhaps she never liked being a star, or perhaps she was more level-headed than most of us. Edith has got a job as a medical secretary. But all of us, the successes and the failures alike, had to go to psychiatrists. It was bloody! How did you start?'

'I had a mother too, but luckily I went to a stage training school.'

'Yes, indeed. Lucky you.'

Anna didn't answer.

One day soon after this, she received a letter from Muriel, and opened it with trepidation. She was touched to find what seemed a humble and affectionate plea for forgiveness. Muriel seemed genuinely delighted at her success, which she had read about in a film magazine, and said she wished Anna all the luck in the world. She was sorry she had treated her so badly in the past, but said that she herself had so longed to have Anna's opportunities that it had 'addled her mind'. She would behave in future and she hoped that, now that Anna was doing so well, she would understand and forgive. Her own news was that

Jacko was very ill, but Charlie was being good for once. She also said that they were all very pushed for money, and even a small amount would be a godsend. She sent much love to Anna from all of them.

Anna read the letter time and time again, trying to make out whether it was a genuine desire for reconciliation or just her mother's normal wish to get cash if there was cash to be got. It mattered very much to her which of these it was, as she had never quite lost her basic desire to obtain her mother's love and approval. In the end she sent some money, but only a brief and impersonal letter.

Then at last she was given a script which she was told would provide a good part for her. She wasn't impressed by the story, but the part was indeed a good one and she gladly accepted it. A renewed outbreak of make-up and publicity sessions followed, and tests began in earnest.

Now Anna felt she belonged in Hollywood. She had made several friends, many of them British expatriates — Stewart Granger and his second wife, Jean Simmons (who had also, like her, just come out), Mike Wilding and his second wife, Elizabeth Taylor, James Mason and his wife, Pamela Kellino, and David Niven — but she had arrived at a curious and uneasy time for the industry. The McCarthy witch-hunt was still operating, though some of the heat had now gone out of it.

The Congressional hearings on Hollywood had begun in 1947, when a group of objecting witnesses who came to be known as the Hollywood ten were cited for contempt of Congress for refusing to answer either yes or no when asked if they were now or ever had been members of the Communist Party. (An eleventh, the playwright Bertolt Brecht, when asked if he was or ever had been a Communist, exclaimed, 'No, no, no, no, no. Never!' and fled the country within hours.) The Ten were given varying prison sentences of up to one year. In 1951 the hearings were resumed, and Larry Parks was the first witness.

The House Committee on Un-American Activities, later known as HUAC, apparently chose Hollywood as a target, firstly, because the Party itself had focussed on Hollywood since 1936 and, secondly, because the entertainment industry — then the dream factory of the world — would ensure wide publicity. During the next few years dozens and dozens of witnesses, some very talented, some world-famous, lost their jobs and were black-listed from getting further work. Senator McCarthy (whose term of office lasted from 1951-1954) was the most vocal anti-Communist of the time and his name became identified with the hearings.

By 1956 when Anna arrived, the situation had calmed considerably, but both Arthur Miller and, in Washington, Paul Robeson had to testify that year and, in 1957, Carl Forman, who with the help of Michael Wilson had written the film script of *The Bridge on the River Kwai*, had to call himself by the pen name of Pierre Boulle to ensure that the film was made.

Although Anna was British, new to the community, and utterly uninterested in politics, she couldn't help being slightly affected by the intensity of the feelings which surrounded her. She was sad that so many gifted people were being banished from Hollywood, but since she as yet knew none of them, the regret was impersonal. She had found that she liked most Americans very much; in her experience they were generous and friendly, and, like actors, a little larger than life. Success was important to them, so that her own small success in *Roman Summer* was a passport to their approval. In England she might have been an object of envy. Here she was an object of pride.

Her new film starred Clark Gable and Walter Pigeon, and a young American, Philip Marsh, was to play opposite her. To be in a film with the great Clark Gable gave her immense satisfaction; and Walter Pigeon, whose work she had always admired, was especially kind to her.

Anna was aware that Philip Marsh was attracted to her but, as with Alex Claverdon, she was still too much in love with Antonio to pay him much attention. She allowed him to date her once or twice, which she enjoyed, but that was all. He was an intellectual, highly articulate and sharply witty. He knew a great deal about a great many subjects and could talk about all of them well. In private he made no bones about his left-wing political views and told her that he might have to leave Hollywood. Anna told him that politics meant nothing to her, which shocked him, and that she was uneducated and very ignorant, but an eager pupil if he'd bother to teach her. Making the film with him, and above all with Clark Gable and Walter Pigeon, helped her to forget Antonio.

The tests had been fruitful, and she was pleased to see that she now looked beautiful rather than pretty on the screen. The part suited her too. It was meaty and sympathetic, and contained a good deal of humour, so she had a real opportunity to show her paces. Everyone assured her that she was doing well, and, as before, she worked with total concentration. When Marilyn and Bob at last returned from their honeymoon, and Anna began to see a good deal of them, she realised that she was finally happy again.

Then she had another letter from her mother. Jacko had died of a massive heart attack after several minor ones, and Muriel and Charlie were broke, so they were setting out to join her in Hollywood. They had found the money for the fare by selling the house. By the time this letter reached her, Muriel said, they would be on their way.

CHAPTER SIXTEEN

Anna was in a turmoil of excitement, mixed with apprehension, but Marilyn was frankly appalled.

'For God's sake don't let them move in with you!' she said. 'Leopards don't change their spots. Charlie will always be bad news, and you haven't gone far enough in your career to cope with such a millstone. That new house of yours will be quite enough responsibility. Muriel is a bitch, and a jealousy as deep-seated as hers doesn't evaporate overnight, I promise you. Be careful, darling. You've managed to escape her, and you do remarkably well on your own. Don't let her ruin everything for you again.' With a generous mortgage, Anna had just bought a spacious house with statutory swimming pool on Mulholland Drive. Marilyn thought her friend had earned some peace and quiet.

But Muriel when she arrived played her cards carefully and well. She was very loving towards Anna, who immediately responded, and she had made herself a wardrobe of simple, quiet, well-cut clothes, which she wore with style. She was still a pretty woman. Her greying hair suited her and her face was remarkably unlined. Charlie seemed to have improved beyond all recognition. He had also become sensationally good looking. On their best behaviour, they positively radiated charm, and both were an instantaneous success.

Anna, relieved and delighted, disregarded Marilyn's advice, and soon installed them in Mulholland Drive. Here Muriel blossomed. She had always been an excellent housekeeper, so the place ran on oiled wheels. Arriving back exhausted from the studio, Anna always found a hot meal waiting for her. Her clothes were kept in perfect order, the linen was spotless, and beautifully arranged flowers were everywhere. The staff Muriel engaged adored her, and fell happily in love with Charlie.

Muriel gave tasteful little parties to which she invited the people she considered important to Anna's career. She took immense care to flatter the women, who, she said, often wielded the most influence. She was the perfect English hostess, and her soirées were considered chic and fashionable. Anna was astonished but filled with pride.

Marilyn was sceptical. 'You're a silly little softie!' she exclaimed, exasperated. 'I tell you, people don't change! It suits her now to behave herself, but you wait! She'll have something up her sleeve, you mark my words.'

Charlie began getting work: plenty of work as an extra, small parts in 'B' pictures and, if he wanted it, any amount of work as a stand-in. Muriel was in seventh heaven. 'Every little helps,' she said proudly, 'and with your looks, Charlie, it won't be long before you're a big star.' Charlie smiled but didn't reply.

He still didn't enjoy acting, though, for someone as idle as he, he recognised that the salary represented a very generous reward for exceedingly small effort. He didn't like getting up early in the morning, and constant proximity to his mother bored him, but he did enjoy the luxury, liked to think of himself as a Hollywood film star, and revelled in the sports that such a good climate could provide. If he really did make the grade, he thought, he would be able to afford a house of his own here, and then life really would be well worth living! Here, the fact that he wasn't a gentleman worried no one — not even himself — and he felt at home in America. Meanwhile he went back to drinking more than was good for him at the many parties he attended. He also slept around indiscriminately.

Gradually Muriel began to overspend the very substantial allowance that Anna was giving her, and Anna began to get worried. She tried to remonstrate, but Muriel became tearful, and Anna was too weak to persevere. 'I have to have clothes to wear in my position, darling,' said Muriel, wiping her eyes carefully. 'What would people think if I was in rags and you in satin? Besides, you haven't been through what Charlie and I have had to suffer. Life has been pretty good to you. Trying to make ends meet by sewing for people, while at the same time trying to take care of Jacko — well, it was a nightmare! So don't spoil my fun, darling! I'll settle down and scrimp and save again, soon enough, never fear. Just let me have my head for a little while more.'

'There's no need to scrimp and save,' replied Anna, anxiously, 'only to go a little steady.'

'Don't worry, my dear. Charlie and I are used to it! We've spent a lifetime doing it, while you've been swanning about in Hollywood and Rome. They tell me you had a wonderful palazzo to live in in Rome, and this is our very first escape from dreary old South London. But never mind, as I say, we're used to it.'

With a guilty sigh, Anna gave up the argument. Weakly, she never remonstrated with her mother either for becoming involved with the other ambitious Hollywood mothers. She disliked this particular Hollywood set intensely. The women were predatory, scandal-loving, competitive and ruthless, and Anna was alarmed at the influence they were having on Muriel. They also drank far too much, and were indiscreet in their cups. They all kow-towed to the two Hollywood gossip-columnist monsters, Hedda Hopper and Louella Parsons. These two were too dangerous to be tangled with as they could make or break careers, but they fascinated Muriel, who was constantly telephoning them with news of Anna. Hedda Hopper, tall, horse-faced, arrogant and witty, and famous for her outrageous hats, was perhaps the more dangerous of the two, though Louella, bloated and simpering, and fond of the bottle, could do her own considerable damage.

Then Charlie got a break, and was cast in a good picture for Twentieth Century-Fox.

There was no holding Muriel. Her excitement was touching, but the façade of affection for Anna which she had maintained so well since her arrival cracked a little. The whole house now had to be run for Charlie, and if this inconvenienced Anna, it couldn't be helped. Anna saw what was happening and was hurt, as she had been as a child, but she recognised that her mother and Charlie had indeed been through a bad time, and so made no fuss.

Unfortunately Charlie couldn't take his small success. He

became conceited and arrogant, and this led to trouble on the set. He was frequently late for his morning call. He stayed out too late at nights and continued to drink too much, so that he was often suffering from a hangover the next day; and, being a lazy young man, he was frequently uncertain of his words. He finished the picture, but was no actor, and had not endeared himself to the studios. He was not given a second chance by Fox. His good looks weren't particularly photogenic, and he wasn't worth the trouble.

Muriel was heartbroken. As usual she didn't blame Charlie, but she audibly began to grudge Anna her 'good luck', as she called it, and her jealousy, never far below the surface, again made itself apparent. The easy happy days of their first arrival in Hollywood passed, and tensions mounted.

Muriel, on the defensive, attacked, as Antonio had done. 'I know you always thought I worked you too hard as a child,' she said, 'but look what it has led to! Your silly old books wouldn't have brought you out here and made you famous and rich, would they?'

'No, mother.'

'Some people said you had no childhood and should have been allowed to play! But you never wanted to play, did you? I've never seen such a studious child.' Anna said nothing, and Muriel went on fiercely. 'Well, say something! You're pretty lucky after all, aren't you?'

Anna sighed.

'What's the martyred sigh for?'

'How often, I wonder, have you told me that I'm lucky?' said Anna. 'I'm sick to death of the word luck!'

'Perhaps you are, but I want to teach you to count your considerable blessings,' said Muriel. 'Everyone should do that!'

'Do you, Mother?'

'What blessings have I had?' There was a pause. 'Did you miss your childhood?'

'Yes,' replied Anna firmly. 'I did. I loved you, Mother, and I still do, but I didn't enjoy myself, and I have a theory that people who miss out as a child have an urgent wish to live irresponsibly later on.'

'Rubbish!'

'Look at Judy Garland, for instance — brilliantly talented, fascinating and wonderful, but longing for love and for a child's life. Like the other child stars, she was given pep pills to help her cope with an overload of work, and she still needs them, and drink, too. And poor Frances Farmer! Years in an asylum! And that's only two out of the dozens and dozens who have been maimed through their parents' ambitions. Half the kids here now are on uppers and downers, hard drugs and drink — all because their parents want to live on their talents. It sickens me!'

'I trust you're not accusing me of giving you drugs and drink!' exclaimed Muriel angrily. 'Dozens and dozens of famous actors started as children and pulled through, and loved it, too. Look at Noël Coward, for one. Or Shirley Temple, for another.'

'Perhaps they were the ones whose mothers loved them,' said Anna firmly. 'Perhaps that's what makes the difference.'

'Perhaps they weren't the snivelling cry-babies,' snapped Muriel contemptuously, 'so their mothers were able to love them.'

'Maybe,' replied Anna quietly. But for the first time in her life she was angry with her mother.

Anna began seeing a good deal more of Philip Marsh.

Muriel didn't like him for two reasons. First he was in love with Anna, and secondly she had an instinctive dislike of intellectuals. She sensed, too, that he didn't like her, and that he had no time at all for Charlie. She did her best to break up the understanding between him and Anna, but failed. Philip was aware of what she was doing and so was unaffected by her scheming, and Anna felt too much at ease with him to take much notice of her mother's warnings. She considered him her best friend in Hollywood, except for Marilyn, and she was happy to know that Marilyn approved of him.

'He's a nice boy,' said Marilyn warmly. 'You'd have to go a long way to find someone more dependable. Forget that silly old Iti of yours, darling. Antonio's no good to anyone — simply not worth wasting your emotions on.'

'I can't help it,' replied Anna. 'You're either hooked or you aren't. Besides, he did do me some good. He made sex possible for me after Jacko, and that was quite something. I think I'm over him, but just sometimes I have a horrible feeling that he was the love of my life. If so, I shall go on remembering him always, I suppose.'

'Phooey!' exclaimed Marilyn. 'You wouldn't be such a fool! He made you so miserable you wanted to kill yourself! Remember?'

'He was a wonderful lover. And he made me happy, too.'

'He's not the only wonderful lover, and sex without love on both sides is always an unhappy business,' said Marilyn.

Philip and Anna went on seeing one another.

CHAPTER SEVENTEEN

One afternoon when Anna was resting after a morning's filming, the telephone rang in her bedroom. She picked up the receiver and almost incredulously heard Antonio's voice.

'How are you, my little English?' he said ebulliantly. 'You are happy to hear me, no?' He sounded pleased with himself, and confident.

'Where are you?' she asked feebly. Exasperated, she realised that her heart was beating heavily and her mouth had gone dry.

'Here in Hollywood. I live in the Garden of Allah.' Even in her state of shock, Anna smiled at this address for him. 'You will come to dinner tonight?'

'Is your wife with you?' asked Anna.

'Certainly not!'

'Why are you here?'

'To make films, like you, my little Susannah.'

'Who with?'

'Your own studio, MGM. Perhaps one day we shall work together again, no? That I should like, wouldn't you?'

'Are you under a long-term contract?' asked Anna, playing for time.

'No. I am on, how you say, on approval. They will see how I make good in my new film, then they will give me a contract. But I shall make good, of course. Antonio does not fail.'

'And then will you bring your wife out here?'

'We shall see.'

'You are happy with her?'

'Of course. I chose her with care.'

'And Gina?'

'Gina?'

'The girl for whom you left me.'

'Oh, yes. Gina. I had forgotten her. Gina has gone, pouf! She was a greedy little girl and she make scenes and upset my poor wife. I did not wish my wife to be upset when she begin to make babies.'

'You have children?'

'Two. A boy and a girl.'

To her dismay Anna found that she was suddenly near to tears. 'How wonderful,' she said shakily. 'I am so glad for you.'

'Yes. You will come out to dinner?'

She thought rapidly then decided that, since he was to be in Hollywood for several months, she might as well get the meeting over as quickly as possible. 'OK,' she said. 'Thank you. What time?'

'Six o'clock.'

'And where?'

'I shall come and fetch you.'

'You know where I live?'

'Of course. I have made it my business to find out.'

'How long have you been here, then?'

'Two weeks.'

Two weeks and he had only just contacted her! And then he had the nerve to expect her to drop everything and dine with him the moment he asked her! She was immediately angry with herself for accepting the invitation.

'I hear very good things of you, my little Susannah,' said Antonio. 'You are working on your second big picture, no?'

'Yes,' said Anna.

'They say you will be a big star.' Antonio sounded almost unctuous, and to her dismay, Anna, discerning something calculating in his voice, became suspicious. Had he only decided to contact her because he thought it might help his career? She didn't like the thought, but instinct insisted it was a possibility.

'All right. Tonight, then,' she said, briskly. 'At six o'clock.'

He murmured seductively, 'And you will wear something very special for me, no? For the sake of the good times in Rome?'

Anna slammed down the receiver.

Antonio was an immediate success with Muriel. He had

brought six dozen red roses for Anna, but the moment he saw Muriel he broke the head off one of them and gave it to her. 'For you to wear, Signora,' he said, kissing her hand. 'For the most beautiful mother of the most beautiful woman in Hollywood.'

Muriel simpered. 'What a charming man,' she whispered to Anna, loudly enough for Antonio to hear. Antonio smirked and Charlie laughed out loud, but Anna said nothing.

In the car Antonio tried to kiss her, but Anna drew away, and in the restaurant he paid her extravagant compliments. He seemed delighted that she knew so many of the stars.

While they were eating, Anna studied him carefully. He was certainly good to look at, and his arrogance gave him a distinguished air, but away from his own surroundings she didn't find him quite so attractive. His brown eyes were set too close together, and there was a certain smugness about him which she hadn't noticed before.

She was in a state of wildly conflicting emotions. She had longed for him for so long that, now that he was here, she was absurdly happy. His presence was the realisation of a dream. But the fact that he had taken so long to contact her was a clear indication of how little she really mattered to him. At the moment he seemed to be overacting the part of an attentive squire to an attractive woman, and it embarrassed her. She found herself looking forward to seeing him with Philip and comparing the two — as indeed she had compared Antonio to Dickie, in Italy. She had a feeling that Philip would come off best. How amazingly foolish she had been to allow Antonio to monopolise her feelings for so long, and how right Marilyn had been!

Antonio leaned forward. 'What are you thinking, my little English?' he asked softly.

'I am thinking how glad I am that you came,' she replied truthfully.

Antonio was pleased with this reply, and he puffed out his chest a little, in the way that had charmed her so often before. It didn't charm her now.

She was utterly astonished. How could all that loving end so quickly and completely, after so long? Had his attraction mainly been proximity, and the attraction of the unattainable?

Marilyn had said that unless both people loved in a physical affair it was an unhappy business. Did despair overwhelm the unloved one simply because pride was hurt and rejection impossible to bear? It seemed that it might well be so. And yet her unhappiness had been terribly real, and she would never have thought of herself as a conceited person. She had certainly loved him, loved him with all her heart. 'But not with all your intelligence, Susannah,' she heard the ghost of Antonio's voice from the past telling her.

Antonio was saying something now, and she pulled herself together to listen to him, but she had missed the remark and she saw the familiar expression of controlled irritation which she had seen so often when she wasn't behaving exactly as he wished. 'I'm sorry,' she said. 'I was dreaming.'

'Of what?' he asked sharply. 'You were miles away.'

'Of Rome,' she replied pacifically, and again she was telling the truth.

He was mollified. 'I was saying, Susannah, that you and I should see a great deal of one another while I am here. I have missed you very much. I was silly to exchange you for Gina. She was a loose girl, and she excited me, but you are a clever girl, and a good friend. We shall be happy here in Hollywood.' She noticed his eyes straying past her even as he was talking, and coming to rest on a lovely blonde at a nearby table. Then he concentrated again. 'Very happy,' he added firmly.

'Let's see how it goes,' she said gently. 'A long time has passed.'

'You forgot me?' he demanded playfully.

'No, I didn't forget you,' she replied slowly.

'There is someone else? Someone special?' He frowned, suddenly anxious, and she realised in astonishment that he was jealous. What conceit! Although he had left her, he yet couldn't bear that he should be superseded!

'I'm not sure,' she said carefully. 'I'm fond of someone, but I don't think I'm in love.'

'Then I shall win your love again,' he said grandly. 'We shall be as before. You are very beautiful, my little Susannah.'

She smiled slightly. 'Thank you,' she said.

From that evening on, he pursued her persistently. He telephoned every day, sent her flowers and presented himself

at the house. Muriel was delighted, Marilyn dismayed, and
Philip became restless.

Knowing that she approved of him, Antonio flattered
Muriel outrageously. She loved it. 'I can't understand why you
go on seeing Philip,' she said, 'when Antonio is so in love with
you. And a nobleman too! Fancy, if he married you, you would
be a Contessa, Susannah! Imagine that!'

'He's already married,' replied Anna. 'And they have two
children.'

'If he was in love with his wife, she'd be here with him,' said
Muriel coldly. 'Anyone can see you have only to crook your
little finger!'

'I'm afraid you don't understand Italian men, Mother,' said
Anna.

Muriel was angry. 'And you do, I suppose! Well, it didn't
make you very happy by all accounts. Besides, men are men the
world over. Antonio would have been a far better choice than
whoever it was in Italy that was such a failure. Believe me!'

'I'm sure, Mother,' said Susannah, and she laughed. All the
same she was immensely relieved that her mother, although
she had clearly heard that Anna had had a lover in Rome, had
not connected the affair with Antonio.

The situation gradually became difficult, and would have
become so quicker had not Anna, Antonio and Philip all been
fully engaged on their various films. Antonio, finding that
Anna really had cooled towards him, became more and more
ardent. He insisted that they should revive their affair, and
that, when they did, she would find him a changed man. As
Anna had suspected, he had realised very clearly how useful she
could be to him, now that she was doing so well and he was
only a small-part player, and it enraged him to sense that he
might have lost her. Anna thankfully found that she had no
temptation to live with him again. The more she saw of him,
the less she liked him. She allowed him to squire her from time
to time, only because she wanted to be totally certain that she
was really free of him for good. His presence had made her
appreciate Philip more, as she had thought it might. Antonio,
seeing that he had a serious rival, became genuinely and
obsessively jealous. When he met Philip he was rude and
boorish, and he was scandalously unpleasant about him behind

his back. Finally Philip told Anna that it was either him or Antonio, and that, if Anna wanted to go on seeing the Italian, he would make himself scarce. So Anna told Antonio that she had no wish to see him again.

Antonio was unable to believe that anyone, least of all Anna, could really resist him if he had made up his mind to charm, and refused to take no for an answer. He redoubled his attentions, and Muriel encouraged him. She insisted on inviting him to the house in spite of the fact that Anna told her that she was through with him, and things became actively unpleasant.

Anna asked Philip to escort her to the première of her latest film, starring Greer Garson and Stewart Granger. (Muriel would be going with Charlie.) Antonio was furious. He had set his heart on being with her on such an important occasion, and had enlisted Muriel's support — which didn't help his cause. Anna was adamant. 'I have asked Philip, and he has accepted,' she said. 'There's no more to be said.'

'Your mother said that you had accepted *me*,' said Antonio.

'Mother had no business to interfere.'

'I shall look a fool. I have told many people that I shall be with you.'

'Then you must tell them that you won't.'

'Do you forget that you were once my mistress, Anna? That we lived together in Rome, and were happy? Because you are now a success, and I am not, have you risen above your true friends?'

'True friends!' exclaimed Anna angrily. 'You have quite a nerve, haven't you Antonio? You left me. You didn't care in the least that I was unhappy, or even that I threatened to kill myself, and if I weren't now a success, as you call it, you wouldn't be hanging around.'

'This is a lie!' shouted Antonio, sincerely believing what he said. 'I love you for yourself. Not for your success. I am far from my home, and lonely, and you could help me very much on such a night by being kind to me.'

'You really are incredible!' exclaimed Anna. 'Such a night happens to be my première. I have asked Philip because I need strength and support. I'm nervous, and the last thing I need is an emotional scene.'

'I am better-looking than Philip! I should do you more
justice!'

'You're behaving like an idiot child,' said Anna. 'Now please
go away and leave me alone.'

Antonio went instead to find Muriel, and Muriel immediately stormed back to see Anna. 'I told him he could go with
you!' she said. 'He'll do you far more credit than Philip. I really
cannot understand what you see in that objectionable young
man!'

'Mother,' said Anna patiently, 'as I've just told Antonio,
this happens to be a première of one of my films. Not yours,
and not Antonio's. Philip is coming with me, and I want to
hear no more about it.'

'I don't like Philip, I tell you!'

'You don't have to like him. You're going with Charlie.'

'Antonio is right. You have a swelled head. I'm beginning to
lose patience with you, Susannah.'

'And I with you,' said Anna calmly.

Muriel could hardly believe her ears. 'What did you say!' she
screamed. 'Did I hear you right? After all I've done for you,
and you turn on me!'

'Look, Mother. Tonight is a big night for me, and I'm
scared. I want to have a quiet day then, in the evening,
dress peacefully, have a drink and go with Philip to see the
film. I want no scenes, no quarrels, no tantrums and no
tears. I need calm and sympathy and understanding — or else
solitude.'

But she got none of these. Muriel (who needed an emotional
outburst to cope with the resentment that was building up
inside her, since the big night was for Anna, not for herself or
Charlie), ranted and raved and followed her round the house
all day, leaving her not a moment to herself. At last Anna
telephoned Marilyn.

'It's me, Anna,' she said. 'May I come round to your place at
once? Mother has got herself into a state, and I can't cope
today.'

'Of course, darling.'

Once she was with Marilyn and Bob, the world resumed
normal proportions, and presently Philip joined them. Anna
had found a ravishing pink-and-silver beaded dress to wear,

and she knew she looked her best. Philip was bowled over by her appearance, and Anna was surprisingly elated.

'You look wonderful,' said Philip. 'Never better. I'm proud to be with you.'

They drove to the cinema. As Anna stepped out of the car, the fans seemed to go mad. They waved, cheered, screamed and ran towards her, and the studio bosses, noticing it all, were delighted.

Antonio, on the other hand, was not. He was there alone, having managed miraculously to get a seat. After leaving Anna's house, he had also had time, most uncharacteristically, to get drunk. The drink had made him morose, and he had brooded on Anna's behaviour until it had assumed the proportions of an unforgivable insult. When he saw her arrive, he decided to have his revenge.

As Anna and Philip walked up the shallow steps, he hurried up to them and deliberately tripped Philip, who fell, pulling Anna down on top of him. Philip managed to rise with difficulty, and as he helped Anna to her feet, he saw Antonio grinning at him. Furiously he lunged at him, and caught him on the jaw. Antonio retaliated and in a moment the two of them were fighting in earnest. Anna watched appalled. So did her famous co-stars, Garson and Granger. The crowd loved it.

The film was well received, and Anna won high praise for her performance — a great feather in her cap with such illustrious colleagues — but it was the brawl that hit the headlines all over the States, and gossip columnists had a field day. MGM was angry as much with Anna as with the two men. All of them were warned that such conduct was prejudicial to their company's good name, and that any further trouble would lead to dismissal.

At the end of his film Antonio's option was not taken up, and with bad grace he returned to Italy. Anna, to Muriel's open disapproval, became engaged to Philip.

CHAPTER EIGHTEEN

Philip had naturally played down his left-wing sympathies because of the McCarthy witch-hunt. He was not a Communist, and never had been. He had no wish to be parted from Anna, nor indeed to end his film career either, but despite his low profile he suddenly found himself appearing before HUAC on the testimony of an anonymous informer. Though he defended himself strenuously, MGM took fright and terminated his contract. Realising that it would be hard to find other work, Philip decided that he must leave Hollywood and headed reluctantly for New York. Anna, shocked and distressed, wanted to follow him but also wanted to continue her film career. Naturally Philip would have liked her with him, but Muriel counselled caution.

She seemed really concerned for once, and, this time, only for Anna's sake. 'You don't want to wreck your career just when it's beginning to go really well, do you?' she urged. 'It's madness, darling! Don't rush things. You're still very young, and Philip is not the only man in the world.'

'You've never liked him,' said Anna doubtfully.

'I've never liked Commies,' retorted Muriel.

'He's not a Communist. He's my fiancé, and he's in trouble,' replied Anna obstinately. 'I can't ditch him just because he's in trouble.'

'Marriage is for a lifetime,' said Muriel sententiously. 'You aren't a Communist. Why get yourself married to one? It won't bring you happiness. You need to have things in common. That's what makes for a happy marriage. You and Philip have a whole area of your lives where you could never agree.'

'Philip isn't a Communist,' repeated Anna angrily. 'Anyway, politics don't interest me.'

'Exactly. And nothing else interests him.'

'Mother, that's simply not true.'

'Listen to me, will you? I know what I'm talking about — even though I'm not famous like you. For left-wing people like Philip, politics are a substitute for religion — a religion in which they are the only God, and they won't be satisfied until they've destroyed the world as we know it and have power over all our lives. They talk about compassion for the underdog. They don't give a fig for the underdog. It's the top dog they care about, because that's what they mean to be. They're hypocrites, dangerous hypocrites — out for revenge.'

Anna looked at her in amazement. 'I've never heard you talk politics before! I thought, like me, you weren't interested.'

'I'm interested when my daughter's whole future is at stake,' said Muriel grandly. 'Philip has been branded as a Commie, and I'd go along with the judgement. You love acting now, and you've made such wonderful progress, why let that man stop you? Don't be a fool! Besides, it's fun being together as a family at last. Surely you don't want to spoil it all?'

'We could all live in New York, Mother,' said Anna. 'I'm sure Philip would agree if I asked him! And I could work in the theatre there with him.'

'Philip doesn't like Charlie and me, as you very well know,' said Muriel. 'If you were married to him, we'd seldom even meet.'

'He wouldn't mind me meeting you. He's not like that.'

'In a marriage, these things are different. The husband calls the tune,' said Muriel, 'or the marriage doesn't work. Besides, darling, you've rescued Charlie and me from a dreary sort of life. D'you want to kick us back into it?'

'Surely Charlie could find something to do out here, and you could too, for that matter?' said Anna. She sounded a little impatient.

She was shaken, though, and touched that her mother should openly acknowledge that she had helped her and Charlie. She also saw that, as far as her career was concerned, it might indeed be madness to leave Hollywood; especially as she would be marrying a man who had left it under a cloud.

Marilyn, with whom she discussed it, refused to make the decision for her. 'You've got to work this out by yourself,' she said, 'but for God's sake do it for your own good, and not for Muriel's! I'm glad that at last she seems to have realised what you have done for her, but it won't change her fundamental attitude towards you, so don't think that it will!'

'Don't you think it has already, if she tells me that she's grateful?'

'No. You have to be generous-minded to have a capacity for gratitude. Even her best friend couldn't call Muriel generous-minded.'

'But what about the other things she says?'

'She's right that it could well finish your career to marry Philip. Your studio is not going to like it, and you've come to Hollywood as a film actress, so you may find it hard to get work in New York on the stage. She's right, too, to say that the happiest marriages are built on compatibility. Are you in love with him? You haven't said so, and that's probably the most important thing of all. Thank God the dreaded Antonio is out of your hair!'

Philip, realising that he was asking a great deal of her to marry him at such a moment, was fully prepared to wait; so, during this interim, Muriel continued to try to prevent it in every way she knew. She was once again at her most charming to Anna and she now began to try and justify her past behaviour. But here, one day, she made a serious mistake.

As well as trying to detach Anna from Philip, Muriel had been doing what she could to come between her and Marilyn, whom she had always considered a bad influence. Over-confident, because she thought she was winning, she said one morning, 'I know Marilyn has never ceased to try and put you against me because I encouraged you to be a child star, Susannah, but you had such talent that it seemed a pity to waste it. When you'd grown up you might have minded very much if I had turned down all your chances for you, mightn't you? As you know, your father left us without any money, and it seemed sensible to make some, while the going was good. Was that really so very wicked? Besides we have all fared very much better than most Coulsdon families, haven't we? You can't deny that.'

'I don't,' said Anna. Then she hesitated and added, 'But I do sometimes wonder if you mightn't have exploited me just as badly as the other ambitious mothers here if we'd been born in America and not England.'

Muriel lost her temper. 'That's a horrible thing to say!' she exclaimed. 'Exploit, indeed! You talk as if I've ruined your life, instead of creating a very successful career for you.'

'You used me, Mother, and we both know it,' said Anna wearily. 'Now, for heaven's sake, let's drop the subject, shall we? You know we never agree!'

'You've never known when you were lucky,' said Muriel acidly, pursing her lips.

'Oh, God!' sighed Anna. 'I'll tell you one thing, Mother. If you ever say those dreaded words to me again, I shall get into the first train going to New York!' She realised rather sadly that at long last her love for Muriel was turning sour.

Muriel didn't like Anna's last remark. 'I bet Marilyn is determined to make you marry Philip just because she knows I don't want it,' she said. 'It would be just like her.'

'Don't be stupid, Mother!' Anna was shocked. 'Marilyn very seldom says anything about you at all, but luckily for me she has always been near when I've needed help. So naturally I love her.'

'Such as that night long ago when Jacko got drunk,' said Muriel, half under her breath.

Anna was stunned. 'What did you say?' she asked icily.

Muriel had the grace to look ashamed of herself, but she said stubbornly, 'I know Jacko drank sometimes, but he wasn't all that bad. There were some good things about him, you know.'

'You can't expect me to be very enthusiastic!' retorted Anna. 'In case you've forgotten, he raped me!'

'He was drunk, and he could never hold his drink,' replied Muriel obstinately. 'And you must admit, it was very unlike him to make a play for you.'

'I certainly don't' said Anna. 'I was terrified of him wanting to paw me every time we were left alone.'

'He loved me, and only me,' said Muriel.

'Maybe, but he never stopped pestering me,' said Anna. 'And I hated it.'

'I believe you encouraged him,' said Muriel spitefully.

'Encouraged him? That revolting little man?' Now Anna was totally outraged.

'How dare you! How dare you!' screamed Muriel. 'I loved him, and you were after him! I saw it! You always were a sexy little piece!' She was so angry that she was shaking.

Giving her a long contemptuous stare, Anna turned on her heel and went out of the room, slamming the door behind her.

CHAPTER NINETEEN

Philip sent letters almost daily from New York. He had found a large apartment in a brownstone in Greenwich Village, and loved the life. 'Immensely mentally stimulating,' he wrote. 'It's great here. Everyone around acts or paints or writes, and there's a continuous artistic dialogue. Wonderful! Far more people to talk to here than in Hollywood, and I'm after a good job with the Method boys and girls. Montgomery Clift is helping me. He's a great guy, and I meet the Strasburgs tomorrow.'

He got the job.

'Interesting play. Interesting part,' he wrote again. 'Do come, darling. I didn't want to persuade you before, because there was nothing to offer you. Now I know there is. You told me once that the play you were in with Marilyn was much more to your taste than filming, so why not take a chance on the theatre over here? You'll get some work, I'm sure, and I love you. Remember?'

Weeks had passed and Anna had become restless. Relations with her mother hadn't improved, and only the fact that she might fatally ruin her acting career had kept her from leaving Hollywood. Then Marilyn told her that she and Bob were going to live in Martha's Vineyard. 'It's a good place for writers,' she said. 'A young man called John Updike has suggested we go. I'm retiring from acting. The parts I'm being offered aren't all that good any more, and Bob is much more important to me than a career. I hate abandoning you, honey, but you'll be getting married to Philip one day soon, won't you? So you'll have what you want.' Anna looked at her, surprised. 'Well, won't you?' she asked.

'Yes,' said Anna. 'I think I will.'

She went to the studios to discuss the situation with Doré Schary, and to her intense surprise he was sympathetic. 'If you're really in love with the guy, there's no use trying to keep you. We'll have to suspend you, of course, and you won't be able to work with another studio without our permission, but you don't hold Marsh's political views, so we've nothing against you.' He smiled wryly. 'Marsh may have told you that I was a well-known liberal writer before I took this job ... '

'Oh, *thank* you!' exclaimed Anna gratefully.

'Also, if we find we need you for a picture, you'll have to come back and do it, until the contract is up.'

'Of course.'

'Right. Then you can go with our blessing. But remember that we've made a considerable investment in your career, and you owe us.'

'I do.'

'Good girl.'

Muriel was furious. 'Don't you understand?' she shouted. 'If you were really doing well they'd never let you go in a million years! You've given them the chance to get rid of you, without them having to pay a cent! And what do you suppose is going to happen to us?'

'To you?' Anna was momentarily taken aback. 'Why, you stay here, of course. You've both settled down well, and you could easily marry again, Mother. You're still awfully pretty. I won't sell the house straight away, so you'll have time to look around.'

'I've had plenty of chances to get married!' returned Muriel venomously, 'but I've turned them down for your sake. So what am I supposed to live on?'

'You're a clever woman, Mother. You'll find something to do.'

'I've concentrated my whole life on you, and now look at what you're doing to me!'

'Mother, I'm young, and I'm going to get married, which at my age is a perfectly normal thing to do. I've told you, you and Charlie can stay in the house until you have found what you both want to do. What more can I say?'

'Charlie!' Muriel was contemptuous. 'What is Charlie going

to do to help? He hasn't got your brains, poor boy, and he needs some help himself.'

'You'll manage,' answered Anna calmly. 'Between the two of you.'

'What sort of work do you suggest that we find?' shouted Muriel. 'Because of you, I'm used to being in a position of some importance! I have been a somebody! Do you want to wreck my life?'

'Certainly not,' replied Anna. 'Any more than you wish to wreck mine, I'm sure. And as I've said already twice, you can stay on in my house for a while.'

'I should think so, when it is I who have made it look so nice!' Muriel was indignant. 'Without me you wouldn't have done anything to it! If you sell it, I ought to have a rake-off!'

'I bought all the furniture,' said Anna mildly, 'and I shall be leaving a good deal of the stuff behind. Also, you and Charlie have lived rent-free, if you remember.'

'I should hope so! Your own mother!'

Anna and Philip were married in front of a Justice of the Peace in New York State. They had no honeymoon, because Philip was acting in an off-Broadway play.

Anna moved happily into Philip's apartment and, although they were very different in character, they were both unpossessive and each respected the freedom, both mental and physical, of the other. Anna had never found life more rewarding.

Her feelings for Philip were a mixture of her feelings for Dickie and for Antonio. Physically she was in love, and she also had a very positive feeling of friendship for him. It was a satisfying combination. She found Philip's body beautiful. Dickie had been short and stocky, and their physical intimacy had been only an extension of their liking for one another. Antonio, although he was attractive and had made magical love, was thin and narrow-shouldered. Philip had the physique of an athlete, with broad shoulders and narrow hips. He was also immensely strong. Making love together, though indeed an extension of their liking for one another, was very much more — ecstasy, lust and love, with happiness as a bonus. With Antonio she had always been too anxious to please, too submissive, somehow diminished as an individual. With Philip she could be herself, but herself radiantly bathed in love, and utterly unselfconscious. Antonio's obsessive need for self-gratification insisted on silence when the love-making was over. Often he had slept immediately. Sometimes he snored. Always he turned away from her. Philip enjoyed talking to her, if she wanted. He also believed that love-making was a joyous business, and that one could even laugh. There was no hint of desperation in their passion, no master-slave relationship. Only freedom.

Anna was still uninterested in the politics which Philip found so absorbing, but strangely, although he felt passionately about such things himself, he was quite willing for her to have her own ideas. 'Politics are part of our youthful brainwashing,' he said. 'You've had one kind of life, darling, I've had another. My father was a College Dean with left-wing ideals, and my mother had been one of his students. I like them both, so I've taken on the beliefs they instilled into me. Your mother is right-wing — practically Fascist I'd say — and you've absorbed her ideas in spite of yourself.'

'She's not in the least Fascist!' exclaimed Anna, laughing. 'She simply isn't interested in politics. Like me. And my father, as far as we know, actually fought against the Fascists, though I expect it was very unwillingly, as he was indeed a Fascist sympathiser. *Your* father wasn't even in the war!' she teased.

The free and easy life of Greenwich Village suited them both. Anna missed the more countrified pleasures of Hollywood, but on the other hand her suppressed wish for an intellectual kind of life was satisfied here at last, although she didn't share Philip's enthusiasm for Method acting which was dominating the New York scene at that time. 'If you can act, you can act by any "method" as long as it suits you,' she protested. 'You might just as well insist that you have to commit murder to act a murderer, and that's ridiculous!' After sitting in at one or two classes as an invited guest at the Strasburg Studio, she gave up, although Philip attended classes as part of the Group almost daily.

She went instead to the art galleries, to art films, to concerts and to the theatre, both on and off Broadway. She read every book she could lay her hands on; and painters, writers, musicians and actors dropped in to their apartment most evenings after the show, or else the Marshes went out to theirs. The talk that Anna now found so fascinating went on into the small hours. She loved it all. Her taste in painting and sculpture never wavered from the pictures and sculptures that Antonio had taught her to love: the Italian Old Masters; the Dutch seventeenth-century and French eighteenth-century masters; Van Gogh, Gaugin, the French Impressionists; English landscape painters and portrait painters of the seventeenth and eighteenth centuries. Sickert, Modigliani, Rodin and Epstein were her most 'modern' loves, but 'new' Americans such as Rothko, Calder and the young Lichtenstein left her cold. On the other hand, some of the most stimulating and interesting people she met were the abstract and action painters; just as, although she might not enjoy Method acting, she enjoyed Method actors. She felt very much the cultural ingenue among the musicians and painters, but she was more than willing to learn, and they were more than willing to give her their time.

In due course Anna was offered a splendid part in a good commercial play on Broadway, and Philip, though it was not his type of play, was as excited as she was at the offer, and indeed at the play's reasonable success. As he had suggested she might, she preferred the theatre to filming; she also enjoyed working at night, which left her day free to be with him.

Then she found she was going to have a baby, and both of them were enormously excited. During the next few years their three children, Maria, and the twins, Sylvie and Philip Junior, were born.

Anna didn't attempt to work during these years. Her own loveless childhood made her determined to be with her children while they were very young. She also found herself to be more maternal than she had expected, which was a joyous bonus, as Philip was a good and affectionate father.

Philip became a well-known actor on Broadway, and, more importantly for himself, also a successful director. This suited his temperament better than acting, and he was in great demand. The house in Greenwich Village grew too small for them, and they moved into a large and luxurious apartment on

Fifth Avenue. There, with the help of a young English girl called Patty to look after the children, Anna was free to resume her career as an actress. In her first big break, a large and rewarding part in a comedy called *Home Town*, she made a hit, and the play had a long run on Broadway.

In all this while she hardly heard a word from her mother or Charlie. She had sold the house in Hollywood, as MGM seemed not to need her services and she, in return, had no deep wish to return there. She gave half the proceeds of the sale to Muriel, and although she received no acknowledgement of her cheque, Anna noticed that it had been cashed very quickly. This worried her in case the family might be in trouble; but she heard through friends that Muriel and Charlie had found a smaller house in West Hollywood, that Charlie had gone back to getting work as a stand-in, and that Muriel was working as a receptionist in a Public Relations firm, and doing well.

Anna was sad that Muriel seemed not the least interested in her grandchildren; but Philip, like Dickie before him, was undisguisedly glad not to have his mother-in-law anywhere near him.

Marilyn and Bob came to New York once or twice a year, and in a way Marilyn came to be looked on as the grandmother the children never saw; in fact, she was Maria's godmother. Anna was delighted to see that the marriage was still extremely happy.

On two occasions, Philip, Anna and the children visited England, a country which Philip Senior adored (though the children far preferred America), and they all descended on Dickie and Eileen, who had two sons of their own. The families got on excellently. Dickie was doing well, but not sensationally, as an actor. Eileen had retired and had already put on weight, but Anna saw that they, too, were happy, which lightened the sense of guilt which she had never quite lost over her behaviour towards Dickie.

All in all, life seemed to be settling into a comfortable, contented and yet creative pattern, which gave Anna a vivid sense of fulfilment.

CHAPTER TWENTY

One morning the porter rang through from downstairs. 'Your mother's here, Mrs Marsh, and your brother. Shall I send them up?'

'Oh God!' exclaimed Philip forcefully. 'It was bound to happen one day, I suppose!'

'Shall I send them up?' repeated the porter.

'Of course!' said Anna warmly. In spite of herself she was pleased. Philip looked angry.

Muriel walked in, flanked by Charlie.

For a bewildered moment, Anna hardly recognised her. The years hadn't been kind to her. Her hair was dyed bright blonde and she held herself well, but her prettiness had faded, leaving her with a lined, narrow, disappointed-looking face and a bad skin. Her chin seemed to have lengthened aggressively, and her neck sagged. Her eyes were still very blue, and she was smartly dressed, but she looked very thin. Charlie had changed very little. He was still spectacularly handsome, though his face, too, had become discontented, and there was something slightly furtive about him which Anna didn't remember. Both were smiling over-charming artificial smiles.

'Good heavens!' exclaimed Anna, running forward to kiss them. 'What a wonderful surprise! Why on earth didn't you let us know you were coming?'

'It's quite a long time since we've seen each other,' replied Muriel sourly. She pursed her lips a little, and looked round the room. 'It's a nice place you've got here,' she said. 'I told Charlie it would be.'

Charlie nodded.

'Where are the children?' demanded Muriel.

141

'They're all at school,' answered Anna. 'It's lovely to see you, Mother. How long are you going to be in New York?'

'Quite a while, I hope.' She darted a look at Charlie, who smirked in return.

'Where are you staying?' asked Anna.

Muriel jutted out her chin in the way that had so frightened Anna when she was a child. 'Surely you don't have to ask that?' she said, flushing angrily.

'You mean here?' asked Anna, astonished.

'Where else?' asked Muriel. 'Charlie will bring the luggage along later. We came by train and stopped off at the Waldorf to freshen up.'

'How long do you propose to be with us?' asked Philip coldly, his dislike of his mother-in-law very evident in his voice.

'We have nowhere else to live!' said Muriel defiantly. 'So unless you can provide somewhere, you'll have to have us here.'

'Nowhere else to live?' echoed Anna. 'Why not?'

'I got into debt,' said Charlie. 'Big debt. It was sell up or go to prison.'

'At least you'd have had a roof over your head,' said Philip unsympathetically.

Anna was shocked. 'Don't, darling!' she said. 'This is serious. They're my family, and they're in trouble.'

'We'll all be in trouble if they stay here,' retorted Philip.

'Then what do you suggest we do?' asked Muriel, suddenly tearful. She had pulled a small lace-edged handkerchief out of her crocodile handbag, and was dabbing gracefully at her eyes.

Philip looked her over deliberately. He stared at her expensive clothes, at the diamond earrings, the diamond brooch and the large diamond rings on her fingers. He gave a long and lingering look at the three-strand choker of real pearls round her neck, and then transferred his gaze to Charlie, who was just as expensively dressed. He turned his back on them both and walked to the window.

Anna was bewildered. 'But I don't understand! How could you lose *all* your money? *Both* of you?'

'It was after Charlie's divorce,' said Muriel. 'The poor boy went to pieces.'

Philip spoke from the window. 'As you never saw fit to communicate the fact that he had married at all, we don't know about the divorce,' he said. 'Perhaps you'd better begin at the beginning.' He was evidently struggling with suppressed rage. 'Will you tell me, Muriel? Or can Charlie speak for himself?'

Charlie reddened. 'Martha was very rich,' he said. (He, like his mother, now spoke with an American accent.) 'She came from a good Philadelphia family and, to quote the family themselves, "They come no better anywhere in the world".'

'Martha being your wife, I take it,' said Philip.

'Yeah,' replied Charlie. He grinned. 'Certainly, they thought themselves the greatest. Martha's family, I mean. Martha was visiting Hollywood on a vacation when we met. We married after a week or two . . . whirlwind romance, eh? . . . We had a honeymoon at Niagara, because she wanted to be "common", as she put it,' he grimaced briefly and un-pleasantly, 'then we went to her home to show me off to her parents.'

He paused.

'Go on,' said Philip.

After a moment, Charlie continued, 'It was quite a palace, that little home. Huge. A sort of museum of modern American art and European antique furniture. Gold trimmings on everything, especially the plumbing, like taps and plugs. Armies of servants; rather surly ones, actually. Troops of dogs, and a stable full of horses. The old man was as hard as nails, but without the charm.' Charlie sounded bitter now. 'His face was made of granite. His heard pumped cement but had to be kept moving with volleys of pills, and if he smiled, the skin cracked so that it hurt, and you could see him wince.' He stopped again.

'Well?' demanded Philip, impatiently.

Charlie glanced at his mother, who seemed to nod slightly. He went on. 'He was small and wizened and mean, that old man,' he said, 'and we loathed each other on sight. He had scads of dough, but it was a real pain to part with it except on his house and his two women. Ma-in-law was worse, if that's possible. So grand that she couldn't look you straight in the eye without lorgnettes because she had spent a lifetime of looking down her nose, and wasn't prepared to give up the habit. Well, as you can imagine, I wasn't their scene, and the rows started. Martha was OK, but her parents were sick. "How are you going to keep my daughter?" the old man asked, sticking his face right next to mine ... "I keep her?" I said. "Why should I keep her? She's so loaded she could keep a stud." He didn't like that and he said, "Are you nothing but a fortune hunter, young man? Where's your pride?" "I'm a B-picture actor," I said, "and I can't afford pride. But I'm not a fortune hunter. Rest easy there. It's her body I'm after." He didn't like that either and said, "So what exactly are you offering my daughter, Charlie?" "Sex and a dicey life in Hollywood," I said. "She knows all about it, and she's settled for it." '

Charlie shook his head sadly. 'It was no go, of course. From the minute Martha hit her own home, the marriage was dead, and in a way she was right. I couldn't have fitted in, and one day she'd have chickened out.' He sighed heavily. 'Luckily, when the crunch came no one mentioned alimony. They were just so relieved to be rid of me. But Martha was a nice girl, and it hurt.' Charlie looked genuinely miserable for a moment, then cheered up and winked. 'They say there's no class snobbery in the States,' he said. 'But there sure is money snobbery, and on a scale you couldn't beat in England! I tell you, that family were snobs, and they had to be my in-laws!' He stopped speaking as suddenly as he had begun.

Anna felt sorry for him. 'So what happened next?' she asked gently.

'Charlie hit the bottle and took to gambling,' said Muriel. 'Poor boy, he really cared.'

'Poor Charlie!' exclaimed Anna.

Muriel pursed her lips again, and they all turned towards Philip.

'So?' asked Muriel.

'So?' returned Philip.

'Are we staying here, or aren't we?'

'Please, Philip!' pleaded Anna. 'As Mother says, they've nowhere else to go!'

'Under the circumstances, I call it colossal nerve!' said Philip.

'What do you mean?' asked Anna, surprised.

'Skip it,' said Philip tersely. 'But understand this, Muriel. If you get up to your little tricks again, you're out on your ear so fast you won't know what's hit you. For the meanwhile, until we can find you somewhere to live in England, you can stay here.'

'I prefer America to England,' said Muriel grandly.

'You'll take what you get, and like it,' said Philip.

Muriel and Charlie moved into the New York apartment.

At first, as always with Muriel, things went well. She was feeling her way, and, knowing that Philip disliked her intensely, was on her best behaviour. She did her best to charm the children, but they were oddly wary of her. Predictably her favourite was the boy, Philip Junior; but he didn't respond, though his twin, Sylvie, who adored him, warmed to Muriel. The children instinctively liked Charlie better. He was good with them, and genuinely liked them. Being an immature human being, he was able to understand them and joined in their activities almost on their own level. He seldom drank, and never gambled. He, too, was on his best behaviour, and he was only too thankful to have found a haven. Anna saw that he was still unhappy about the divorce, sometimes almost depressive.

Imperceptibly, Muriel took over running the apartment and again, as always, she made a success of this. The staff liked her. She was a splendid cook, and the tradesmen spoiled her. She rapidly made a number of friends (though she was never at ease with Philip and Anna's circle) and in quite a short time seemed to have settled into the household as though she had always been a part of it.

Trouble began when Philip announced that he had received particulars of several houses and apartments in England which he thought might be suitable.

'I have no wish to live in England,' said Muriel. 'You can't make me go.'

'I'm certainly not going to buy you a place over here,' said Philip.

'Why not, if here is where I want to live? It needn't cost you any more.'

'Except peace of mind,' replied Philip drily. 'If I'm paying, that's what I'm paying for.'

'I don't understand,' said Muriel.

'You're a born mischief-maker, Mother-in-Law,' said Philip. 'I don't trust you an inch. For the moment you're being an angel, but it won't last. When you think you're immovable, you'll start stirring things, and I won't have it.'

'Anna is my daughter. Your children are my grandchildren.'

'You took a long time to remember that,' said Philip. 'Anyway, I won't change my mind, and considering all things you're very lucky to be here at all.'

Muriel went to find Anna, and when she saw her she burst into heartbroken sobs. Anna was distressed. 'What on earth is the matter, darling?' she asked, horrified.

'Philip has found some houses and flats for Charlie and me in England, and I don't want to go! I quite understand that we're unwanted here,' she sounded utterly desolate, 'and we'd leave New York if we had to, although we both love it — but Philip won't have it. He says we've not only got to leave you and the children, but we've got to leave the country, too.'

'But that's absurd,' said Anna. 'Of course you must stay in America if you want to! I'll have a talk with him.'

'Oh thank you, darling!' sobbed Muriel. 'It has given me such tremendous happiness being with you again! A mother needs her child, and I need you.'

Something in the way she had said all this didn't ring quite true, and Anna, who had been heading for the door, stopped and turned to look at her mother. 'Did he give any reason?' she asked.

'None that I could understand,' said Muriel innocently.

This sounded unlike Philip. Anna studied her mother carefully. How many thousands of times in her life had she tried to search out the meaning or mood behind her mother's words? During their stay, she had accepted so gratefully that both Muriel and Charlie had behaved well that she had barely questioned their motive, except for the obvious one. She knew Philip hated her mother with what she could only think of as an unreasoning hatred, but Muriel's reaction had been so affectionate and dignified that Anna had hoped that all would finally be well. Muriel had also been very loving to Anna;

Anna, fooled too often, could no longer take this at face value, but she had enjoyed Muriel's company, and had found a new affinity with Charlie. She would be sorry to see them go.

'I'll do my best,' she said finally, and went to Philip's study.

She found him leafing through the brochures from the English estate agencies. He smiled on seeing her, and said cheerfully, 'Hi, there! There are some quite cute places among this lot! One of them should do very well.'

'Mother has just been talking to me. She's in floods of tears about leaving America,' said Anna.'

'Too bad!' said Philip, unruffled.

'But darling, you can't just pack her out of the country if she doesn't want to go!'

'Can't I just?'

'But it's so extreme! America is a huge country. Why must she leave?'

'She gave me hell in Hollywood, and I want out,' said Philip.

'Surely she's been nice to you here?'

'Sure.'

'Then why not forgive and forget?'

'Because I've told her, I don't trust her.'

'She's changed a great deal,' said Anna earnestly. 'Really she has!'

'There's a cliché about leopards that I won't bore you with,' said Philip.

'Surely some people do change?'

'Not people like Muriel.'

The two of them argued until it was almost time for Anna to go to the theatre. At last Anna became exasperated. 'All right. Have it your own way, but I think it's extremely unkind. And I don't like you very much at the moment.'

'That's not fair!' exclaimed Philip. 'I wouldn't be sending her away just for a whim!'

'What else are you sending her away for?'

'I've told you, I don't trust her.'

'About what?'

'Anything!' he said. 'She might take it into her head to come between you and me, or she might get up to some other sort of mischief — who's to know? I don't want to have her around until she decides which.'

'That's silly!' said Anna. 'You hold the purse strings, remember? She can't get up to anything! She has to behave.'

'Want to bet?' asked Philip.

They agreed to compromise. 'Let's offer them another two months here,' said Anna, 'and if she still behaves well, and well enough for even you to think she's changed, then let her stay in the US.'

Philip shrugged his shoulders. 'If that's the way you want it,' he said, 'it's OK by me.'

CHAPTER TWENTY-ONE

Muriel didn't like being on approval for the second time. While supposedly on her best behaviour, she showed her displeasure in numerous small but significant ways. Anna was unhappily aware of what she was about, having seen the same manoeuvres only too often before. Philip seemed not to notice. The children however both saw and disliked what was happening. Criticism of any sort was anathema to Muriel, spoiled from birth and too entrenched in self-love to grow up, so when she realised that she was losing face with the children she became very carefully spiteful.

She began by referring to Philip as 'your dear Commie' whenever she was alone with Anna. As Anna said nothing, she became emboldened, and told the children exaggerated stories of the wonderful career in films that their mother had had to give up because their father was drummed out of Hollywood. This proved quite successful, as none of them had been told that Philip had been banished. When they asked their mother why not, Anna said it was old and unimportant history. Even so the story had its effect.

Cheered by this small victory, Muriel cast about for new worlds to conquer, and soon began spreading the tale of Philip's banishment to her own circle of gossip-loving friends. In a short while the 'Commie' nickname became widespread. Emboldened further, she retold the tale of Anna's lost opportunities, embellishing it with a few innuendos to the effect that Anna had to bear more than she should as a wife. This, though vague, sounded intriguing and in next to no time rumours about Anna's unhappy marriage began to gather momentum. Inevitably the rumours got back to the victims, and Philip at once knew from whom they emanated. Although angry, he tried to be fair. He went to Muriel, told her what he had been hearing, and said that if she didn't pull herself together he was through with her. Muriel gazed at him innocently with her enormous blue eyes, but he could see that she was furious. He expected the worst.

Muriel had indeed felt herself belittled and insulted by what she considered Philip's 'attack', and the next morning she rang up one of her gossip-column friends in New York, mentioning in passing that it was so clever of Philip to have made such a successful career after his Hollywood banishment. For good measure she added that Anna now regretted her film career but was loyal for his sake and the children. Ornamented a little by the columnist, this tasty morsel duly appeared the following day in the form of a feature article. Philip not only read it but was telephoned about it several times by friends and by other newspapers. He was very angry indeed.

The scene that finally exiled Muriel from his house, and indeed from America, took place that very evening. Philip had been to see a writer about the next play he was going to direct, and came back tired and dispirited from a long and unfruitful interview. Charlie was 'n for the evening, which was unusual, and Anna's play in Broadway had folded the previous Saturday, so she was at home too, as were Maria and Sylvie. Philip Junior was spending the evening with friends.

Walking into the living room to fix himself a much-needed drink, Philip found Muriel and a crony of hers talking animatedly together on the sofa. As soon as he came in, they stopped and the friend turned her back ostentatiously. Philip bade her a pleasant 'Good evening', to which she didn't reply. When he repeated his greeting, she got up out of the sofa, saying loudly, 'Well, dear, I'll take myself off', and as she passed Philip she gave an unmistakable sniff. Embarrassed, Muriel replied fussily, 'I'll see you to the door, Olive,' but Olive declined the offer and went out red-faced and self-righteous, with her head in the air.

Philip took a swig at his drink, then said slowly, 'I read your article, Muriel, and considered it most unwise.'

Muriel pointed her chin at him. 'I've no idea what you're talking about,' she said.

'Not only do I think it unwise, but so do all my friends,' said Philip.

'I don't write articles,' answered Muriel.

'You promoted this one,' said Philip. 'I can detect your style a mile off.'

Anna came brightly into the room and kissed her husband affectionately. 'Had a good day, darling?' she asked.

'Terrible.'

'It must have been,' murmured Muriel acidly, 'since he's been accusing me of writing newspaper articles.'

'Inspiring them, to be correct,' said Philip.

'What on earth are you two talking about?' asked Anna, bewildered.

Philip said grimly, 'I warned your mother the other day that, if she couldn't behave, I was through.'

'What has she been doing?' asked Anna anxiously.

'Slandering her son-in-law.'

He was interrupted by the arrival of the two girls with Charlie. Uncharacteristically, Charlie went straight to the drinks table and gave himself a large Scotch on the rocks.

'Hi, Phil!' he said expansively. 'How's the world treating you?'

'Your mother has been playing silly games as usual,' said Philip. He tossed the morning paper to Anna. 'Read that.'

'What sort of games?' asked Charlie cheerfully.

'Did you read the paper this morning?' demanded Philip.

'Oh, that!' exclaimed Charlie, looking extremely uncomfortable. 'What's that got to do with Mother?' He spoke blusteringly.

'Don't you start playing games too, Charlie. You know what, as well as I do.'

Charlie sighed and sat down.

Anna read the article with a sinking heart. Finally she threw the paper to the ground and turned to face her mother: she was so shocked that she was almost crying.

'This is horrible!' she said. 'How could you, Mother! It's vile and untrue! Disgraceful!'

'Oh, God!' murmured Charlie unhappily.

Muriel said nothing, but stared expressionlessly at her daughter.

'I told you she couldn't behave herself!' exclaimed Philip, angrily. 'I didn't tell you this before, because I love you and I didn't want to wreck your illusions about the goddam bitch you call your mother, but it was Muriel who got me drummed out of Hollywood.'

'Philip, that can't be true!' Anna was white with rage.

Both girls were staring at their grandmother with open dislike. Muriel saw it and said ingratiatingly, 'Don't you believe a word of it, girls. Your father feels bad because of what I told you he did to Anna.' She had been drinking fairly heavily with her crony and, as always with her, this was making her incautious and aggressive.

'And what am I supposed to have done to your mother, Maria?' asked Philip dangerously.

'Like it says in the paper — ruined her film career by getting turned out of Hollywood during the witch-hunt,' said Maria. 'Don't bother, Dad. The girls at school think it's an honour.'

'You told them that, Mother?' demanded Anna.

'She sure did,' agreed Sylvie.

'She didn't tell you that she engineered it though, I bet,' said Philip.

'I can't believe it!' said Anna. 'I simply can't.'

'Well you'd better, because it's true. This pussyfooting, prurient-minded, bloodsucking little lush of a leech, Muriel, did exactly that,' said Philip. 'Didn't you, Muriel? You tell them straight! You always tell us you like to say what you really *think* when you're in your cups. So say what you really *did*.'

'I'm not in my cups,' retorted Muriel haughtily. 'What a vulgar expression!'

'You should know,' said Philip.

'This is far too serious for you two to have a slanging match,' said Anna coldly. 'Is Philip telling the truth, Mother? I want to hear it from your own lips.'

'Would you rather believe him than me?' asked Muriel pathetically.

'Yes,' said Maria.

'No one was asking you!' snapped Muriel. 'Philip has always hated me,' she said, turning back to Anna.

'In spite of the fact that you have always loved me, I

suppose,' said Philip. 'It's true that I can't stand her, though, God knows, for your sake I've tried, Anna, but when I found out who had blown the whistle, I naturally didn't feel very affectionate.'

'Who told you?' demanded Muriel.

'Hedda Hopper, and in writing,' said Philip. 'I still have the letter.'

Muriel walked unsteadily to the drinks table and gave herself her third large Scotch. 'He was ruining your career, Anna. How could I let him? I so wanted you to have the best of everything! Philip was standing in your way!'

'*My God . . . !*' said Anna. 'You knew perfectly well I was in love with him! What a revolting thing to do.'

'I was doing it for your own good,' said Muriel. 'You were doing so well, and everyone said you had such a wonderful future.'

'Philip was doing well, too,' said Anna. 'No wonder he has always detested you!' She saw Charlie sitting miserably by himself in a chair by the window. 'Did you know about this, Charlie?' she demanded.

'Don't bring me into it!' said Charlie. 'You know as well as I do that I couldn't have stopped her if I tried.'

'Now you know why I didn't want her hanging around!' exclaimed Philip. 'I didn't trust her, as I said, and I was right. Today's paper proves it. Though today is a far cry from the McCarthy era and she won't harm me except with a few old reptiles like herself.'

'Are you going to stand there and let your husband insult me?' demanded Muriel.

'I certainly am,' said Anna with feeling, 'and when he stops, I'll start.'

'One day you'll regret this,' said Muriel. 'Both of you. I shan't rest until I've had my own back!'

'Anna hasn't done anything,' said Charlie, worried. 'Except produce the dough that keeps us going!'

'That's enough, Charlie!' said Muriel grandly. 'Come along. You and I will go out somewhere to have a bite to eat. We probably shan't see the rest of this charming family until the morning, and that will be soon enough, I can tell you.'

With enormous dignity, and in a zig-zag course, she made

for the door, and stood beside it until Charlie had opened it for
her. Then she swept out saying loudly, 'The trouble with
Communists is that they haven't got any manners.'

Anna saw her mother off to England on the Queen Elizabeth.
It was a farewell gift from her that she should travel back to
England in style. Muriel had already gone up the gangway;
Charlie stood dejectedly beside Anna, waiting to board. His
misery touched her heart and she said kindly, 'I wish you didn't
hate going back home so much, Charlie. Why don't you break
away from Mother and live a life of your own?'
   'I did once, and look where it got me!' said Charlie wryly.
   'But that's absurd!' said Anna. 'You're a big boy now!
Surely you can go it alone?'
   'I'll try,' said Charlie, 'but you wouldn't understand. I've
left it too late.' He paused, then added, 'In all sorts of ways.'
   'You don't mean you're going to hang on to her coat tails for
ever!' exclaimed Anna.
   'I might,' said Charlie. 'I shall have to see.'
   Muriel shouted from the deck, 'Come along, Charlie,' and
he waved and shouted back, 'Coming,' then grinned sheepishly
at Anna.
   'But it's so feeble, Charlie!'
   'I know,' said Charlie, 'but then, I am feeble. In a way you've
been lucky that Mother never liked you. She's a strong personality, you know, and you're apt to get engulfed if she loves
you. Besides, you've been on the winning side in the great wide
world for some time, old girl, and it makes a difference — I
mean, the fact that you have been on the winning side and not
me. It shouldn't have, but it has. I know you've always been
very good to us. A bloody miracle, really, after what you've
been through. But you being so much cleverer than me has
made me feel a failure, deep down, in a way that would astound
you, and I don't suppose I can eradicate that now. In Mother's
eyes I'm the wonder child, and I always have been, and it
gives me reassurance. Whatever I did, however idiotic, she'd
find an excuse — and as she always has, I need it. They say
that a complete mother-relationship can give one assurance.
Not always. It can maim you and you become queer, or it
can maim you and you're emasculated but still some sort of

a man. My marriage was my run for freedom. I bodged it.'

'It was only a first marriage,' quipped Anna faintly.

'Martha mattered a great deal to me. Still does.' Charlie sounded tense.

Muriel was organising their luggage; with a steward in tow, she shouted down to Charlie that she was going to vet their cabins. Then she disappeared out of sight.

Charlie and Anna began walking up the gangway, side by side.

'I wish we were closer, Charlie,' said Anna. 'I'm so fond of you!'

'Really?' asked Charlie, genuinely touched. 'Me too. I used to be hellishly jealous, and I used to hate you, too. I don't now. I know I can't compete, so I've taken to liking you.' He grinned.

'But you've got so much!' exclaimed Anna. 'For a start, don't you know you're marvellous to look at?'

'Having good looks is no good without vanity or conceit or, better still, self-confidence,' said Charlie. 'That's why I've spent a lifetime laying all the girls . . . to give my self-confidence a boost. It won't work after this — I mean, after my marriage — not unless someone falls for *me*, *Charlie*, rather than my looks.'

'Perhaps they will in England,' said Anna, trying to sound encouraging.

'I shall hate England. I know where I belong in England — Coulsdon,' said Charlie. 'After America, I shall hate it.' He was staring wretchedly ahead. 'I loathe Coulsdon.' He sighed.

'But you're not going to Coulsdon, you're going to Hampstead!' said Anna. They had stopped on the gangway and other passengers were impatiently pushing by.

'What does that matter?' demanded Charlie bitterly. 'I've been thinking over a lot of things since Mother spilled the beans to Philip. She'll probably be all right. There's something indestructable about her, and the actress she never was comes in quite handy when she wants to fool the people around her. Besides, she'll have me, and that's her main concern. She nearly went off her head when I got married. The trouble for me, though, is that I need her but I don't want her. It's a bore.'

'It's so funny,' Anna mused, 'I've spent three-quarters of

my life envying you! And now it seems I've wasted my time!'

'I sometimes think close relationships are more trouble than they're worth,' said Charlie. 'If you hadn't been my sister, I wouldn't have wanted to compete, so I probably wouldn't have felt such a failure. Mind you, if you hadn't been my sister, I should never have left Coulsdon, and I've had a good few years in America on the whole, so it's swings and roundabouts, as they say.' He stepped aside to let another passenger pass.

'I wish we'd talked like this before,' said Anna. 'I've never been able to get near you until now!'

'No,' said Charlie. 'We're not very alike.' They had now reached the deck together.

'I wish I'd known you were unhappy too,' said Anna. 'I might have been able to do something about it.'

'Such as what?' asked Charlie. 'As you say, I'm a big boy and it's up to me.'

Muriel reappeared. 'The cabins are OK,' she said grudgingly, 'and my steward and I have already had a little talk.'

'Are the flowers I sent you in the cabin?' asked Anna.

Muriel pressed her lips into a thin sour line. 'Yes, thank you,' she said. She turned to Charlie. 'You got everything, Charlie?' she asked.

'I've got my overnight bag,' said Charlie. 'What else am I supposed to have? You've just seen to all the rest.'

'I hate goodbyes,' said Muriel, 'so if you don't mind, Anna, I'll be getting along.'

'I wish all this hadn't happened!' said Anna sadly.

'Well it has,' said Muriel, 'and that's that.'

'What is it that bugs you most, Mother?' asked Anna. 'That I was born at all, or that I've been a successful actress?'

'I shall never forgive Philip for sending us out of the country,' said Muriel, side-stepping the question.

Sadly Anna bent forward to kiss her mother. 'Goodbye, Mother,' she said. 'Take care of yourself.'

'I shall have to, won't I?' said Muriel, grudgingly allowing herself to be embraced, 'because if I don't, no one else will.'

Anna looked at the spiteful worn face of the indomitable little woman with whom she had waged an almost ceaseless war ever since she was a child, and sighed. It seemed absurd that, with so much good will on her side, hostilities were never to end. 'Let's be friends, Mother,' she said impulsively. 'Forgive me for whatever sin I committed that turned you against me, and I'll forgive you about Philip, even if he never does. Let's start all over again.' She felt disloyal to Philip, and disliked herself, but she also wanted her mother's forgiveness.

'Come along, Charlie,' said Muriel. 'As I told you, I don't like goodbyes.'

She turned and walked away from them both until she was lost to sight around the corner of the deck.

'Sorry for that, old girl,' said Charlie sheepishly, 'but she's right about goodbyes. They're hell. Thanks, Anna, for everything, and thank Philip for providing us with a roof over our heads.'

'I do hope things come all right for you, Charlie,' said Anna warmly.

'I dare say I shall keep going.' He kissed her affectionately and rather shyly. 'Cheers,' he said. And he slowly followed his mother.

Anna waited on the quayside as the great ship moved away, but neither Muriel nor Charlie reappeared on deck.

She drove home sadly, realising that the rift between her mother and herself had grown almost too wide to bridge, certainly for many many years — and, if Philip had anything to do with it, for ever. She realised, too, that she and Charlie had found a form of peace at last.

To her amusement, Philip and the children treated her touchingly as something of an invalid after Muriel's departure. Eventually the house settled back into its old routine, and even Anna found that she missed her mother and Charlie very seldom.

CHAPTER TWENTY-TWO

The years passed. There were domestic upsets and stresses of various kinds, but the love between Philip and Anna remained sure and true. Some years they were lucky in their careers, others — in the nature of things — not. On the whole they did remarkably well. Philip gave up acting altogether for directing, Anna found a great deal of theatre work. The children grew up into three very different personalities. Maria, dark and beautiful, was otherwise very like her father: incisive, clever, tolerant. She had no wish to become an actress, and showed instead an aptitude for drawing and painting. Philip Junior looked just like his father, and very much wanted to follow in his footsteps to the stage. The fair-haired Sylvie, although his twin, was very different. She was gentle and sunny-tempered. She still adored her brother above all else, but she was a domesticated little creature, never happier than at home surrounded by her family. She looked like a fair version of Anna and, unlike the rest, was not particularly bright scholastically.

Muriel never wrote, but Charlie communicated from time to time. The two of them seemed to be getting along quite well. They both missed America, but Muriel had solved the problem by assuming an American persona among the British. As usual, she was running their pretty new house to perfection. She had found a job as a receptionist at one of the big London hotels and seemed to be coping splendidly, according to Charlie.

Charlie himself went through a variety of jobs, but seemed to keep going. After their last talk together, Anna felt less impatient with him for never keeping down a job for long. He had found a girl-friend. Muriel disapproved and said she was 'loud', but Charlie thought her restful. He had no wish to repeat his failure with a girl who came from 'any kind of drawer' as he put it. He didn't consider her loud, and was grateful for her unaffected adoration.

In 1976, when Maria was sixteen, and the twins fourteen, Anna was offered a good play in London and, after some hesitation, accepted it. It was a big starring part, by an interesting new British writer; her last few plays in New York had offered her little challenge. Philip urged her to take it.

The play was to tour the provinces for six weeks then come into London; and rehearsals were to take place in London. She wrote at once to her mother telling her what had happened, but it was Charlie who replied, saying that Muriel had no wish to see Anna again and would be out if Anna ever called at the house. Charlie, on the other hand, said that he was looking forward to seeing her, and that he would come to the play in London, but not on the first night.

Anna booked into the Savoy for the rehearsal period. She found it strange to be living in England in such luxury; strange, but satisfying.

The play was directed by Nigel (Paddy) Patrick — a well-known British stage and film star who was also a good director, meticulous in his work and funny and friendly off-stage. The rest of the cast were more than capable, and rehearsals proceeded smoothly enough. Being a woman on her own in a hotel was a lonely business, but the fact that she was so busy kept boredom at bay. She telephoned the family most evenings, and wrote to them nearly every day. It was her first absence from Philip, and she missed him more than she had thought possible.

Philip himself had a new play under way, and the children, whose summer vacation was just coming up, had made their own plans for the holiday. Maria was to spend three weeks with Marilyn and Joe at Martha's Vineyard; Philip Junior was to spend three weeks camping in the mountains with friends, and then go on to other friends in Dallas; Sylvie was staying at home with her father until his latest production had opened in New York, after which the two of them had accepted an invitation to join friends with a son of Sylvie's age, on a yachting holiday in the Caribbean.

During her rehearsal period, Anna met Noël Coward, who was also staying at the Savoy. He was over from Switzerland for a week, after major abdominal surgery, to visit Lorne Lorraine — his friend for forty-seven years, once his secretary, now his representative and adviser, who had helped him run the Actors' Orphanage, as it was then called. A large, thick-legged, sensible woman, utterly direct and honest and as loyal as she was dependable, Lorne was dying, and both she and Coward knew it.

To Anna's generation, Noël Coward was one of the theatrical gods. Known throughout the profession as 'the Master', he was urbane, witty, brusque and invariably entertaining. His versatility was prodigious, his status unique: Coward's personality was seen as the epitome of amused sophistication and his fans were as loyal to him as he himself was to his friends. About his own plays (some of which, as comedies of manners, can take their historical place alongside Wilde and Sheridan, Congreve and Shaw) he was unexpectedly nervous and self-deprecating. But what surprised Anna most was his kindness. In spite of his present unhappiness, he seemed to have time and consideration for anyone he liked, and whose work he admired.

Noël's 'family', as he called it, was vast, but his closest and most constant companions were Joyce Carey (actress daughter of Dame Lilian Braithwaite, who had played for him in his first great *succès de scandale*, *The Vortex*), Graham Payne, the actor and singer, and Cole Lesley, who with Graham shared Coward's house in Switzerland. Other old friends who happily surrounded him during that week in London included Laurence Olivier ('a lion among men; a giant among midgets', Noël called him), Johnnie Mills with his playwright wife, Mary Hayley Bell, Marlene Dietrich, Evelyn Laye, Joan Sutherland and her husband, Richard Boynynge, and Vivien Leigh — now unwell, and living with Jack Merrivale.

Queen Elizabeth the Queen Mother, the Queen herself and other members of the Royal family showered invitations on Coward. His social round would have exhausted most people half his age, but for a man supposedly convalescing from a serious operation it was astonishing. Yet he also had time to make a new and enduring friendship. He welcomed Anna into his devoted circle, and Anna joined it with joy. He talked to her with great interest and enthusiasm about her play, as well as about the work on which he himself was engaged (two novels); and one night, in his room at the Savoy, he talked to her about his dread of the British press.

'They were suddenly wonderful to me about "Suite in Two Keys" last year,' he said, 'but if they had stopped attacking me earlier, I would have had the courage to write more serious plays. As it was, I had to live through a barrage of ill-will every time I returned to this country. I lost my nerve, so I played safe and wrote popular pieces. It was a sad waste of time. Luckily my success in cabaret in Las Vegas, two years ago, was too great even for the British press to ignore, so I and, with me, incidentally, plays which were formerly dismissed as of no worth, have all been resuscitated.'

'Surely it can't have been that bad!' exclaimed Anna.

'Worse,' he said tersely. 'Tito Gobbi once told me that the British press never gave Gigli a good notice until he was too old to sing well. Then, when every other country in the world said he no longer had a voice, the British, with their passion for longevity, took him to their hearts and "discovered" him. Marlene dreads coming here. She's utterly sick of being labelled a glamorous grandmother. And why not? She's still one of the most beautiful women in the world, grandmother or not, and has put quite a nifty little cabaret act together as well as made some memorable films, so why harp on the fact that she's a grandmother? It's absurd. Anyhow,' he ended cheerfully, 'I'm getting old myself now, and though I shall never be a grandfather, maybe from now on they will love me too.'

After three and a half weeks in rehearsal, Anna's play went on tour; but, although it received rave reviews, the company itself began falling apart. The leading man professed himself in love with her, and the juvenile girl, who was in love with him, spent her time either in hysterics or in tears. Fortunately Paddy Patrick made it his business to visit them wherever they went, and when he saw what was happening, under the guise of 'director's notes', he gave them a forceful pep-talk, reminding them that the play had to be in good shape for the London opening in two weeks.

In Newcastle, Anna received shattering news.

She had enjoyed her first few days there. The Theatre Royal is a magnificent old late-Victorian theatre in Newcastle's most lovely street, Gray Street. She had also been given an introduction to friends of Dickie's and Eileen's in Hexham and, accustomed now to the difference in scale between the English and American countryside, was charmed by the dead-straight little Roman road which climbed up and down the hills on its way to the high ridge where they lived, even though it was toy-like in comparison with the great freeways she was used to. The friends themselves were hospitable and amusing, and the weather sunny and hot for a change. In the play, the leading man was now more or less behaving himself, and the juvenile girl had nearly stopped crying. Added to this, the audiences at every performance were enthusiastic and gratifyingly large, so it seemed as though they might be going to have a hit on their hands in London.

On the Thursday evening, after the show, Anna retired to her room in the Turk's Head Hotel after supper, with the comfortable feeling that all was well with the world, and with the play. She also entertained a reasonable hope that the leading man wouldn't try to get into her bedroom, and that his lovesick adorer wouldn't be crying loudly in the passage outside. As she reached her door, the telephone shrilled, startling her. It was late for an English call, and an unusual time for her family to ring. With a premonition of disaster, she ran across the room, and picked up the receiver.

The line was so clear that she could have been talking to someone next door, but Marilyn — the imperturbable and always comforting Marilyn — was speaking so quietly that Anna could scarcely hear what she was saying. Anna thought she was crying.

'Be brave, darling. Be brave. It's terrible, but be brave. The others will need all your strength.'

Immediately she was frightened. 'What's the matter?' she asked almost frantically. 'I can't hear you properly. What am I to be brave about? Are you all right? What's happened?'

It slowly transpired that Sylvie and the young son of Philip's yachting friends had gone surf-boarding by moonlight the previous evening, while the adults were dining. Sylvie's board had overturned and Sylvie had vanished from sight.

Panic-stricken, the boy had returned to the yacht to report what had happened, and a distraught Philip had swum out to look for her. He had just eaten a heavy meal, and developed cramp. Both he and Sylvie were drowned.

At first, Anna couldn't take it in.

'Both drowned? You mean they're *dead*?' she asked, stunned. '*Both* of them?'

'Yes, darling.'

'I simply can't believe it!'

'It's true.'

'Oh, my God!' said Anna, and instinctively she put down the telephone. She was shaking all over, and felt sick.

The telephone rang again. 'Oh, darling, I wish I were near you ... There was absolutely no way of saving them,' said Marilyn. 'Don't cry!'

'*Both* Philip and Sylvie! I don't understand. Dead! It just doesn't seem possible!'

'Bob and I are driving up to New York with Maria right away,' said Marilyn. 'The children will be staying with us until you can get here.'

Philip and Sylvie dead! It was final, and senseless, and cruel. But Marilyn was right, the children would need her. She must indeed be brave.

CHAPTER TWENTY-THREE

Anna flew down to London on the next plane, early the next morning. Charlie was at Heathrow to meet her. He had heard what had happened on the late-night news, and at once took control. He saw to her arrangements for the flight back to New York and telephoned Marilyn, who had already collected Philip Junior and agreed to take the two children straight to the Marshes' New York apartment, ready for Anna's return. He spoke also to the manager of the play, made Anna's apologies and told him of her plans. He was sympathetic, unexpectedly brisk, and steady as a rock.

Marilyn met Anna at Idlewild (now Kennedy Airport) and drove her home. She and Bob made the funeral arrangements, and then stayed on in the apartment for a further three weeks to comfort and help look after the family. Philip Junior missed Sylvie even more than his father, as he had had the special love and understanding with her that twins experience. Maria missed her father more; she had always been especially near to him, as first daughters so often are. Anna was once again close to despair. Her marriage had given her the sense of security she had needed so passionately after her bleak and unchildish childhood. Unlike the despair she had undergone through Antonio's rejection, however, it contained no loss of self-respect, and so left room for the future.

There were endless discussions as to what to do next. Anna had an urgent wish to leave America for Europe. America suddenly seemed to her alien and cruel, and the apartment a daily reminder of her lost happiness. A move to Europe, even if not back to England, might provide a more sympathetic environment, and one close to her own origins. She telephoned her British agent and he was against it, feeling that it might harm the career she had made for herself in America.

Marilyn too was against it. 'Why add to your traumas by uprooting yourselves even further?' she asked. 'You all belong here now. It is where you have all your friends.'

But Anna's instinctive wish to leave was too strong.

Eventually it was agreed to try Switzerland — at least for a while. Noël Coward, to whom Anna wrote thanking him for a letter of warm sympathy, at once suggested that he should look for a house for them, and they thankfully accepted his offer.

Switzerland proved a success. Its unfamiliarity took the edge off their sorrow and Anna liked its blandness. She found it enchantingly pretty and the people kind, undemanding and efficient. Her new home, a châlet near Vevey, stood high among vineyards, overlooking Lake Geneva. Arranging it gave her a great deal to attend to.

To the back of the house, beyond the vineyards, ran a small railway; behind this again there were lush meadows and a few scattered farms. Pretty fawn-coloured cows with tinkling cowbells wandered over the hills most of the year round and, early in the morning, small brilliantly-feathered cockerels crowed their excitable welcome to each new day. The local country people were kind, if taciturn, and Anna found a pretty and cheerful little Swiss maid to live in, and a woman from the village to come and cook for her daily. Philip Junior enjoyed having a swimming pool in the garden once again, even though at this time of year he couldn't use it, and much of his time was spent learning to ski, which soon became a passion. Maria approved of the finishing school to which she was to be sent in Les Avants, and was delighted that it was only a short way from Noël's house, as she had taken an immediate and strong liking to him. The school had a large number of American and English pupils and, with Anna living near by, she felt she wouldn't be too homesick.

Philip Junior's education was more difficult to arrange but, as ever, Marilyn came to the rescue. Through friends of hers, he was allowed to sit for a Harrow scholarship, and though he failed to win one, he was accepted on the strength of his papers.

Through Noël, and his friends, Cole Lesley, and Graham Payne, Anna, Maria and Philip came to know a number of entertaining and interesting people. Stewart Granger, now living in Geneva, put Anna in touch with several directors of European film companies, and the London management with whom she had been working when the tragedy struck offered to employ her whenever they could find a suitable play for her.

Marilyn and Bob came over on a visit to satisfy themselves that all was well, and left relieved. Charlie, too, paid them a visit — with his new girlfriend, a pliable and adoring young woman, but evidently no real substitute for his lost love. He was drinking heavily again, and the slightly furtive air that Anna had noticed before now seemed permanent. His good looks were beginning to go.

Throughout all this time, Anna had heard nothing from Muriel, but this neither surprised nor hurt her.

For almost a year, emotional numbness combined with the novelty of her new home to make it possible for her to get through her waking hours almost pleasantly. But as the numbness wore off and feelings returned, Anna was immersed once again in despair. When the children were at school, boredom compounded the problem and, in spite of the efforts of her new friends, she was desolate.

She obtained a certain amount of film work, but not enough. For a time, a film in Austria provided her with a good part — but it was ruined in the finish, in her eyes, by an unsuitable German voice dubbed in place of hers to obviate language difficulties. Equally frustrating was a film she made in Berlin, which relied too heavily on improvisation instead of rehearsal and a finished script. She found herself seriously considering a return to America, but Maria and Philip Junior had now settled down too well for further upheavals.

And so another year went by — and yet another — slowly, doggedly, and, for her, without meaning. When she wasn't filming she threw herself into the social whirl provided for her; but no one could fill the void left by Philip and Sylvie, and she found it hard to believe that the effort was worth it.

Then suddenly a miracle happened. One day, three years after the tragedy, when holidaying in Gstaad, she met a playboy called Jacques François, many years her junior. The attraction was immediate and violent. It was also mutual. Anna did her best to resist it, but failed. And so an affair began. She was jolted into life and feeling again, with a rapidity she was unable to fight.

In Jacques' company, she was a different woman. He was immensely rich. He was clever, spoilt, funny and magnetic. He was also sincerely loving. He made her laugh more than anyone she had ever met since fat little Tony Falk in her first play in London all those years ago; and her passion for him, though strongly maternal, was yet so profoundly sensual that life became intensely and obsessively exciting once again. When she was with him, time, place, other people and all sense of responsibility faded. He was like a brilliant child, precocious and wilful, but to her infinitely endearing, and with him she became both the mother she sensed he needed, and the child her mother had never allowed her to be. They were totally absorbed in one another, and completely companionable. Day and night fused. They made love drowning in happiness, and the love-making never sated them; on the contrary, it constantly renewed them.

Because of the disparity in their ages, Jacques' friends gave the affair three months. They were wrong. This time he was really in love. Anna was all he needed, as he was for her — a rare thing in love affairs. Both were satisfied, and both were astounded by their good fortune.

When the children were home, Jacques understood and respected Anna's wish to be with them. He loved them because they were hers, and they liked him because he was good to their mother and provided them with constant amusement. Jacques flew his own plane, and was a surprisingly responsible pilot. After the first qualms, Anna allowed him to take Philip and Maria with him on hops to Paris or Holland or Italy. When they were back at school, he took Anna alone. Flying beside him, with the prospect of a month in the south of France, ten days in Morocco, or a week in Bangkok, she watched with loving respect his care and professional conduct. Reckless and extravagant in all else, in his plane he was meticulous. She saw the world under ideal conditions.

In return, Anna took him to see the people she cared about. She lunched at Les Avants, when visiting Maria at school, and introduced Jacques to Noël. She thought Noël looked ill, but he was in excellent spirits as he had just been awarded a knighthood. It was to be the last time she ever saw him.

She went to England with Jacques and saw Charlie, and was horrified at the change in him. He was now hooked on drugs and seemed to live in another world, hardly aware of her — or indeed of Jacques.

She also wrote to Marilyn and, on her return to Switzerland, Marilyn and Bob came over for a second time — this time for a three-month stay. They both loved Jacques, who reciprocated their affection. Happiness had returned.

'It's mad, isn't it?' exclaimed Anna excitedly. 'Jacques and I are tempting fate, Marilyn, and I know it, but Jacques won't have it that the Gods will be jealous. I'm frightened that they'll never allow such a wonderful second chance to last!'

'They've allowed mine,' replied Marilyn seriously.

'It will all end in tears,' laughed Anna. 'I know it, but I don't care. It's worth it!'

Marilyn kissed her. 'Darling little Anna!' she said. 'If you only knew how much pleasure it gives me to see you so happy!'

'And me, you!' retorted Anna. 'What a wonderful friend you've been to me, Marilyn!'

'You're my surrogate daughter!' replied Marilyn. 'And a very satisfactory one, too!'

'It's all so good at the moment,' said Anna. 'All of us such good friends, and all of us so happy — and Bob, of course, so distinguished and successful! It's extraordinary isn't it? I mean, the number of different lives some of us seem to live? I so wonder why ...'

'Yes, it's extraordinary,' agreed Marilyn. 'I'm not religious-minded, and I have no idea what we're all doing on this curious earth of ours, but I'm certainly appreciating my life right now.'

When she and Bob left, Anna missed them; but Jacques so filled her life that she needed little more than him — and her children, though she knew they would soon be leaving her.

Maria finished at her school and opted for a course in the history of art, to be taken in London, Florence and Rome. When Philip Junior finished at Harrow he managed to scrape into Oxford, to study Modern Languages (he hadn't quite committed himself yet to a life in the theatre). Muriel, surprisingly, wrote to Anna once or twice; she never mentioned Jacques, or the life Anna was now leading, but she asked for news of the grandchildren and was looking forward to seeing something of Maria. (Philip made no contact with Muriel and, surprisingly, she seemed to accept this with stoicism.) There were no requests for money and, except for a deepening worry over Charlie's behaviour, she seemed, even if remotely, to have accepted her role as a mother and grandmother at last. She did once remark, and it touched Anna, that she had been only twenty when Anna had been born, and so, probably, unsuited for motherhood. This letter seemed to Anna to contain some kind of apology.

Jacques asked Anna to marry him, twice. The first time he was hesitant and slightly nervous, which made Anna suspect that he was proposing for her sake. The second time he was insistent. Both times Anna gently reminded him that she was very much older than he, and that one day the disparity in their ages might come to matter.

'You're not saying that because you're getting tired of me?' he asked anxiously.

'No, darling. I don't think I shall ever tire of you. We suit each other so well.'

'You said Philip suited you.'

'So he did, but in a different way. That's one of the magical things for me. The way I love you is so different that I don't feel I'm letting Philip's memory down.'

'I wish you had never loved anyone else but me,' he said.

'Loving always teaches one to love even better,' smiled Anna.

He seemed content, and didn't persist in the proposal. He did however take her to see his parents in Paris and, though they were extremely polite, she could see that she wasn't what they had had in mind for the wife of their only son. She liked them both, though, indeed, neither of them was what she had expected. Their extreme age surprised her. Père François was an industrialist who had made all his money in ball-bearings. He was tall and aristocratic-looking, with heavy eyebrows over sunken eyes. His smile was charming, and he had an excellent and well-cultivated mind. Madame was also tall, with beautiful white hair and a natural grace. She was clever and shrewd but, though a good conversationalist, entirely without a sense of humour. (Jacques certainly hadn't inherited his from her.) They lived in a house which, although it was almost in the centre of Paris, had a garden behind a high wall, with an enormous wrought-iron gate barring a short drive. It was dark and gloomy, with very old soft-footed servants who had been with the family for many years. The meals were taken with great solemnity; they were protracted affairs with innumerable courses, the food of gourmet standard, and the wines superb. Jacques had said that he had found his home life imprisoning. She could see why; she could also see why he had rebelled against their way of life, although it was for entirely different reasons from those she had imagined. 'I need sun and air and travel and young friends,' he had told her. 'My parents are too old for me just now.'

'Then why pick on me?' Anna had asked, laughing, teasing him that perhaps he had needed a mother-substitute.

'Because you attract me as no one else has ever done,' he replied simply.

Yet he had a great sense of family, and from time to time they went to visit what she thought of as an overabundance of aunts and uncles, all of whom lived as imposingly as his parents, in great châteaux, or in huge modern mansions in the South of France.

One day when they were staying with his parents, Madame François said to Anna, 'I have come to be glad that you are my son's companion. At first I was worried — although, as you know, in France many young men are taught to love by older women. Now I am pleased. With you my son has found peace. He is a strange one, this Jacques. We were not young when he was born, and he is the apple of our eye. One day he will take over my husband's business, and he has said he will do so willingly — if he lives to see the day. He has a preoccupation with death. You have noticed it?'

'I can't say that I have.' Anna was astonished.

'That is surprising,' said Madame François. 'It has always been a part of his nature and it has worried his father and me. This is why we allow him to live exactly as he chooses until the day he has to shoulder his responsibilities.' She stopped talking and looked searchingly at Anna. 'It is interesting that, in these years that you have been with him, he has not showed you this side of him.'

'I've noticed how intensely he lives for each day,' said Anna.

'Ah, yes,' she nodded. 'I too have noticed this, and sometimes I am thankful.'

'I don't think I quite understand,' said Anna.

'In case he is right to have a preoccupation with death,' said Madame François gravely.

'What an extraordinary thing to say!' exclaimed Anna. 'You mean, you think he may have a premonition of his own early death?' She suddenly remembered with chilly dread her own premonition just before she had picked up the telephone in Newcastle and heard of Philip and Sylvie's death.

'Who knows?' said Madame François sadly. 'It is possible.' She shrugged her shoulders and gave a bleak smile. 'All things are possible, in this far from easy world.'

CHAPTER TWENTY-FOUR

Muriel wrote one day to say that Charlie had been sent to gaol. 'Poor Charlie!' she said. 'He doesn't have an easy time. He's too good-natured for his own good. That horrid little Brenda hasn't been loyal to him, and she has left him. I never liked her, and now I have been proved right. Someone got him hooked on drugs and I had rather a difficult time with him. He was telephoning people all over the world ... America ... Japan ... Holland ... everywhere. The bills were enormous, but if I complained he became upset ... really terribly excitable. Then one day he went over to Holland with a friend, and when he came back alone, the customs men caught him at Heathrow with heroin in the false bottom of his suitcase. He was accused of being a courier, and admitted it. He hasn't been well lately, and I'm worried about the effect prison will have on him. He has chronic bronchitis now, and gets alarming depressions. Really, that marriage brought nothing but disaster — and I thought at the beginning it would be so wonderful for him! He has never got over Martha, and I'm afraid he never will.

'Your children never come and see me, though Maria does telephone sometimes. She seems to like her present course, doesn't she? I shall miss her when she goes to Italy. Philip doesn't seem to want to get in touch at all, but I hear he is doing quite well at Oxford and working quite hard.

'I haven't seen your name in the papers lately, but perhaps that's a good thing as you seem to have been running around with a man half your age. Not a very good example to your children, and unsettling for them, too, I should imagine. *You* may have lost a husband and daughter, but *they* have been bereaved too. However, you've always gone your own way,

and I daresay you always will. Is this why you're not
concentrating on your career? Because he can well afford to
keep you (and, I trust, the children)? Do you expect to marry
him?'

Anna wrote at once to Charlie, suggesting that she return to
England for a bit so as to be near enough to visit him; but he
wrote by return to dissuade her. 'Thanks for the thought, old
girl, but for God's sake don't put it into action! *I* don't want
the press connecting us, even if *you* don't mind, as then I'd
never get back to being anonymous again when I get out of
here. It's not too bad, all things considered, and I'm having
plenty of time to think.'

Anna discussed her family with Jacques, including her long-
ago conversation with Charlie at the quayside, when he and
Muriel were leaving America for England.

'Don't blame yourself for succeeding in life,' said Jacques.
'With your home background it is courageous.'

'Courageous is the very last thing I am!' laughed Anna

'Most success needs a courage of the spirit, I think,' he said
seriously. 'Courage of the spirit gives a certain inner
confidence that even lack of love in the family cannot quite
destroy. It makes the winners in life. The others are the losers.'

'Don't forget, I tried to kill myself over Antonio!' said
Anna.

'I won't! This so-silly Antonio! How lucky for you that he
did not love you! Think of the life you would have spent with
him! The English can seldom make good Italian wives, I think.
Their expectation of some sort of equality between husband
and wife is fatal — and Italian husbands are still dominated by
their mothers. Besides, this Antonio was spoilt from birth.
Spoilt to the point of damage.'

'And you weren't spoilt?' teased Anna.

Jacques ducked the question.

'Anyway, my parents — whom you like, I think — are clever
people. Antonio's people are nonentities.'

Anna laughed again. 'Your command of English is becoming
spectacular!' she said. 'Antonio's parents are very well-born.
They certainly don't think of themselves as nonentities!'

'From what you say, it was their forebears who were the
clever ones. Not they. They simply have to live with rigidity,

and they will be respected. My parents are old, but they live with a sense of purpose, and, although I cannot live near them, I respect them. I realise, too, that I may well grow like them, when I am older.'

'That wouldn't worry me!' said Anna.

'You are the one and only Anna Starr,' said Jacques, kissing her passionately. 'You are the most beautiful and the most understanding woman in the world.'

Suddenly Anna decided to tell him of the conversation she had had with his mother about his obsession with death.

'Yes, she is right,' said Jacques solemnly. 'You see how clever she is? We do not talk about this often, my mother and I, yet she realises that death is an obsession with me. I live on — how do you call it? — borrowed time, and so I respect time. If I am wrong, I am glad to have respected time; the small amount of it we are given on this earth is an anxiety to me. If I live until I am a hundred, I will still be grateful that my obsession taught me to value each day. And why not? Each day is important. Very important.'

'It doesn't worry you that you live without doing any work? That you are so much richer than so many people? That you live a life of luxury and ease, and you don't try to achieve anything?'

'Consider the lilies of the field,' laughed Jacques. 'They toil not, neither do they spin! I give work, because I am rich, to many people. I try to cheat no one. I live with you because you are special, and I see this as my destiny. I cannot forego my destiny, I believe in my destiny.'

'And you really think of death, often?'

'Oh, yes. Often and often.'

'I don't like the idea of predestination,' said Anna, with a shiver.

'Whether you like it or not, if we are predestined, then we are predestined.'

'You don't believe in free will?'

'Of course. This has nothing to do with it. It is all a question of time-span, and the milestones — isn't that how you call them? — on the way. What we do about the time-span and the milestones, is our business. The rest will be as it has been ordained.'

'I hate that thought!'

'I am accustomed to it. It is my belief,' said Jacques.

'Has achievement no interest for you?'

'For some of us, what life is about is what we do. For others, it is what we are.'

'How much does your religion really mean to you?' asked Anna suddenly. Having little feeling for religion herself, the question of faith had often puzzled her.

'Like all Catholics, I cannot escape my religious teaching,' said Jacques. 'It is a part of me.'

'I don't know whether I wish it were a part of me or not,' she said.

'That will manifest itself to you in time,' replied Jacques.

'Do you mind that I care about it so little?'

'How do you know that you care about it so little? You will only find that out when the testing time comes. That is, if you are one of the ones to be tested.'

'Dear Jacques! How wise you sound!'

'I am wise,' he laughed. 'You should always remember that! And now, I have a suggestion to make. I should like very much to go to Kenya, and to take you with me. Will you come?'

'When?'

'The day after tomorrow?'

'Good heavens! For how long?'

'Six weeks. Maria will be here at the end of July, and Philip soon after, so we must be back by then.'

'I haven't got any clothes,' objected Anna.

'You have too many clothes! I like you best with no clothes!' he said fondly.

'How wonderful! Yes, I'll come. I'd adore it.'

'Good. After this one last time, I shall have to settle down,' said Jacques. 'My mother has written to say my father is not well, and we shall have to go to Paris, you and I, where I can learn how to help him. He has said I can be free until he needs me. Now he needs me, and Maman too. So now I must grow up and stop being La Fontaine's cricket.'

'La Fontaine's cricket?' echoed Anna. 'What is that?'

'The *Fables de La Fontaine*. How does it go? "A silly young cricket accustomed to sing, through the warm sunny months of September and Spring ... " '

'Yes?'

'I forget the rest, but the cricket he leave it too late. I must not do that. I have written to tell them I shall be with them in seven weeks' time.'

Anna felt her heart sink. 'So soon?' she asked sadly.

'But yes.'

'Then we have to leave each other?'

'Certainly not! You will stay here for the children while they are here, then you will come to Paris.'

'Things may be so different there.'

'They will be different. Of course! You want all life to be the same?'

'Of course not, but you will have serious work to do in Paris, and you will be with your family. Perhaps we shall drift apart in such circumstances.'

'Foolish one. Love does not drift apart. You remember this beautiful sonnet by your Shakespeare?:

Let me not to the marriage of true minds
Admit impediments. Love is not love
Which alters when it alteration finds,
Or bends with the remover to remove:
O, no! it is an ever-fixed mark,
That looks on tempests and is never shaken;
It is the star to every wandering bark,
Whose worth's unknown, although his height
                            be taken ...

then I can't remember how it goes until it ends:

Love alters not with his brief hours and weeks,
But bears it out even to the edge of doom.
  If this be error and upon me prov'd,
  I never writ, nor no man ever lov'd.'

'Yes, it's a beautiful sonnet. What an extraordinary man you are, Jacques! Where did you learn that?"

'At the Sorbonne.'

'One day our affair will finish, and, oh, how I shall miss you!'

'This I do not believe. That our affair will finish.' He spoke quietly but with finality. She stopped arguing.

*   *   *

Two days later they set off for Africa, heading for Nairobi. Though fortunately neither of them knew it, it was to be the last flight Jacques ever took, and the abrupt end for Anna of an unclouded love affair. The plane ran into a violent storm and went out of control over Mount Kenya. They crashed into the mountainside and Jacques was killed outright.

Anna was found by a rescue party and taken to hospital. Her face was smashed to pieces, and her back was broken, but she was alive.

For a week she lay in a coma. Surgeons operated several times on her back and on her face, and for months they were afraid she would never walk again. She didn't care. She cared about nothing. She was eventually flown back to Switzerland to a clinic in Basle. Philip and Maria, who had both flown to Nairobi to be near her, were in attendance here, too. Surgeons were still operating. She was so dazed with grief and drugs that she hardly seemed to feel pain; hardly knew what was happening to her. In her lucid moments, she cried helplessly. She had terrible dreams; nightmares in which Philip's accident became mixed with the aircrash, and somehow — as often in nightmares, when time becomes violently awry — she dreamed of Jacko, too.

Her mother cabled once or twice, but made no offer to come to Switzerland. Marilyn, loving as always, came over for an indefinite stay, promising that Bob would follow after the publication of his latest book.

Charlie wrote from prison. 'I wish I could be with you, old girl, though it won't be too long before I'm let out now. I know I shall have to pull myself together when I do get out, but God knows how! I'll have to go back to Mother, of course ... yes, I know what you'll say ... and it will all be the same as before, except that Brenda has gone ... but that's my life. Brenda leaving me was hard to take, though I expect she didn't seem much to you, and Mother never liked her. I really did think she cared for me ... more fool me! Well, so much for Brenda! Glad they're looking after you well, and that you're getting better.'

Her room was a bower of flowers all the time she was at the clinic. She had been headline news in every European newspaper. The Swiss press hung round the hospital constantly, ready to report progress. Friends came and went, and gradually, bit by bit, she recovered. The surgeons had done a wonderful job on her face and back, and she was now walking for short distances, with a stick.

Every day, Philip, Maria or Marilyn were at the clinic, anxiously and lovingly doing their best to give her courage and hope.

Eventually, for their sake, she began to wish to live; and once she had started, the improvement was rapid. She had lost a second German film, but an Italian one was on offer for December if she had completely recovered. She looked into the mirror at the face which had been so miraculously repaired and, blankly, her beautiful new face stared back at her — herself ten years younger, unlined and perfect. She still cried feebly for hours on end when she thought of Jacques, and his mother and father sent her flowers every week, which also made her cry; but the doctors, comforting her, told her that such tears were beneficial.

At last the day came when she was allowed home. Philip had had to return to Oxford, and Marilyn was back in America since Bob had developed an attack of shingles, but Maria was staying in Switzerland to be with her.

'Darling,' said Anna one day to Maria, 'How can I ever thank you enough for all your care and concern? You and Philip have been wonderful! No mother ever had more marvellous children — and yet, my affair with Jacques must have upset you dreadfully sometimes.'

'It would have if you'd ever let it interfere with what you were doing for us,' said Maria gravely. 'We talked it over a lot, and knew it was good for you, and that Father and Sylvie would have understood.'

'I told Jacques that the way I loved him never for one moment made me feel I was letting your father down,' said Anna. 'It was such a very different way of loving.'

'Of course,' replied Maria softly. 'Don't worry, Mummy. I told you we understood.'

'But *you* didn't have anyone to help make you forget,' said Anna.

'The three of us were still a family,' said Maria. 'That was the most important thing. We knew you loved us, and Jacques did too, which was sweet of him. That mattered, because it meant we mattered to you, or he wouldn't have cared.'

'I know what you mean,' said Anna, 'because that's what made me want to get better — that you and Philip Junior and I were a family.'

'Jacques was a nice man,' said Maria, 'and Father and Sylvie were the best, so it's better than never having known nice people.'

'Yes,' said Anna. 'It's a great deal better,' and she felt much happier.

While they were living together quietly at Vevey, they were able to discuss Maria's work and her ambitions in a way that they might never have thought of doing otherwise, and this brought the two of them very close. Anna marvelled at Maria's strength and good sense. 'You're years older than I was at your age,' she said. 'I was so feeble and indecisive.'

'We might have been too, if Muriel had been our mother!' laughed Maria.

'You were so good at painting, darling,' said Anna, on another occasion. 'You don't think that working at an auction house will be too restricting and uncreative?' Maria had expressed a wish to join Sotheby's or Christie's.

'If either of them will have me, I'll be over the moon!' exclaimed Maria.

'Has Philip decided yet what he wants?'

'Yes. A drama school, then the stage.'

'Well, I'm glad! And what about marriage?'

'No one I want to marry yet, though I may set up with a boy I know, if it all turns out OK.'

'If what turns out OK?'

'Oh, things,' said Maria vaguely.

'May I meet him?'

'Of course.'

'And what about Philip?'

'He's going steady with a girl at Oxford,' said Maria. 'She's a nice girl, and very clever.'

'Serious?'

'It might be.'

'But he's so young!' exclaimed Anna.

'He's old enough to take care of himself,' replied Maria firmly.

'I suppose so,' answered Anna wistfully. 'Yet it seems only yesterday ... '

'It always does,' interrupted Maria. 'It's always only yesterday. That's what the past does for you.'

Anna looked at her, surprised. 'You say that with such a sense of loss,' she said, wonderingly.

'Do I?' Maria suddenly sounded brisk. 'The past is always loss, isn't it?'

CHAPTER TWENTY-FIVE

By the autumn, Anna had fully recovered her physical health. Maria returned to art school in London. Anna had accepted the film in Rome and the film company had booked her into the Hilton from December. She was thankful to be going. She thought it unlikely that she would see Antonio, and knew that, if she did, he could affect her no longer; Switzerland, by contrast, reminded her too much of Jacques, just as America had reminded her too much of Philip.

'I'm just a coward,' she thought guiltily. 'Jacques' idea that you have to be courageous to be successful is wrong as far as I'm concerned.'

Rome seemed to her as beautiful as it had always done. There were changes, of course, but the heart of it was there — the ravishing architecture in the centre of the city, the grave and splendid clamour of the great church bells, the elegance of the women, the flowers everywhere, the singing and the laughter, even though the streets now were dangerous at night. The film was a co-production, with Americans and English and Italian actors. The foreign stars were all staying at the Hilton, and it was with these that she spent her free time.

At work, she could quite often forget her tragedies; and she enjoyed being in harness once more, especially since she was acting in a particularly literate comedy. Again she blessed her mother for choosing this particular life for her. That she spoke Italian so well also increased her enjoyment of the city, and she felt at home here now, in a way that she had not when she'd been Antonio's mistress.

She asked after him. It appeared that he had completely given up the theatre and was living in the country on the family estates. He was still very rich, as was his wife, and they now had three children who were all nearly grown up. She thought of telephoning him, but resisted the idea.

Meanwhile, so that she could be of help to Maria in her chosen career, she made friends with the sort of Italians who could show her daughter around when she came to Italy for the Italian part of her art course — though in fact Maria would be spending most of her time in Florence, not Rome.

Both children came to Rome at Christmas; she was touched to hear that both of them had visited Charlie. They said he was in remarkably good spirits and putting up a brave front, but they thought he was almost afraid of the future. They both thought he didn't trust himself to be able to pull himself together. Maria had kept in fairly constant touch with Muriel and reported that she was well, but lonely for Charlie. Philip, on the other hand, still had not forgiven her for her treatment of his father and did not like seeing her.

Philip was very like his father now: sandy-haired, slim but well-built, and with a devastatingly caustic wit. His girl friend, Evie, came out to join him for a few days after Christmas, and to meet Anna. Anna noticed that, although Philip pretended to be indifferent to their effect on one another, he watched Evie and his mother closely when they were together. He evidently cared strongly about Evie, and the two of them were good friends. Evie was probably the cleverer and perhaps the dominant partner, but the girl loved Philip, of that there was no doubt. Her ambition was to be a writer. She had already had a couple of short stories published, which, considering her age and the narrowing market, was quite an achievement; and she wanted to get into a publishing house meanwhile, to 'get the feel' as she called it, of the book world.

Although young men swarmed round Maria, she seemed to take no interest in them, which made Anna wonder if perhaps the boy with whom her daughter had thought of sharing a flat had either left her, or was playing her up. When she asked Maria about it, Maria refused to discuss it.

'It's only that perhaps I might be able to help you, if you're unhappy,' said Anna.

'I don't need your help,' answered Maria firmly. 'I'm OK.'

Philip also refused to talk about his sister's affairs.

They did, however, all discuss Anna's future — though the children made it plain that the actual decision about where to live rested with her. 'We've both more or less left the nest,' said Philip, gently, 'so it will matter more to you than to us.'

Anna acknowledged bleakly that they were right. As she had after Philip's death, though, she urgently wished to leave her present home.

Maria said forcibly, 'You can't run away every time something awful happens, Mother. It does no good. And why move from Vevey? What for?'

'We moved when your father died.'

'Quite.'

'Did you think of it as running away then?'

'I wasn't old enough to think in those terms.'

'No, I suppose not.'

'Financially, surely Switzerland is much the best bet,' urged Maria sensibly. 'And it's marvellously central for the rest of Europe. That is, unless you wish to return to America?'

'I don't know where I want to be,' answered Anna. 'I'm just restless, that's all.'

'Why not stay put until the shock has really worn off?' suggested Philip. 'I'm sure that many people move away from their surroundings too soon when someone has died. They end up cutting themselves off from their memories and their friends, and it's a bad idea. Wait two or three years.'

'You think the pain will only last two or three years?' asked Anna.

'Let's hope so,' said Philip, again very gently.

'It did last time,' said Maria. 'For all of us!' And Anna thought she spoke bitterly.

The children went back to England. When the film finished, Anna herself returned to Switzerland, where she received an invitation to stay with Jacques' parents in Paris. She decided to accept. Both were as utterly devastated as she was about his death and clung on to her as the daughter-in-law that perhaps she might have been. Since Père François was now terminally ill, a nephew had come to take Jacques' place as the head of the company and he too was staying in the house temporarily. Though Jacques' parents both thought he would be good at the job, he got on their nerves as a house guest.

'He is insensitive and arrogant,' complained Maman. 'He regards my husband as already dead, and this is not comfortable.' She spoke without a trace of humour, but Anna understood and was fiercely on her side.

'He has perhaps good and practical ideas for the firm,' said Père François, 'but he wishes to move in too much of a hurry. The previous generation may now be a little out of date, but they weren't stupid or the firm would never have come into being. It was, after all, my brain-child, and although I am no longer young, I have never been, nor am I now, a stupid man.'

They openly mourned the death of their only son, and with them Anna could openly mourn him too. She found it therapeutic. She also knew that she had found in them new friends whom she loved.

The nephew tried to subvert her to his own cause, but she didn't like him, and wholeheartedly agreed with Maman that he was arrogant. She also found him insensitive, and although he might perhaps be good with money, she felt he wouldn't be good with people, and this, Anna thought, boded ill for the future of the firm.

One day, when Anna and the two old people were talking, Anna said impulsively, 'You're wonderful to be so kind to me! Over and over again I have wished that I hadn't said I would go to Kenya with him. I've said to myself, over and over, if only . . .'

'It would have made no difference,' interrupted Maman. 'There would have been other dangers. I explained to you that he knew he would die young.'

'So in a way, we were prepared,' nodded Père François. 'We were a good family together, and this is an achievement in today's world. It gives us now, as it gave us then, great happiness.'

'Yes. He loved you both very deeply,' agreed Anna. 'He once told me that he looked forward to taking on his responsibilities when the time came.'

Père François looked pleased. 'This was true,' he said. 'He was a good son.'

'A good son,' echoed Maman. And they smiled at one another.

*				*				*

Back in Switzerland, time dragged. It was spring. Both
children would be visiting Anna again soon. She had many
friends. She loved her house. The nearby village was within
walking distance, and now that the snow had melted she could
wander along a valley, at this moment alight with spring
flowers, among those pretty fawn-coloured cows with tinkling
cow-bells. But she was restless. She was heading towards her
fiftieth birthday, and suddenly she felt old.

Surely her best days were over now? What could the future
hold? As an actress, certainly, she had work which she enjoyed.
But although she was known internationally through the
success of her early films, as a stage actress she had never
reached the heights, and since Philip's death it hadn't seemed
important. Her 'time out', as Jacques had called it, had been an
experience she wouldn't have missed for the world, or for any
of its material rewards; but now both her men were dead, and
the children, as Philip Junior had so gently reminded her, were
grown up.

Philip would come down from Oxford soon, and had
written to say that he had already passed his audition for
RADA and had been accepted. He was still with Evie, and
although Anna thought it unwise for them to marry while he
was still a student, she had a feeling that he would disregard her
advice. Anna liked Evie but would find it hard to love her, she
thought. She was so self-sufficient, so reserved, and indeed so
tough. And Maria, now in Florence, no longer confided in her
mother. So what should she do next?

Her agent sent her a play to be put on in England in the
autumn. It had a cast of six, and an excellent part for her. It was
a domestic comedy, but written with a welcome amount of
intelligence, and she liked it. But she hadn't done a play since
Philip's accident, and the thought of touring again made her
nervous. What should she do?

The agent settled matters for her. He telephoned Anna.
'Well?' he asked. 'What do you think of it?'

'I like it.'

'Good,' said the agent briskly. 'I'll talk money and billing
tomorrow.'

'Not so fast!' exclaimed Anna. 'Give me time to think, for
heaven's sake!'

'What about?'

'Whether I want to do it.'

'Well, don't you?'

'I haven't decided.'

'What's worrying you?'

'Nothing in particular. I just haven't made up my mind.'

'There isn't even a nibble in any other direction, darling,' said the agent, 'and the management is a good one. Caldecott is going places. He's already got two plays running in the West End, and a lot of good ideas. You get in with him now and it will do you no harm. Besides, you'll like him. He's a nice man.'

'Don't rush me.'

'Look, darling, it's a good part in a good play with a good management. You still look marvellous, but you're no longer a juvenile, and work isn't all that easy to get for women of your age. I'm not trying to be rude, but it's a fact. Women don't have it all that easy, anyway — not with a ratio of work eight-to-one in men's favour! And the young women are certainly the luckiest. Tony Falk is directing, by the way.'

'Who?' Anna almost shouted the word.

'Don't blast my ear off, ducky. Tony Falk, and he's a damned good director.'

'Tony Falk? What age is he?'

'About your age, I should think.'

'Good God! I didn't know he was still on the stage! I thought he was going to be a vet!'

'I don't know what you're on about, but he's not a vet. He was a good steady actor for years. Then he turned director, and he's absolutely first class.'

'How extraordinary! I wonder if it's the same one?'

'The same one as what?'

'When I was fourteen I did my first play in London with Marilyn de la Roche, and the other kid in it was Tony Falk. He was a dear! Frightfully sophisticated and self-confident, with a huge shock of brown hair, and tiny brown eyes. He was rather short, and a bit portly then.'

'It sounds the same, though he's quite tall now, and not particularly fat. He's still got a mop of hair, but it's gone a bit grey.'

'Well well well!'

'Has that made up your mind for you?'

'Yes, I think it has. I really think it has.'

'Good girl,' said the agent. 'I'll keep in touch.'

Anna immediately wrote to Marilyn to tell her the news.

Anna had a card from Tony Falk. 'Well what a turn up!' he wrote. 'Looking forward to seeing you. Hope we still get on as well as we did.'

The fact that he was going to be her director somehow transformed the situation for Anna. She wrote to her mother, telling her what had happened and saying that she was looking forward to seeing her; and her mother wrote back quite warmly, saying that she remembered Tony well and would be glad for Anna to see the house, though she had no room for her to stay, she was afraid, as Charlie would come out of prison during the summer and had to have a home waiting for him.

Maria came up to Switzerland for a month from Italy. She looked brown and fit and happy. She was full of her studies, which she was relishing, and had begun to paint again. She had brought some of her canvasses to Switzerland, and Anna proudly thought she had considerable talent. Whatever it was that had been distressing her at Christmas evidently distressed her no longer and, once again, she and Anna were able to talk freely to one another. Anna didn't refer to the change in her, though, or ask what had upset her so much, and she thought this was a relief to Maria.

Philip arrived with Evie. He had taken his exams at Oxford, and was awaiting the results, as indeed was Evie for her own. They were living together, and had decided against marriage for the time being. They didn't give any explanation, but Anna guessed that both realised that an early marriage might interfere with their careers. She got slightly closer to Evie this time, but not much. Evie had been brought up by her grandmother and wasn't really used to families, she said. She had a theory that families could stunt each other if they lived too much in each other's pockets. She needed freedom to breathe, she said, and had evidently either received it or made it for herself. Her parents had split up early, and her father had married another woman as soon as the divorce was through. He didn't parti-cularly want her with him, and her mother had become an alcoholic, so her grandmother had taken charge, and all had been well. She said that it didn't matter who loved you when you were young, but that you had to have someone or you had no self-respect later. Anna agreed that this was correct so far as she was concerned, but said that she believed you could learn self-respect over the years if you found love. She also said that no one had ever been more loved than Charlie, and that he continually felt a failure. Evie replied that there were always exceptions. She was, in her way, egotistical and didactic and slightly bossy, but she suited Philip. He never used his sharp tongue on her, and although Evie was seldom amused by anyone, including Philip, Philip was amused and entertained by Evie.

Anna found that, as the autumn drew near, she was excited to be going back to England to do the play. She had studied the part at some length, and had learned most of the lines in spite of a warning from Tony that there were to be changes in the script. She frankly preferred theatre work to films, and quite suddenly she realised that, through this offer, she felt as though, at last, she were going home.

CHAPTER TWENTY-SIX

Philip met Anna at Heathrow, and to her surprise Tony was with him. She recognised him at once, even after such a long time-gap. He was indeed tall and slim, but his little brown eyes twinkled as they always had in the now lined face, and his ears stuck out boldly from the great mop of greying hair. They hugged and kissed enthusiastically, then the three of them had lunch at Tony's expense at the Dorchester.

To Philip's amusement, his mother and Tony hardly drew breath. They each wanted to know everything about the other, and both were delighted that the years seemed to have made no difference to their liking for one another. Tony's mother had now died. As in Anna's case, it had been his mother, not he, who had wanted him to stay in the theatre. While he was still a child, he had had no choice, and after the play he had done with Anna had finished, he had managed to get a succession of jobs. As his father had been killed in the war, money in the family was tight, and he, again like Anna, had been the financial mainstay. Later, when he could choose, he had never trained to be a vet after all.

Anna laughed. 'I remember so well you asking me scornfully if I'd got a mind of my own, and saying you'd never earn your living in such a soppy way at the theatre, and now here you are! D'you mind?'

'I love it, but I prefer directing to acting.'

'Like Father,' said Philip. 'Why, I wonder?'

'To begin with, unlike what I heard of your father, I wasn't all that hot as an actor; and then, I hated the fact that I wasn't in control of my own career. An actor has to be chosen by both the management and the director. The director only has to be approved by the management. An actor may well know more or less how he wants to play the part, and have a great many excellent ideas to contribute as well as himself, but a director has the final say about the overall shape. I like that. You're very beautiful still,' he said suddenly, turning to Anna. 'I'm glad. I was tremendously in love with you, you know, all those years ago. I was so shy, I could hardly say a word.'

'What rubbish!' replied Anna. 'You never stopped talking, and you were so poised and worldly-wise that I was in awe of you!'

'Keep it that way for the play,' laughed Tony. 'I'm a rather tough director they say, and really like to have my own way. That's only as far as work is concerned, though.'

She noted with pleasure that he was genuinely interested in other people, and was enquiring searchingly into Philip's life. Philip, instead of clamming up as he was quite liable to do with inquisitive strangers, was actually blossoming. He had told Tony that he wanted to be an actor, and Tony was saying how pleased he was. 'It's strange,' he said. 'Without being aware of it, these theatrical dynasties are often founded by people who had had nothing to do with the theatre before. Look at Johnnie Mills, for instance. He was the son of a schoolmaster, and Mary was the daughter of a Colonel who held the position of Commissioner of Chinese Maritime Customs in Tientsen, but now that his dynasty has been started — with Juliet and Hayley — it will probably go on.'

'I would never have suspected you of sentimentality!' exclaimed Anna.

'Nor would I,' said Tony. 'It's meeting up with old friends that does it, I expect.'

'Oh, by the way,' interrupted Philip, 'Charlie rang to say that Grannie would like you to go and see her as soon as possible for tea or a drink. She gave up her job as a receptionist, you know, and lives only at home now.'

'Is Muriel still a tartar?' asked Tony.

'She certainly is!' replied Philip. 'For my money, she's a pain.'

'Philip, please!' said Anna, pretending to be shocked.

'What's Charlie doing now?' said Tony hastily. 'You see? I even remember his name!'

'Working in a pub in Hampstead. As a waiter,' said Philip.
'Poor old Charlie! I like him, but he's pathetic.'

The two men took Anna back to the Savoy, where she was
to stay until she moved into the flat in Chelsea which Philip
had found for her. As he left, Tony said, 'See you on Monday,
then. A read-through at ten at the Apollo. The designer will be
there as well as the management, and we'll get wigs and clothes
settled as soon as possible. O.K.?'

'Fine,' said Anna. 'I can't wait to get started.'

'Oh, and there'll be the author of course. I told you he had
made changes. I'm not giving you a new script, as I want us all
to feel free to discuss them.'

'Do you agree with them?' asked Anna.

'I suggested them,' said Tony, briskly. 'So long, darling.
Lovely we're to be together again.'

'See you Monday,' replied Anna happily.

After he had gone, Philip said enthusiastically, 'I like him,
Ma! They say he's an ace director.'

'Glad you approve,' answered Anna.

'I hope I get to work with him one day!'

'I'm so happy you're going to be an actor!' answered Anna.
'It means a lot to me. I know it's what Philip would have
wanted.'

'Yeah, I guess so,' said Philip.

'Though perhaps it's a waste of a good degree at
Oxford?'

'I don't think so.'

'You and Evie still OK?'

'Yeah. I told you she sends her love.'

'Bring her to the flat on Monday after rehearsal,' said Anna.
'I'll be feeling a bit lonesome on my own there, and a bit keyed-
up after the first reading.'

'Fine,' said Philip. 'We'll be there.' He hesitated, then said,
'I'm real happy about this job of yours, Ma. Haven't seen you
look this relaxed for many moons.'

'Thank you, darling. That's very understanding of you.' She
smiled. 'I'm pretty blessed in my children,' she said.

He smiled back. 'Now then! Don't get maudlin! It's not
your style.' He kissed her lovingly. 'Be seeing you.'

Anna unpacked a suitcase, then telephoned her mother and

arranged to be with her for drinks on Thursday evening.
Muriel sounded almost pleased at the thought of seeing her,
which Anna found encouraging. There were no snide remarks,
and no signs of self-pity. She then telephoned Maria in Florence,
and all seemed well there, so she went to bed more easy in her
mind than she had been for some time. She slept soundly
without having to take pills; a thing she hadn't done since her
accident.

Anna moved into the Chelsea flat over the weekend. It was
pleasant enough but had the bleak, rather defensive, air of all
rented accommodation. The furniture was the kind that could
be easily replaced if damaged. The curtains and upholstery
were charming without being inviting, and in sensible colours
which wouldn't show the dirt, and the windows looked over a
fair-sized garden at the back. At the moment, as it was late
Setpember, there was only a ragged lawn with some bedraggled
roses and chrysanthemums, but with a little effort the garden
could be made pretty in the spring if Anna were still here. A
girl would be coming in to help her in the house, and as a part-
time secretary as well. She was due to arrive before rehearsal on
Monday, but Anna started in straightaway, busying herself
with a duster and polish; by the time she had arranged a few of
the garden flowers in vases, she thought that, with a few good
bits of china and a few new cushions, she might come to feel
quite at home.

From Monday onwards she was fully occupied with the
rehearsals and had no time for moping. She liked the cast,
thought the play read well, approved of most of the changes,
found the set ingenious and enjoyed working with Tony. He
was a hard worker, but so was she. He was articulate and clear
in his direction, and had a good sense of comedy. He had the
slight paternalism of most good directors, but knew very well
indeed what he wanted.

On the Thursday, she took a taxi to Hampstead, realising
wryly that she was nervous. She was still very slighly frightened
of her mother and was fully aware that Muriel always called the
tune. At a deeper level, her feelings for Muriel were ambivalent. The most she hoped for was that she would get through
the visit with no unpleasantness. On the other hand, she still,

in spite of everything, had the last lingering longings for acceptance.

Muriel met her at the door and for a moment, as in New York, Anna hardly recognised her. She had aged even more dramatically than between Hollywood and New York. She had let her hair grow grey again and wore no make-up except for a rather heavy red lipstick. Her once-fair skin had become dun-coloured, but the blue eyes were as blue as ever. She was still slim, still had the remnants of elegance, and she was dressed smartly in black, with diamond earrings and several diamond rings on her fingers. Her hands had roughened, and the veins stood out on the back of them. Her legs were very thin, and she was tottering on absurdly high heels. Inappropriately there was a coquettish air about her, mixed with some sort of defiance. She kissed Anna, and Anna was startled to smell gin on her breath.

The house was small and Georgian — very pretty from the outside. There was a short path leading to it, with flower beds on either side. Inside it was quite richly furnished, but without much taste; though, as usual with Muriel, everything was spotless and shining. She led the way into a sitting room at the back of the house, where there was a small but neatly kept garden in which a man was working industriously. Muriel looked a little embarrassed when she saw him, but gave no explanation, so Anna didn't like to comment on him either.

'This is my den,' Muriel said archly. 'Charlie will be down in a minute. The drawing room is being used by friends for a little while, I'm afraid, but I'll show you the house after we've had a tipple.'

Anna looked round for an empty glass as an explanation for the smell of gin (she thought her mother might have been fortifying herself for the visit), but there was no sign of one. Instead Muriel opened a well-stocked cupboard and brought out two clean glasses, some gin, some vermouth and some lemon. 'This do you?' she asked. 'It's my favourite these days.'

'Fine thanks. How are you, Mother?'

'Fine. Just fine,' said Muriel, with a trace of her American accent.

'This is a dear little house. I hope you like it?'

'Yes, thank you. It suits us well.' She might have been

talking to a stranger, but there was no edge to her voice.

'Everything sparkles in your houses, Mother. I've never seen one thing out of place ever, even in the old days when things were hard.'

'Well, naturally,' said Muriel rather grandly. 'I've always prided myself on my housekeeping.'

'And with every reason,' said Anna, and thought how absurd such a conversation was, after so many years apart.

Muriel was mixing the drinks with extreme care. 'How are you enjoying the play?' she asked.

'I think it may be good.'

'I presume you'll have tickets for me and Charlie on the London first night?'

'Of course, if you'd like them.'

'I miss that sort of thing,' said Muriel. 'I'm rather wasted here, but I have found diversions.'

'Good. Have you friends round here?'

'Oh, certainly. Many. I play bridge now, and that gives one an entrée into a certain kind of circle.'

'I suppose it does.'

'The accident doesn't seem to have hurt your looks,' said Muriel abruptly, assessing Anna.

'The plastic surgeons were marvellous,' said Anna. 'So were the doctors. In that way I was very lucky.'

'You were indeed.' Muriel sipped her own drink, nodded in approval, then handed Anna hers. 'I hope you'll like this,' she said.

The gin was practically neat, but Anna smiled and answered, 'Couldn't be better.'

'How's Tony? Still fat and pushy?'

'No. Rather slim and reserved.'

'My, that's a turn up! And that hair?'

'That hasn't altered.'

Muriel laughed. 'And his mother? I didn't like her much.'

'She's dead.'

'Everyone speaks very highly of Tony as a director,' said Muriel. 'What do you think?'

'He seems excellent.'

'That's fine.' She stopped talking and cocked her head on one side, listening, then she got up and tottered to the door.

'I'll call Charlie,' she said. 'I don't know what he's doing! Charlie! Charlie! She's here! In the den! Come and join us!'

She came back from the door, and before she sat down gestured towards the window and added, 'Colonel Smith will be in as soon as he's finished with the asters.' (She made the flowers sound like visitors.) 'He's a dear friend; very good to me. I don't know what I should have done without him.'

'I look forward to meeting him,' said Anna.

Muriel downed her drink quickly and went roguishly back to the drinks cupboard. 'Drink up, drink up!' she said. 'It's not every day I see my famous daughter! I'm having another gin, so don't let me drink alone.'

Had her mother taken to drink in earnest, in order to keep Charlie company? It looked very like it.

Charlie came into the room, greeting Anna affectionately. He had lost a lot of weight and his face was a bad colour. His quite good suit was hanging off him and, though he had made an effort, he hadn't succeeded in masking an air of defeat. He was obviously pleased to see Anna. Sentimental tears came into his eyes as he patted her murmuring, 'Wonderful, old girl. Wonderful to have you here!' He finished mixing his mother yet another drink, gave it to her, and poured himself a Scotch. Then he sat down heavily in the armchair beside Anna.

The door opened again almost immediately, and the man who had been working in the garden appeared.

Anna was shocked. He could almost have been Jacko's double! A little up the social ladder, perhaps — slightly better clothes, a real air of authority, a more educated voice, and less chin — but he had the same watery eyes, the same slack, surprisingly red, mouth, and the same blue-veining in the nose. 'Not intrudin' am I?' he asked playfully as he entered. 'You told me to come and get a tipple, didn't you, old girl, what?'

'Certainly, Fawcett,' replied Muriel. She looked coy. 'I want you to meet Anna. This is Colonel Smith, Anna. I told you how good he has been to me. He's Fawcett to his friends.'

'Fawcett!' thought Anna. 'Some name!'

'Oh, I say, what? Done nothin', Miss Starr! Nothin' at all. A feller has ter help a lady in distress, dontcher know, especially a charmin' little woman like our Muriel.' He too helped himself to a Scotch, and Muriel simpered. He had put on a jacket and

tie, and had brushed his hair since he'd been in the garden, but
Anna could swear that he'd also given himself a swift shot of
whisky before arriving.

She had always been an outsider in the family, but now
indeed she felt the stranger that Muriel had so quickly devined
her to be. Yet, in a way, paradoxically, it was her own intensely
lived past that she was seeing before her once again. Her
mother and Jacko, thirty years on. As Anna looked at them all,
she had a sense of helpless bewilderment. Was this really what
life was about? A curious obstacle race, full of bizarre coin-
cidences and urgent emotions, with death as the goal from the
moment of birth? If you were Christian, you believed that
eternity was the post-mortal prize. If you had no religion, life
was an intricate zig-zag course to destruction. Charlie had said
that Muriel was a survivor, and here she was in her seventies, a
grotesque old woman still trying to ingratiate herself with a
pseudo-gentleman — in order, perhaps to prettify the trollop
in her soul? During the entire time she had spent in Hollywood with Anna, she had shown no signs of this part of her
nature; nor indeed, for all her vagaries, had she shown it in
New York. Why then in England? Was it because her need to
be a somebody was so passionate that, when circumstances
relegated her to being a nonentity, she could manage only by
appearing important to some man whom she would pretend to
admire — however dismally unworthy of admiration?

Colonel Smith was saying something, and Anna pulled
herself together. She must find Hampstead very small after the
vastness of America? ... Well, yes ... but why Hampstead?
Why not England? She felt a little light-headed. How long
could she stand this? She hadn't seen Muriel for years, so she
must spend a little time with her; but the Colonel's nightmare
likeness to Jacko had brought back the old terror, and with it
feelings of suffocation and disgust. Besides, when Muriel had
drunk too much she always became aggresive, and she certainly
looked as if she might be going to drink too much this evening!
Anna tried to concentrate and, with a sweet smile, agreed that
America certainly was vast, and perhaps glossier, too, than
Hampstead, but that she hadn't been in America for years, and
that England was home, and you couldn't beat England when
it came to real living.

She caught Charlie's eye, and saw that Charlie appreciated what she felt. Dear old Charlie! The whole business was a crying shame! At least, unlike all those years ago, he was on her side! She wished she could do something to help him, but of course he was right. She couldn't. And usually when you thought you were acting for another's good, you were only making matters worse anyway.

The Colonel was saying that Muriel was a wonderful house-keeper and cook — so he was a fixture evidently.

'Where do you live?' she asked him.

He looked surprised. 'Why, here, of course!' he said.

Muriel looked down her nose. 'I have selected guests here,' she said. 'I'm afraid that, what with inflation and everything, your husband's far-from-generous allowance didn't go far.'

The Colonel stroked his chin. 'I'm sure your beautiful daughter will help out,' he said. 'After all, she's a very success-ful little lady.' He grinned at Anna ingratiatingly.

'We haven't talked about it, Fawce,' said Muriel, embar-rassed. 'If you remember, Anna and I haven't seen each other for some time.'

The Colonel nodded in a sagacious way, and looked up at the ceiling, humming a little tune under his breath.

The fact that her mother was embarrassed made Anna wonder if this whole meeting had been contrived so that she should be made to feel guilty that she wasn't giving her mother money. She felt indignant and hurt. She would have helped if need be, without this stupid and roundabout way of pressuris-ing her! Then she realised that none of it was for her benefit at all. It was all aimed at the dreadful Colonel. Did her mother hope to re-marry? It almost looked like it.

There was a long silence. Then, as Anna said nothing, Muriel rose to her feet. 'You haven't seen the place, my dear,' she said. 'I keep forgetting. I'll take you round.'

There were three people in the sitting room — two elderly men, and a youngish woman. They all gushed over Anna and were deferential to Muriel. She was shown the large kitchen, where surprisingly a girl of about twenty was cooking the dinner. She was shown the dining room, where one table was laid for four, and a smaller table laid for three (for Muriel, the Colonel and Charlie, she supposed). She was taken upstairs to

Muriel's bedroom, which was large and Hollywood-in-the-Thirties in style, decorated in pink and white with an adjoining bathroom. She was shown Charlie's room, which was small and untidy, and then she was returned to the 'den'.

'Well?' asked Muriel. 'How d'you like it?'

'You've done it marvellously, Mother.'

'A bit of a comedown, but it's not as bad,' said Muriel. She sounded self-satisfied. 'I wish I could ask you to stay on for a meal,' she continued, 'but, as you can see, it's not very easy and I don't think you would enjoy it after living so grandly for so long.'

'How long have you been taking in lodgers?' asked Anna.

'For some time now.' Muriel sounded vague. 'I need the money, as I told you. Charlie helps out,' she added, and for the first time there was acid in her voice. 'I thought perhaps that you might like to, too.'

'Charlie lives here,' said Anna sharply, feeling a little sick.

Muriel flushed. 'Yes, Charlie lives here. He's been a good son to me.'

Charlie came to Anna's rescue. 'Anna's been a wonderful daughter,' he said firmly. 'More than others might have been in her place.'

Muriel flicked a helpless but at the same time meaningful glance at the Colonel. 'Yes, of course,' she agreed, with a martyred air. 'I'm sure I don't deserve anything more.' She paused, then said brightly. 'Another drink dear?'

'No, thanks,' said Anna. 'I must be going.'

'I'm sure,' said Muriel. 'Nothing to tempt you to stay.'

'I wanted to see you so much,' said Anna. 'You'll never believe how nervous I have been!'

Muriel smiled her neat little smile. 'My clever daughter always exaggerates so much,' she said.

She slurred the last three words, and Anna was glad that she had said she must go. The Colonel was already looking raffish, and his face was beginning to sweat ... as Jacko's used to. Charlie seemed to be holding his drink, but he was on his third large neat whisky. All of them were smoking, and no window was open. They stood up and Muriel walked to the door. The Colonel gallantly kissed Anna's hand and then gave it a little squeeze. 'Anna Starr!' he breathed ecstatically. 'Anna Starr!

Fancy a pooped-out old military man having a couple of drinks with a real live star!' He made it sound like a pun, and barked with laughter at his own joke, then he was serious again. 'Don't you worry your little head about old Muriel, what? I may not carry quite the clout I did in the army, what? But I'm not finished yet! Not by a long chalk.'

'How kind!' said Anna uncomfortably.

Charlie kissed her warmly. 'See you soon,' he said, 'and good luck.'

Muriel walked Anna to the front door. 'So now you see how the poor live!' she exclaimed vivaciously. 'Down but not out, what?'

Anna looked at her in surprise, thinking she might be taking off the Colonel as a joke, but she had evidently decided to mimic him as a compliment. She suddenly seemed pathetic as Anna stooped down to hug her. 'I'll ring you tomorrow, Mother,' she said, 'and perhaps we can see a little more of one another.'

'Who knows?' asked Muriel skittishly. 'Who knows anything about anything, if it comes to that?' And with a sudden little lurch she shut the door in Anna's face.

CHAPTER TWENTY-SEVEN

Anna had terrifying dreams both that night and the night following. She dreamt that her mother was a witch riding the night sky on a broomstick, with Charlie disguised as a cat, sitting behind her. She herself was holding on to her mother's tattered clothing, and it was ripping apart in her hands as she swept through the sky. It was cold and she was scared, and suddenly the material she was holding came away and she hurtled down to destruction. She managed to look up as she was falling. The cat had disappeared, and only the Cheshire-cat grin was left behind, but the witch was staring straight ahead, apparently oblivious of what had happened to Anna. In another dream she was wrestling under bedclothes with Jacko, and he was winning. As he threw her to the floor she woke up sobbing. The third dream was the worst of all. Her mother was standing, naked and very old, in front of Anna, beckoning. Anna set off hopefully to reach her, but her mother slowly glided backwards, laughing, with the tears rolling down her face, until Anna missed her footing and fell an endless and horrifying fall ...

Rehearsals rattled along at a good pace. Anna grew to admire Tony more and more. He knew what he was doing, and the company were happy and inventive in his care. He usually ate with them at lunchtime, and Anna found his good temper and tart conversation much to her liking.

They opened to excellent notices on the road, and Tony came to each place they played.

The opening night in London had its hazards for Anna, as Muriel first said she would come, then said she wouldn't, and then didn't like the tickets Anna had bought for her. Tony placated his box-office, explaining what Muriel was like, and he exchanged his tickets for hers.

Marilyn had cabled to say that she and Bob would be over for the first night, which delighted both Anna and Tony.

Among the quantities of flowers that graced her dressing room on the night was a bouquet from Marilyn, and with it a velvet box enclosing a small diamond watch. The card read, 'To remind you, darling, of that first night so long ago, when you and Tony and I all worked together, and to tell you how proud I am that I was in at the start of your career.'

Anna was more touched by this than she could have imagined possible, and decided to wear the watch for the play. It would be entirely in keeping, and a talisman for her and Tony.

The audience enjoyed what they saw; so did Tony, who told the cast he was confident they had a hit on their hands.

Anna's dressing room was full afterwards. Marilyn and Bob were the first people round, and both were ecstatic. 'It's a smash!' said Marilyn. 'You're away. I know it.' Muriel came in, nodded coldly at Marilyn, then sat in the only armchair. She was dressed in black and wearing her diamonds, and she greeted the rest of visitors graciously, pointedly ignoring Marilyn from then on. Charlie, however, who had come in with her, made a point of hailing Marilyn enthusiastically, but Anna thought he looked the worse for wear.

To Anna's astonishment, among the crowds of actors, directors, managers, friends and hangers-on was Alex Claverdon, whom Anna had last seen with Marilyn in France all those years ago, after her disastrous affair with Antonio. He was remarkably unchanged, and Anna was surprised at how delighted she was to see him again. He was evidently charmed to see her, too, and had been vastly impressed by her performance. His hair had greyed, but he was still a handsome man. With him was his daughter, Jane, and her husband Hugo. Though she was unable to concentrate on them among such a mass of people Anne had the impression that Jane was looking a little sour. Muriel, too, was restless at the amount of attention that Anna was getting. Fortunately, and to Anna's relief, Tony Falk had noticed this and was making a great fuss of her, while Marilyn was kindly concentrating on Jane.

In spite of the tensions, there was a sense of victory in the air. It was quite obvious that Anna's friends had genuinely enjoyed the play. This didn't necessarily mean that the critics would be kind, but it did mean that, if the critics liked it, it had a good chance of a run.

Presently the room began to empty, and Jane exclaimed impatiently to her father, 'Come on Father, or we'll be last!'

Alex took Anna's hands in his and said ardently, 'I suppose it's too late to ask you to dine with us, Anna? We'd so love it!'

'I'm afraid so,' said Anna.

'Far too late,' agreed Muriel spitefully. 'I can't even dine with her myself, and I'm her mother.'

Jane shot a malicious look at her husband, and the other people in the room stopped talking.

'People never realise that, for actors and actresses, and their directors and managers, a first night, far from being a glamorous social occasion, is a business evening,' said Tony, cheerfully. 'On its success depends the livelihood of everyone connected with it. Anna and I will be having dinner with the management, and we'll be conducting a serious post mortem.' He forebore to say that Marilyn and Bob would be with them, too.

'I'm awfully sorry, Mother,' said Anna. 'I wish I *could* be with you, but I've told Charlie to look after you.'

'Charlie always does,' said Muriel. 'It's you who don't seem to have time for me.'

'I thought I had explained,' said Tony, and Anna could see that he was now angry. 'This is an important night for Anna and me.'

'Tony was a boy actor in Anna's first play in London, Lord Claverdon,' said Muriel. 'He was fat and very boring. He wasn't very good either. It's wonderful what a success he had managed to make under the circumstances.'

Alex looked unimpressed by this display of bitchery. Jane again tugged at his arm.

'He's one of the best directors around,' replied Anna fiercely.

'Thank you, darling,' murmured Tony.

'I was only trying to tell Lord Claverdon that, although no one would realise it, I've been in the business as long as either of you,' said Muriel. 'And I don't like being patronised.'

'No one is patronising you, Mother,' said Anna. 'Tony was simply explaining the situation.'

'Come along, Charlie,' said Muriel. 'It seems that we're not wanted here. Goodbye, Lord Claverdon. Anna has told me so much about you.' Anna looked astonished. Jane looked even more sour, and Alex looked pleased.

Charlie laughed. 'Right you are, Mother,' he said. 'It's time to get you home anyway.'

But Muriel hadn't quite finished. Her passion for titles had been unrequited since Antonio's day, and she went on, 'If Hampstead is not too far off your way, Lord Claverdon, Charlie and I would always love to give you a drink. Anna might even deign to visit us if *you* came!'

'Thank you very much,' said Alex. 'How kind.' He looked uncomfortable.

'Come *on*, Mother!' urged Charlie.

'And I do so hope you enjoy that business dinner of yours, Anna,' added Muriel, with a bright and mirthless smile. 'One excuse is as good as another.' And she went.

'She's a caution, is Muriel!' said Tony. 'Get dressed, Anna, darling, or we'll be late.'

'May I ring you some time?' asked Alex.

'Any time,' said Anna, and she meant it. 'Here's my number.'

Alex bent forward and shyly kissed her on the cheek, while Jane and her husband looked on with disapproval.

The general feeling at the supper party on that first night was that the play was a winner. Next day, the press and box-office bookings confirmed it, and Anna now settled down to a life in England. She took a long lease on the flat, made arrangements to leave Switzerland for good, and re-opened contact with Dickie and Eileen. Sadly Marilyn and Bob had had to return to Martha's Vineyard.

Maria, who was flowering in the Italian sun and extremely happy, came backwards and forwards to see her mother. She had a boyfriend in Italy, with whom she was living (shades of Antonio, thought Anna — but this boy made Maria happy); and, when her course finished, she wanted to stay in Florence — at least for a while, if Anna would give her permission — to continue her painting. Anna was pleased that her daughter had, for the moment, given up the idea of working for Sotheby's or Christies. She believed her to have real talent, and Maria was young enough to change her mind later, if she couldn't make the grade.

Philip and Evie were constant visitors, too, though Anna felt that Evie was a slightly reluctant one. They still seemed to be getting on well together, although Evie complained that Philip was spending more and more time at the drama school. She herself had found a job at a publisher's, where she was already making herself indispensable.

Both Tony and Alex were squiring Anna at this time, and she knew both of them were fond of her. Neither made any sort of proposal however, which relieved her; she was happy with her life as it was, and had no wish either to change it, or indeed to make decisions. She carefully refrained from comparing her feelings towards them; simply accepted the fact that she found pleasure in their company. The success of the play meant that her social calendar was full. She had redecorated the flat, and quite often entertained on Sundays, and all in all, she enjoyed herself. It was a recuperative time after all that she had suffered.

The play ran for two years and, as it drew to a close, so the attitudes of both Tony and Alex subtly changed.

Alex invited her to his house in Lincolnshire. Anna accepted.

It was a magnificent building designed by Inigo Jones in the seventeenth century, with beautifully decorated ceilings and fireplaces. Anna was enchanted by it. The grounds were equally resplendent with a formal garden and, beyond it, a landscape designed by Repton. Alex's father had been a keen gardener, passionately fond of trees: he had planted a particularly fine arboretum with many rare specimens (though, in the cold climate of the north, he had been unable to grow the more exotic kinds, which in some ways he had loved best), and it was famous among the cognoscenti. Alex had inherited his father's green fingers. His own speciality — orchids in a series of enormous greenhouses in the kitchen gardens — had acquired a similar reputation. The house and grounds were open to the public several days a week.

It turned out that Jane and her husband lived with Alex, and Anna suspected that this was why they had instinctively disliked her. They were clearly afraid of being turned out if Alex married, and they had seen at once how attracted he had been. She thought their behaviour ill-judged since, if she did marry Alex, their surliness would indeed tempt her to reject them. They were barely civil to her, which angered Alex, and embarrassed Anna on his account.

Anna loved the place. Her passion for beauty was fully satisfied here, and although the opulence of the furnishings and the quality of the paintings reminded her sometimes of Antonio, Alex himself was so different that she could relax and savour it all. Several times she thought he was on the verge of a proposal, but each time he drew back, and each time Anna was not entirely sorry.

When she returned to London, Tony was more attentive than ever.

How strange! she thought. When she was young, fifty had seemed an immense age — a milestone on the long march to the grave. Yet here she was with two men wooing her, and herself reluctant to commit herself! Although, to be honest, it seemed as if neither man was quite able to commit himself, either! This still relieved her, because she had no idea which one she would choose. Marriage entailed a change of direction, a life geared to the wishes of someone else. If she married Alex, Wintershill would be her life. Keeping it up would be her main preoccupation, as indeed it was Alex's. She would spend her life as a countrywoman, with obligations to the staff and to the neighbours, and she would spend a great deal of her time showing strangers round her home. She was not a country-woman. She was used to a very different kind of work, work she enjoyed. And Jane's presence would always worry her.

Alex she loved. She admired his character. He was kind, he had a sense of duty and he was clever. His business acumen was astonishing, they said, and all that he made he ploughed back into his house, which swallowed the money in an instant. Anna was happy in his company, and he gave her the most vital gift that any one person gives to another: a feeling of total trust.

Except in that respect, Tony was very different. The world to which he belonged was more febrile, but to Anna more exciting. He would never earn the money that Alex earned so effortlessly. But he came from a background she understood well. He was her own sort. He was as clever as Alex, but ambitious for himself, not for anything outside him. He and Anna had a friendship which embraced almost a lifetime. Sexually she found him more attractive, too. And this, to Anna, was still important. Jacko was dead — Antonio, Philip and, finally, Jacques had entirely exorcised him — and almost to her own dismay she still had a sexual appetite. Friendship even now was not quite enough for her, for marriage.

Suddenly, one morning, some weeks later, Charlie telephoned her, sounding agitated. 'Mother is getting married again.'

'To that ghastly Colonel?' asked Anna.

'Yes.'

'When?'

'On Saturday week.'

'Will they stay on at the house in Hampstead?'

'Oh, yes.'

'Will you be all right, Charlie?'

'Yes. Perfectly all right. There'll be no changes, really. Only that she'll be making it all legitimate, as she calls it. She wants you to come to the wedding. It's to be at the Hampstead Registry Office.'

'Of course I'll be there. I'm not working.'

'Good. She's set great store by you being at the wedding. She wants photographs and everything. You'll never believe it, but she's in love with the old crasher!'

'I'm not really surprised,' said Anna. 'He's got a look of Jacko, don't you think?'

'Yes. Yes, I do.' He still sounded agitated.

'What's the matter, Charlie? You sound worried. Don't you approve of the wedding?'

'Oh, yes. It's not that.' He stopped.

'Well? What's wrong?'

'I don't know if Mother would want you to know.'

'Know what?'

'It's rather serious,' said Charlie, and again he stopped.

'What is, Charlie? Come on! Out with it, for heaven's sake!'

'She's ill,' said Charlie. 'Very ill.'

'You mean, terminal?'

'Yes.'

'What's wrong with her? D'you mean she's got cancer or something?'

'Yes.'

'Does she know?'

'Oh, yes. That's why she wants to get married. To tell the truth, I think that's why the old bastard has agreed to marry her.'

'How long has she got?'

'A few months at most. Certainly less than a year.'

'Good God!'

'Yes. She's pathetically thin, but she's still the same as ever. Still bosses us about. Still keeps the house like a new pin. Still cares passionately about everyone and everything ...' His voice broke. 'It isn't painful, luckily — or else the doctor is keeping the pain down.'

'Thank God for that!'

'Yes.'

'Would she like me to come and see her before the wedding?'

'Yes, I think she would. She's been talking quite a lot about you lately.'

'I'll be there tomorrow,' said Anna.

When she put the receiver down she realised there was a lump in her throat.

Muriel dying! She could hardly believe it. The long and painful duel between them was drawing to a close. What a waste it had all been! With so much love, for so long, on her side, it need never have happened. But then that, of course, was to reckon without Muriel's character. Muriel was competitive in a way that Anna had never been. Jealousy had been her abiding weakness and, as Marilyn had said so long ago, jealously as deep-seated as Muriel's never lessens. Anna herself had probably aggravated it by her weakness. Things were never one-sided in a relationship.

Muriel dying! What would Charlie do? How would she herself feel, when her mother was no longer there? Suddenly she began crying in earnest.

CHAPTER TWENTY-EIGHT

Muriel's registry-office wedding was a sad affair, but she seemed delighted with it. She wore a new pink suit with a veiled hat and pink gloves. She looked, as Charlie had said, desperately thin, but still managed her kind of raddled elegance. To please her mother, Anna had also dressed up, and Charlie and the Colonel were resplendent in new grey suits and silk ties. Tony accompanied Anna, but there were no other guests. The service was perfunctory, and Anna was very aware that they were on an assembly line of couples. Those who had been married were in various little ante-rooms, taking photographs, and those about to be married were waiting, usually nervously, in a large hall just off the office.

Anna had telephoned Alex to tell him about the wedding. To her surprise he had sounded cool and somewhat evasive. He apologised for not being able to be with her on the day, and gave as his excuse that he had to go up to Wintershill on urgent business.

'Are you all right, Alex?' she asked.

'Of course.' He sounded very slightly irritated.

'Nothing wrong at Wintershill, is there?'

'No, no. Just a few things that need seeing to.' He didn't explain, and she was surprised. He had discussed all his problems with her until now.

'Nothing I can do?'

'No. How could there be?'

This indeed was a curious answer.

'When will you be back in London?' she asked.

'Three weeks,' he said. 'I wondered if perhaps you could dine with me then, one night.'

'But of course. Any suggestions?'

'How about the Wednesday?'

'Tuesday or Thursday, not Wednesday, I'm afraid.'

'Shall we make it Thursday?'

'Sure.'

Muriel was put out that he was not present at the wedding. 'Where is he?' she demanded.

Anna explained as best she could.

'You haven't quarrelled with him, have you?' asked Muriel beadily. 'You never have known what is best for you, have you? He's a charming man, and very much in love with you, so what more do you want? You can't go on being an actress until you're ninety. You may have lost your memory by then. Far better to settle for a good man with plenty of money. And a title never comes amiss either. I only wish I had had your chances!'

'That's an odd thing to say on your wedding day!' laughed Anna kindly.

'You know quite well what I mean!' retorted Muriel. 'You are just being obstinate as usual.'

Anna had arranged a reception in her flat, with professional caterers in charge, and her girl to help out. There were flowers in profusion and photographers as well. Maria and Philip were present, as well as Evie, and Anna had invited several of her famous friends so that the occasion would have a touch of glamour. Muriel was pleased by this and enjoyed herself hugely, introducing her new husband to them grandly, and with a touch of patronage. Presently, however, she became a little drunk, and soon both the Colonel and Charlie became very drunk. Most of the guests fled; but a hard core remained, and they settled down to a drinking sesion which lasted for several hours.

As the afternoon turned to evening, Muriel and the Colonel became more and more sentimental and, in Anna's eyes, Fawcett became more and more like Jacko. This sickened her to such an extent that she finally couldn't bear to watch it any more, and went by herself into the kitchen.

Tony joined her. 'What's up?' he said.

'It's my new step-father,' replied Anna, wryly. 'He reminds me too much of Jacko. D'you remember him?'

'Not sure that I do,' said Tony.

'He was ghastly,' said Anna, 'and on one never-to-be-forgotten night he raped me.'

'Good God!'

Anna told him the story. 'It was such a trauma that even after all these years I can hardly bear to think of it. I've been lucky enough to meet one or two wonderful men who have made it possible for me to live a normal life, but his ghost is always there, right at the back of my mind. I can't ever entirely rid myself of the horror, or the terrible feeling of degradation. Just imagine what it must be like for someone with a less fulfilled life than mine, to have gone through such a thing! There must be hundreds of women who have, I suppose, and I sometimes worry about them.'

Tony kissed the top of her head lightly. 'We'll get away from here as soon as we can,' he said. 'Why don't we go to my place and ask Charlie to ring us when they're through here?'

'We can't possibly!' exclaimed Anna. 'Muriel and the Colonel are meant to be catching a plane to Marbella tonight, and they'll never get it if I don't put them on it!'

'We'll both put them on it,' said Tony. 'Meanwhile, we deserve a breather!'

At Tony's place, she felt at home as usual. It was untidy, and filled with books which overflowed the bookcases and were lying about on every conceivable flat surface. His few pieces of furniture were good, and the pictures (several of them Old Master drawings) were very good. There were shelves of play scripts, a desk stacked with papers, two huge and comfortable armchairs, a battered sofa and some coloured rugs. Tony made them both mugs of tea, put some music on the recorder, and they sat easily and happily together, talking and at peace with one another. Finally he said, 'How's Alex? Like Muriel, I expected to see him today.'

'Me, too,' said Anna. 'He rang to say he wouldn't be here, as there are problems at Wintershill.'

He looked at her sharply. 'Only at Wintershill?' he asked.

'I don't know,' she replied truthfully. 'I'm seeing him in ten days' time.'

'Will you let me know what happens?'

'What do you mean, what happens?'

'Just that,' said Tony. 'I need to know.'

Anna looked at him in surprise. 'Do you know something I don't?'

He was equally surprised. 'No. Certainly not! Why should I?'

'I'll tell you anything there is to tell,' she said, smiling.

'OK,' said Tony. He leaned forward and kissed her very gently on the lips. 'And now we must help those lovebirds to the plane.'

On the Thursday as arranged, Alex took Anna to dinner at one of their favourite restaurants. He looked ill-at-ease and nervous. Anna had never seen him look either before, and she in turn became nervous. As soon as they'd ordered the meal, she said, 'What's happened, darling? Something's wrong, I can tell.'

'Not really wrong,' he said uncomfortably. 'In fact, I am very happy, but it's a little awkward to explain.'

'Try,' she said gently.

'You may not like what I have to say.'

'Never mind.'

'I'm going to get married, and I wanted you to be one of the first to know.'

Anna felt winded, but she managed to smile. 'That's wonderful, Alex!' she said. 'Do I know her? Who is she?'

'No, you don't know her. I haven't known her all that long myself. She's very young — young enough to be my daughter — but we're in love.'

'That's marvellous.'

'Yes. Marvellous.' He nodded solemnly. 'It's something I never expected to happen. As you must have known, I was in love with *you* for years. But when you made your life in America, I married Patricia, and we had a good time together. She had all my interests ... very important, don't you think?'

Anna assented. 'And it worked. Our greatest sorrow was that we had no sons, only Jane. And Jane has no children either.'

Anna studied him carefully. Was he still hoping for a son? It was possible, though perhaps unlikely. 'Does Jane like her?' she asked.

'I don't know,' he replied. 'I haven't risked telling her. She made no secret of the fact that she didn't like you — I suppose she considered you a rival for the estate — so I haven't told her about Arabella.'

'Are you going to?'

'I'm announcing the engagement tomorrow. I'll tell Jane tonight. She's in London, at my London flat.'

'You thought I might object, too?' asked Anna. 'I mean, you have left it a little late to tell me, too, haven't you, and I always considered we were friends.'

'We were ... we are,' he corrected himself. 'But I'm on tenterhooks in case something goes wrong.' He smiled apologetically. 'I'm really bowled over this time, and I couldn't take it.'

'What can go wrong if she has agreed to marry you? You've told *her* family, I imagine?'

'Certainly. And they're all for it, in spite of the age difference.'

'Then surely you have nothing to fear?'

'No. I suppose I haven't.'

'Well, congratulations,' said Anna. She raised her glass. 'To your great happiness, dear Alex,' she said.

He looked immensely relieved. 'Thank you, my dear,' he answered earnestly. 'That's very sporting of you.'

Anna felt very slightly nettled. He had evidently taken it very much for granted that, if he had proposed, she would have accepted. Would she? What did she feel, now that marriage to him was no longer a possibility? Was she upset? Unhappy? Relieved? Indifferent? No, not indifferent. Some kind of emotion, and a fairly strong one, was struggling to the surface, but at the moment her chief feeling was of surprise, followed closely by this niggling feeling of resentment that he had taken her acceptance of him as a foregone conclusion.

'I hope you find someone, too, my dear,' he went on. 'Women shouldn't be left on their own as they get older.'

'Millions of them are,' she replied drily. 'Since most women live longer than men.'

'You've always got your career, which you'd have had to give up, had you married me,' he said.

She bit back any sort of retort, and answered gently, 'That's true.'

'So perhaps it's all for the best,' he said.

This went too far. 'You are very certain that I'd have married you if you'd asked me, aren't you?' she asked quietly.

He was quite obviously astonished. 'Why, yes,' he said. 'That's why I was so worried about telling you.'

'It was an unnecessary worry,' she said. 'Of course I've thought about it many times, but although I like you very much, and I like money, and the title, and beautiful Wintershill, it really would never have done. I don't come from your world, and if truth were to be known, I don't particularly like it. Some of your kind are all right, and some aren't — as with actors. But I'm used to actors, and the world of the theatre. My son will be an actor. My husband was an actor. I'm at home with actors — and if one marries, it is to have a home, basically, isn't it?'

'Yes, I suppose it is.' She could see that he didn't quite approve of the way the conversation was going. 'Well, I'm glad. I dreaded hurting you.'

'You hurt me by not taking me into your confidence.'

'I'm sorry.'

'But in no other way. When is the wedding to be?'

'Six and a half weeks from now. At Kensington Registry Office. Can you come?'

'May I let you know?'

'Of course.'

A constraint now fell between them and in the silence Anna once more tried to work out how exactly she felt. Then she recognised the emotion. She felt free! Free, because what he had to offer her had been a severe and constant temptation, and one for which she might have fallen. Free, because what she had just been saying was the truth. His world wasn't her world, and she preferred her own. She'd had enough of being an outsider. If she married again, it would be to someone of her own kind. Free, because she knew at last and with great force, that it was Tony she loved. Not Alex. And if Tony wanted her, she was free to go to him.

CHAPTER TWENTY-NINE

The following morning she lay in bed, propped against pillows, reading *The Times*. Alex was to marry the Hon. Arabella Montagu Fitz-Montagu, a pretty blonde of twenty-eight. Photographs of them both stared out of the paper at her. Alex was smiling broadly and happily. Arabella was looking demure. She also looked determined. She had been running a boutique, but said she would be giving it up to run Wintershill and to look after a family. (Jane wouldn't like any of this: Anna wondered how she had taken the news the night before.) She and Alex had met at a dance and had fallen for each other at first sight. Both were very very happy, and Arabella would go back to keeping the dogs and horses which she adored but had had to forego when she was working in London.

The telephone bell rang. It was Tony.

'Well, well!' he said. 'So that's what it was all about!'

'Yes.'

'Do you mind?'

'Not a bit.'

'I was afraid you might. I always thought you'd marry him yourself. He had a lot to offer.'

'Not enough,' she said cheerfully.

'I must say, I'm pretty relieved!'

'Are you?'

'Yes. Enormously! Doing anything for lunch?'

'Not a thing.'

'How about the Dorchester?'

'Isn't that a little extravagant?'

'I'm feeling a little extravagant. To begin with, I've got a wonderful play to direct, with a sensational part for you in it. And secondly ...' He stopped.

'Secondly?' she prompted.

'Tell you when I see you,' he said abruptly. 'Could you come first to my office behind the Globe?'

'Sure.'

'Twelve o'clock?'

'Sure.'

In the highest of spirits, she was just getting into the bath when the telephone rang again. It was Jane.

'Hullo,' she said. 'Have you seen the news?'

'Yes. I'm delighted for him.'

'Are you?' Jane sounded astonished. 'I thought you'd be upset.'

'Why should I be upset? Is there something wrong with the girl?'

'Only that she's about half his age. She's a year younger than I am!'

'Sometimes those kinds of marriages work very well,' said Anna.

'I'm disappointed in you,' retorted Jane. 'I'd hoped you might be an ally.'

'In what way?'

'Make him see sense.'

'From what he told me last night, he's in love. It's a marvellous feeling, but hardly to do with being sensible.'

'He's too old to marry again.'

'He's certainly old enough to know what he wants,' said Anna.

'My father's a fool about women!' said Jane. 'At one time I thought he wanted to marry you.'

'Did you?'

'Yes. Did you turn him down?'

'No. He never asked me.'

'Oh! Well I hoped perhaps you could come and see me with him, to persuade him not to go through with this.'

'No. I'm afraid not,' said Anna firmly. 'I wouldn't dream of interfering. Or, indeed, standing in the way of his happiness.'

'It's absurd at his age!'

'He may have been very lonely since your mother died.'

'He's got us,' said Jane.

'Not quite the same thing,' replied Anna. 'Now, if you'll excuse me, Jane, I must get ready. I have an appointment at the Dorchester.' As she said it, she felt a sudden surge of pure happiness.

'Oh, very well,' said Jane sulkily. 'If you won't help, you won't!'

'I have one suggestion to make, though,' said Anna.

'What's that?'

'That you let your father mind his own business. You may be trying to enlist my help now, but you didn't want your father to marry me and you made it very obvious.'

'You're a far better companion as regards age,' said Jane.

'Your father's life is his own. He's a very nice man, and a very clever one. Let him be.'

Jane put down the receiver as abruptly as Tony had done.

Anna had a long and lazy bath, dressed and made up carefully, then settled down to read the rest of the paper until it was time to go out to lunch.

She heard a rattle at her letter box and went to see what had arrived. There was a postcard from her mother. 'Having a wonderful time. We're living it up in style. Muriel.'

Another letter was on the mat, in a handwriting that Anna didn't recognise. She picked it up and opened it. It was signed Fawcett. With a sinking heart she read what it had to say. 'Dear Anna,' he wrote. 'I think the little lady is enjoying herself. She's certainly the life and soul of the party, but I think you ought to know that she's failing pretty fast, and I'm worried about whether we ought to get her home. She'd make the devil of a fuss at going back before the month is up but I don't want anything to happen out here, away from her doctors.'

The telephone shrilled again. Anna numbly lifted the receiver, scared by how shocked she felt. Charlie was on the line. 'I've had a letter from Fawce,' he said.

'Me too,' replied Anna. She found that she was shaking, and had to sit down.

'It's ghastly, isn't it? What are we to do?' He sounded panic-stricken.

'Do you think one of us should go out and see how bad she

is?' asked Anna. 'As Fawcett says, she'd make the devil of a fuss if we insisted on her coming back over here.'

'That's a good idea!' exclaimed Charlie. 'I wouldn't mind going, if you like. I don't mean this badly, old girl, but I think she'd take it better if it was me and not you.'

'Thanks, Charlie. It would be most awfully kind. What about your job at the pub, though? Wouldn't they mind?'

'I don't think so,' said Charlie. 'I'm on pretty good terms with them, and they know about Mother.'

'When could you go?'

'Any time ... if you could help with the cash.' He was evidently embarrassed. 'I'd see to everything else.'

'Of course!' exclaimed Anna. 'Bless you, Charlie!' She hesitated. 'You'll send for me if it's really bad, won't you?'

'Sure.' He sounded desolate. 'Poor old Muriel,' he said. 'She's got her faults but she's a doughty fighter.'

'Yes,' agreed Anna. 'She certainly is. I do hope Fawcett was exaggerating.'

'Me, too.'

'Whatever will you do, when the time comes?' asked Anna. 'I wonder about it sometimes, and I get awfully worried for you.'

'Don't be, old girl,' said Charlie. 'I've done all my own worrying, and I'll be OK. You see, for one thing, I'll be free.' His voice was utterly bleak.

'Free?' echoed Anna, astonished. So Charlie too would be 'free'!

'Yeah,' he said. 'Free. I love the old girl, but she's been one hell of an albatross. Not financially, of course, but through the emotions. While she's around, I'm bound to her. I can't help it. It's an emotional fact. When she goes, nothing will be the same again for me, but at least I can grow up.'

Anna found this too difficult for unconsidered comment, so she changed the subject. 'How will you explain the fact that you've decided to join them on their honeymoon?' she asked.

'I'll say Fawce thought she'd like it.'

'Fair enough. Good luck, Charlie.'

'Shall I come by for the money?'

'Do. I'm going to the Dorchester for lunch with Tony, but

going to his office first. He's got a new play for me, and he says
it's good.'

'Great.'

'I'll be leaving here at about eleven-thirty.'

'Right. I'll be straight round. Congratulations about the
play. Oh, by the way — you've seen about Alex?'

'Yes. He told me about it last night.'

'Hope he'll be happy.'

'So do I.'

'You don't mind?'

'Not in the least.'

'Good for you.' He rang off.

He came to the flat not long afterwards, and Anna thought
he looked haunted and also defeated; but, in view of his
conversation on the telephone, she hoped this was only temporary. He was very affectionate and a little drunk, but with it
all there was a pathetic air of resolution. When he left, she saw
him hunched against the wind, in a dirty mackintosh, lurching
down the road, and had a vivid revelation of his almost
desperate loneliness. Then she put on her coat and drove to
Tony's office.

Tony was on the telephone, but he looked delighted to see
her, and waved at her to sit down.

She sat and waited.

The telephone conversation finished, and he came round to
where she was sitting and kissed her long and hard. 'I've sent
for champagne,' he said. 'In celebration. It's in the office
fridge. I'll ring through and tell them to bring it.'

She laughed. 'You must be certain you've found a good
play!' she exclaimed.

'In celebration of Alex's engagement,' Tony said firmly.
'It's the best news I've had in years! I wish him all the luck in
the world.'

'So do I,' said Anna.

'I couldn't ask you while he was hanging around, because of
his money and his title and all that — but now I can. Will you
marry me Susannah?'

'Susannah!' she exclaimed. 'What a long time since anyone
called me that!'

'Well?'

'Of course, darling. Thank you.'

'After all these years!' he said wonderingly.

'After all these years!' she replied.

'My first and second marriages didn't work,' he said. 'You've got courage!'

'In a way we belong to each other,' said Anna. 'We started together, and the theatre is our home. I think we'll make it.'

'If you like the play,' he said, 'it will be quite a coincidence. I've got the Globe for it, where we both started, and as you'll be the sole star, you and I will have top billing. Quite a turn-up! It's taken a long long time for us to get together again at the same old theatre, but there we'll be! Let's cable Marilyn and ask her very specially to be with us on the first night, shall we? I'm sure she'll make it. Just think of it! The three of us, forty years on! Not bad, eh?'

'Not bad,' echoed Anna. A feeling of immense peace came over her. 'Not bad at all!'

There was a knock on the door and Tony's assistant appeared, grinning broadly, with the champagne bottle already opened, and two glasses. He put the tray on the table, then went straight out again, with a cheerful wink.

Tony poured out the champagne, and when he had filled both their glasses he said with a wry smile, 'To your mother, and mine. After all, they made this possible.'

'Amen,' said Anna.

And she hoped that Charlie would get to Muriel in time.